THEY BOTH DIE AT THE END

ALSO BY

ADAM SILVERA

More Happy Than Not

History Is All You Left Me

They Both Die at the End

What If It's Us (with Becky Albertalli)

Here's To Us (with Becky Albertalli)

The Infinity Cycle

Infinity Son

Infinity Reaper

ADAM SILVERA

THEY BOTH DIE AT THE END

SIMON & SCHUSTER

First published in Great Britain in 2017 by Simon & Schuster UK Ltd
This edition published in Great Britain in 2021 by Simon & Schuster UK Ltd.

First published in the USA in 2017 by HarperCollins Children's Books,
a division of HarperCollins Publishers, 195 Broadway, New York, NY 10007.

1 3 5 7 9 10 8 6 4 2

Simon & Schuster UK Ltd
1st Floor, 222 Gray's Inn Road
London WC1X 8HB

www.simonandschuster.co.uk
www.simonandschuster.com.au
www.simonandschuster.co.in

Simon & Schuster Australia, Sydney
Simon & Schuster India, New Delhi

A CIP catalogue record for this book
is available from the British Library.

ISBN 978-1-3985-1440-9
eBook ISBN 978-1-4711-6621-1

Printed and bound by CPI Group (UK) Ltd, Croydon, CR0 4YY

FSC
www.fsc.org
MIX
Paper from
responsible sources
FSC® C020471

For those who need a reminder to make every day count.

Shout-out to Mom for all the love and
Cecilia for all the tough love. I've always needed both.

PART ONE

Death-Cast

To live is the rarest thing in the world.

Most people exist, that's all.

—Oscar Wilde

September 5, 2017

MATEO TORREZ

12:22 a.m.

Death-Cast is calling with the warning of a lifetime—I'm going to die today. Forget that, "warning" is too strong a word since warnings suggest something can be avoided, like a car honking at someone who's crossing the street when it isn't their light, giving them the chance to step back; this is more of a heads-up. The alert, a distinctive and endless gong, like a church bell one block away, is blasting from my phone on the other side of the room. I'm freaking out already, a hundred thoughts immediately drowning out everything around me. I bet this chaos is what a first-time skydiver feels as she's plummeting out of a plane, or a pianist playing his first concert. Not that I will ever know for sure.

It's crazy. One minute ago I was reading yesterday's blog entry from *CountDowners*—where Deckers chronicle their final hours through statuses and photos via live feeds, this particular one about a college junior trying to find a home for his golden retriever—and now I'm going to die.

I'm going to . . . no . . . yes. Yes.

My chest tightens. I'm dying today.

I've always been afraid of dying. I don't know why I thought this would jinx it from actually happening. Not forever, obviously, but long enough so I could grow up. Dad has even been drilling it into my head that I should pretend I'm the main character of a story that nothing bad ever happens to, most especially death, because the hero has to be around to save the day. But the noise in my head is quieting down and there's a Death-Cast herald on the other end of the phone waiting to tell me I'm going to die today at eighteen years old.

Wow, I'm actually . . .

I don't want to pick up the phone. I'd rather run into Dad's bedroom and curse into a pillow because he chose the wrong time to land himself in intensive care, or punch a wall because my mom marked me for an early death when she died giving birth to me. The phone rings for what's got to be the thirtieth time, and I can't avoid it any more than I can avoid what's going down sometime today.

I slide my laptop off my crossed legs and get up from my bed, swaying to the side, feeling really faint. I'm like a zombie moving toward my desk, slow and walking-dead.

The caller ID reads *DEATH-CAST*, of course.

I'm shaking but manage to press *Talk*. I don't say anything.

I'm not sure what to say. I just breathe because I have fewer than twenty-eight thousand breaths left in me—the average number of breaths a nondying person takes per day—and I might as well use them up while I can.

"Hello, I'm calling from Death-Cast. I'm Andrea. You there, Timothy?"

Timothy.

My name isn't Timothy.

"You've got the wrong person," I tell Andrea. My heart settles down, even though I feel for this Timothy person. I truly do. "My name is Mateo." I got the name from my father and he wants me to pass it down eventually. Now I can, if having a kid is a thing that happens for me.

Computer keys are tapping on her end, probably correcting the entry or something in her database. "Oh, apologies. Timothy is the gentleman I just got off the phone with; he didn't take the news very well, poor thing. You're Mateo Torrez, right?"

And just like that, my last hope is obliterated.

"Mateo, kindly confirm this is indeed you. I'm afraid I have many other calls to make tonight."

I always imagined my herald—their official name, not mine—would sound sympathetic and ease me into this news, maybe even harp on how it's especially tragic because I'm so young. To be honest, I would've been okay with her being chipper, telling me how I should have fun and make the most of the day since I at least know what's going to happen. That way I'm not stuck at home starting one-thousand-piece puzzles I'll never finish or masturbating because sex with an actual person scares me. But this herald makes me feel like I should stop wasting her time because, unlike me, she has so much of it.

"Okay. Mateo's me. I'm Mateo."

"Mateo, I regret to inform you that sometime in the next twenty-four hours you'll be meeting an untimely death. And while there isn't anything we can do to suspend that, you still have a chance to live." The herald goes on about how life isn't always fair, then lists some events I could participate in today. I shouldn't be mad at her, but it's obvious she's bored reciting these lines that have been burned into memory from telling hundreds, maybe thousands, about how they'll soon be dead. She has no sympathy to offer me. She's probably filing her nails or playing tic-tac-toe against herself as she talks to me.

On *CountDowners*, Deckers post entries about everything from their phone call to how they're spending their End Day. It's basically Twitter for Deckers. I've read tons of feeds where Deckers admitted to asking their heralds how they would die, but it's basic knowledge that those specifics aren't available to anyone, not even former President Reynolds, who tried to hide from Death in an underground bunker four years ago and was assassinated by one of his own secret service agents. Death-Cast can only provide a date for when someone is going to die, but not the exact minute or how it'll happen.

". . . Do you understand all of this?"

"Yeah."

"Log on to death-cast.com and fill out any special requests you may have for your funeral in addition to the inscription you'd like engraved on your headstone. Or perhaps you would like to be cremated, in which case . . ."

I've only ever been to one funeral. My grandmother died when I was seven, and at her funeral I threw a tantrum because she wasn't waking up. Fast-forward five years when Death-Cast came into the picture and suddenly everyone *was* awake at their own funerals. Having the chance to say goodbye before you die is an incredible opportunity, but isn't that time better spent actually living? Maybe I would feel differently if I could count on people showing up to my funeral. If I had more friends than I do fingers.

"And Timothy, on behalf of everyone here at Death-Cast, we are so sorry to lose you. Live this day to the fullest, okay?"

"I'm Mateo."

"Sorry about that, Mateo. I'm mortified. It's been a long day and these calls can be so stressful and—"

I hang up, which is rude, I know. I know. But I can't listen to someone tell me what a stressful day she's been having when I might drop dead in the next hour, or even the next ten minutes: I could choke on a cough drop; I could leave my apartment to do something with myself and fall down the stairs and snap my neck before I even make it outside; someone could break in and murder me. The only thing I can confidently rule out is dying of old age.

I sink to the floor, on my knees. It's all ending today and there is absolutely nothing I can do about it. I can't journey across dragon-infested lands to retrieve scepters that can halt death. I can't hop onto a flying carpet in search of a genie to grant my wish for a full and simple life. I could maybe find some mad scientist to cryogenically freeze me, but chances are I'd die in the middle of that wacky experiment. Death is inevitable for everyone and it's absolute for me today.

The list of people I will miss, if the dead can miss anyone, is so short I shouldn't even call it a list: there's Dad, for doing his best; my best friend, Lidia, not only for not ignoring me in the hallways, but for actually sitting down across from me in lunch, partnering with me in earth science, and talking to me about how she wants to become an environmentalist who will save the world and I can repay her by living in it. And that's it.

If someone were interested in my list of people I *won't* miss, I'd have nothing for them. No one has ever wronged me. And I even get why some people didn't take a shot on me. Really, I do. I'm such a paranoid mess. The few times I was invited to do something fun with classmates, like roller-skating in the park or going for a drive late at night, I bowed out because we *might* be setting ourselves up for death, *maybe*. I guess what I'll miss most are the wasted opportunities to live my life and the lost potential to make great friends with everyone I sat next to for four years. I'll miss how we never got to bond over sleepovers where everyone stayed up and played Xbox Infinity and board games all night, all because I was too scared.

The number one person I'll miss the most is Future Mateo, who maybe loosened up and lived. It's hard to picture him clearly, but I imagine Future Mateo trying out new things, like smoking pot with friends, getting a driver's license, and hopping on a plane to Puerto Rico to learn more about his roots. Maybe he's dating someone, and maybe he likes that company. He probably plays piano for his friends, sings in front of them, and he would definitely have a crowded funeral service, one that would stretch over an entire weekend after he's gone—one where the room is packed with new people who didn't get a chance to hug him one last time.

Future Mateo would have a longer list of friends he'll miss.

But I will never grow up to be Future Mateo. No one will ever get high with me, no one will be my audience as I play piano, and no one will sit shotgun in my dad's car after I get my license. I'll never fight with friends over who gets the better bowling shoes or who gets to be Wolverine when we play video games.

I collapse back onto the floor, thinking about how it's do or die now. Not even that.

Do, and then die.

12:42 a.m.

Dad takes hot showers to cool down whenever he's upset or disappointed in himself. I copied him around the time I turned thirteen because confusing Mateo Thoughts surfaced and I needed tons of Mateo Time to sort through them. I'm showering now because I feel guilty for hoping the world, or some part of it beyond Lidia and my dad, will be sad to see me go. Because I refused to live invincibly on all the days I didn't get an alert, I wasted all those yesterdays and am completely out of tomorrows.

I'm not going to tell anyone. Except Dad, but he's not even awake so it doesn't really count. I don't want to spend my last day wondering if people are being genuine when they throw sad words at me. No one should spend their last hours second-guessing people.

I've got to get out into the world, though, trick myself into thinking it is any other day. I've got to see Dad at the hospital and hold his hand for the first time since I was a kid and for what will be the last . . . wow, the last time ever.

I'll be gone before I can adjust to my mortality.

I also have to see Lidia and her one-year-old, Penny. Lidia

named me Penny's godfather when the baby was born, and it sucks how I'm the person expected to take care of her in case Lidia passes away since Lidia's boyfriend, Christian, died a little over a year ago. Sure, how is an eighteen-year-old with no income going to take care of a baby? Short answer: He isn't. But I was supposed to get older and tell Penny stories of her world-saving mother and chill father and welcome her into my home when I was financially secure and emotionally prepared to do so. Now I'm being whisked out of her life before I can become more than some guy in a photo album who Lidia may tell stories about, during which Penny will nod her head, maybe make fun of my glasses, and then flip the page to family she actually knows and cares about. I won't even be a ghost to her. But that's no reason to not go tickle her one more time or wipe squash and green peas off her face, or give Lidia a little break so she can focus on studying for her GED or brush her teeth or comb her hair or take a nap.

After that, I will somehow pull myself away from my best friend and her daughter, and I will have to go and live.

I turn off the faucet and the water stops raining down on me; today isn't the day for an hour shower. I grab my glasses off the sink and put them on. I step out of the tub, slipping on a puddle of water, and while falling backward I'm expecting to see if that theory of your life flashing before your eyes carries any truth to it when I grab hold of the towel rack and catch myself. I breathe in and out, in and out, because dying this way would just be an extremely unfortunate way to go; someone would add me to the "Shower KO" feed on the *DumbDeaths* blog, a high-traffic site that grosses me out on so many levels.

I need to get out of here and live—but first I have to make it out of this apartment alive.

12:56 a.m.

I write thank-you notes for my neighbors in 4F and 4A, telling them it's my End Day. With Dad in the hospital, Elliot in 4F has been checking in on me, bringing me dinner, especially since our stove has been busted for the past week after I tried making Dad's empanadas. Sean in 4A was planning on stopping by on Saturday to fix the stove's burner, but it's not necessary anymore. Dad will know how to fix it and might need a distraction when I'm gone.

I go into my closet and pull out the blue-and-gray flannel shirt Lidia got me for my eighteenth birthday, then put it on over my white T-shirt. I haven't worn it outside yet. The shirt is how I get to keep Lidia close today.

I check my watch—an old one of Dad's he gave me after buying a digital one that could glow, for his bad eyes—and it's close to 1:00 a.m. On a regular day, I would be playing video games until late at night, even if it meant going to school exhausted. At least I could fall asleep during my free periods. I shouldn't have taken those frees for granted. I should've taken up another class, like art, even though I can't draw to save my life. (Or do anything to save my life, obviously, and I want to say that's neither here nor there, but it pretty much is everything, isn't it?) Maybe I should've joined band and played piano, gotten some recognition before working my way up to singing in the chorus, then maybe a duet with someone cool, and then maybe braving a solo. Heck, even theater could've been fun if I'd gotten to play a role that forced me to break out. But no, I elected for another free period where I could shut down and nap.

It's 12:58 a.m. When it hits 1:00 I am forcing myself out of this apartment. It has been both my sanctuary and my prison and for once I need to go breathe in the outside air instead of tearing through it to get from Point A to Point B. I have to count trees, maybe sing a favorite song while dipping my feet in the Hudson, and just do my best to be remembered as the young man who died too early.

It's 1:00 a.m.

I can't believe I'm never returning to my bedroom.

I unlock the front door, turn the knob, and pull the door open.

I shake my head and slam the door shut.

I'm not walking out into a world that will kill me before my time.

RUFUS EMETERIO

1:05 a.m.

Death-Cast is hitting me up as I'm beating my ex-girlfriend's new boyfriend to death. I'm still on top of this dude, pinning his shoulders down with my knees, and the only reason I'm not clocking him in the eye again is because of the ringing coming from my pocket, that loud Death-Cast ringtone everyone knows too damn well either from personal experience, the news, or every shitty show using the alert for that *dun-dun-dun* effect. My boys, Tagoe and Malcolm, are no longer cheering on the beat-down. They're dead quiet and I'm waiting for this punk Peck's phone to go off too. But nothing, just my phone. Maybe the call telling me I'm about to lose my life just saved his.

"You gotta pick it up, Roof," Tagoe says. He was recording the beat-down because watching fights online is his thing, but now he's staring at his phone like he's scared a call is coming for him too.

"The hell I do," I say. My heart is pounding mad fast, even faster than when I first moved up on Peck, even faster than when I first decked him and laid him out. Peck's left eye is swollen already, and there's still nothing but pure terror in his right eye. These Death-Cast calls go strong until three. He don't know for sure if I'm about to take him down with me.

I don't know either.

My phone stops ringing.

"Maybe it was a mistake," Malcolm says.

My phone rings again.

Malcolm stays shut.

I wasn't hopeful. I don't know stats or nothing like that, but Death-Cast fucking up alerts isn't exactly common news. And we Emeterios haven't exactly been lucky with staying alive. But meeting our maker way ahead of time? We're your guys.

I'm shaking and that buzzing panic is in my head, like someone is punching me nonstop, because I have no idea how I'm gonna go, just that I am. And my life isn't exactly flashing before my eyes, not that I expect it to later on when I'm actually at death's edge.

Peck squirms from underneath me and I raise my fist so he calms the hell down.

"Maybe he got a weapon on him," Malcolm says. He's the giant of our group, the kind of guy who would've been helpful to have around when my sister couldn't get her seat belt off as our car flipped into the Hudson River.

Before the call, I would've bet anything Peck doesn't have any weapon on him, since we're the ones who jumped him when he was coming out of work. But I'm not betting my life, not like this. I drop my phone. I pat him down and flip him over, checking his waistband for a pocketknife. I stand and he stays down.

Malcolm drags Peck's backpack out from under the blue car where Tagoe threw it. He unzips the backpack and flips it over, letting some Black Panther and Hawkeye comics hit the ground. "Nothing."

Tagoe rushes toward Peck and I swear he's about to kick him like his head's a soccer ball, but he grabs my phone off the ground and answers the call. "Who you calling for?" His neck twitch surprises no one. "Hold up, hold up. I ain't him. *Hold up.* Wait a sec." He holds out the phone. "You want me to hang up, Roof?"

I don't know. I still have Peck, bloodied and beat, in the parking lot of this elementary school, and it's not like I need to take this call to make sure Death-Cast isn't actually calling to tell me I won the lottery. I snatch the phone from Tagoe, pissed and confused, and I might throw up but my parents and sister didn't so maybe I won't either.

"Watch him," I tell Tagoe and Malcolm. They nod. I don't know how I became the alpha dog. I ended up in the foster home years after them.

I give myself some distance, as if privacy actually matters, and make sure I stay out of the light coming from the exit sign. Not trying to get caught in the middle of the night with blood on my knuckles. "Yeah?"

"Hello. This is Victor from Death-Cast calling to speak with Rufus Emmy-terio."

He butchers my last name, but there's no point correcting him. No one else is around to carry on the Emeterio name. "Yeah, it's me."

"Rufus, I regret to inform you that sometime in the next twenty-four hours—"

"Twenty-three hours," I interrupt, pacing back and forth from one end of this car to the other. "You're calling after one." It's bullshit. Other Deckers got their alert an hour ago. Maybe if Death-Cast called an hour ago I wouldn't have been waiting outside the restaurant where freshman-year college-dropout Peck works so I could chase him into this parking lot.

"Yes, you're right. I'm sorry," Victor says.

I'm trying to stay shut 'cause I don't wanna take my problems out on some guy doing his job, even though I have no idea why the hell anyone applies for this position in the first place. Let's pretend I got a future for a second, entertain me—in no universe am I ever waking up and saying, "I think I'll get a twelve-to-three shift where I do nothing but tell people their lives are over." But Victor and others did. I don't wanna hear none of that don't-kill-the-messenger business either, especially when the messenger is calling to tell me I'll be straight wrecked by day's end.

"Rufus, I regret to inform you that sometime in the next twenty-three hours you'll be meeting an untimely death. While there isn't anything I can do to suspend that, I'm calling to inform you of your options for the day. First of all, how are you doing? It took a while for you to answer. Is everything okay?"

He wants to know how I'm doing, yeah right. I can hear it in the stunted way he asked me, he doesn't actually care about me any more than he does the other Deckers he gotta call tonight. These calls are probably monitored and he's not trying to lose his job by speeding through this.

"I don't know how I'm doing." I squeeze my phone so I don't throw it against the wall painted with little white and brown kids holding hands underneath a rainbow. I look over my shoulder and Peck is still face-first on the ground as Malcolm and Tagoe stare at me; they better make sure he doesn't run away before we can figure out what we're doing with him. "Just tell me my options." This should be good.

Victor tells me the forecast for the day (supposed to rain before noon and later on as well if I make it that long), special festivals I have zero interest in attending (especially not a yoga class on the High Line, rain or no rain), formal funeral arrangements, and restaurants with the best Decker discounts if I use today's code. I zone out on everything else 'cause I'm anxious on how the rest of my End Day is gonna play out.

"How do you guys know?" I interrupt. Maybe this dude will take pity on me and I can clue in Tagoe and Malcolm on this huge mystery. "The End Days. How do you know? Some list? Crystal ball? Calendar from the future?" Everyone stays speculating on how Death-Cast receives this life-changing information. Tagoe told me about all these crazy theories he read online, like Death-Cast consulting a band of legit psychics and a really ridiculous one with an alien shackled to a bathtub and forced by the government to report End Days. There are mad things wrong with that theory, but I don't have time to comment on them right now.

"I'm afraid that information isn't available to heralds either," Victor claims. "We're equally curious, but it's not knowledge we need to perform our job." Another flat answer. I bet you anything he knows and can't say if he wants to keep his job.

Screw this guy. "Yo, Victor, be a person for one minute. I don't know if you know, but I'm seventeen. Three weeks from my eighteenth birthday. Doesn't it piss you off that I'll never go to college? Get married? Have kids? Travel? Doubt it. You're just chilling on your little throne in your little office because you know you got another few decades ahead of you, right?"

Victor clears his throat. "You want me to be a person,

Rufus? You want me to get off my throne and get real with you? Okay. An hour ago I got off the phone with a woman who cried over how she won't be a mother anymore after her four-year-old daughter dies today. She begged me to tell her how she can save her daughter's life, but no one has that power. And then I had to put in a request to the Youth Department to dispatch a cop just in case the mother is responsible, which, believe it or not, is not the most disgusting thing I've done for this job. Rufus, I feel for you, I do. But I'm not at fault for your death, and I unfortunately have many more of these calls to make tonight. Can you do me a solid and cooperate?"

Damn.

I cooperate for the rest of the call, even though this dude has no business telling me anyone else's, but all I can think about is the mother whose daughter will never attend the school right behind me. At the end of the call Victor gives me that company line I've grown used to hearing from all the new TV shows and movies incorporating Death-Cast into the characters' day-to-days: "On behalf of Death-Cast, we are sorry to lose you. Live this day to the fullest."

I can't tell you who hangs up first, but it doesn't matter. The damage is done—will be done. Today is my End Day, a straight-up Rufus Armageddon. I don't know how this is gonna go down. I'm praying I don't drown like my parents and sis. The only person I've done dirty is Peck, for real, so

I'm counting on not getting shot, but who knows, misfires happen too. The how doesn't matter as much as what I do before it goes down, but not knowing is still freaking shaking me; you only die once, after all.

Maybe Peck *is* gonna be responsible for this.

I walk back over to the three of them, fast. I pick Peck up by the back of his collar and then slam him against the brick wall. Blood slides from an open wound on his forehead, and I can't believe this dude threw me over the edge like this. He should've never run his mouth about all the reasons Aimee didn't want me anymore. If that'd never gotten back to me, my hand wouldn't be around his throat right now, getting him even more scared than I am.

"You didn't 'beat' me, okay? Aimee didn't split with me because of you, so get that out of your head right now. She loved me and we got complicated, and she would've taken me back eventually." I know this is legit—Malcolm and Tagoe think so too. I lean in on Peck, looking him dead-on in his only good eye. "I better never see you again for the rest of my life." Yeah, yeah. Not much life left. But this dude is a fucking clown and might get funny. "You feel me?"

Peck nods.

I let go of his throat and grab his phone out of his pocket. I hurl it against the wall and the screen is totaled. Malcolm stomps it out.

"Get the hell out of here."

Malcolm grabs my shoulder. "Don't let him go. He's got those connections."

Peck slides along the wall, nervous, like he's scaling across some windows high up in the city.

I shake Malcolm off my shoulder. "I said *get the hell out of here*."

Peck takes off, running in a dizzying zigzag. He never looks back once to see if we're coming for him or stops for his comics and backpack.

"I thought you said he's got friends in some gang," Malcolm says. "What if they come for you?"

"They're not a real gang, and he was the gang reject. I got no reason to get scared of a gang that let Peck in. He can't even call them or Aimee, we took care of that." I wouldn't want him reaching out to Aimee before I can. I gotta explain myself, and, I don't know, she may not wanna see me if she figures out what I did, End Day or not.

"Death-Cast can't call him either," Tagoe says, his neck twitching twice.

"I wasn't gonna kill him."

Malcolm and Tagoe are quiet. They saw the way I was laying into him, like I had no off button.

I can't stop shaking.

I could've killed him, even if I didn't mean to. I don't know if I would've been able to live with myself or not if I did end up snuffing him gone. Nah, that's a lie and I know it, I'm just trying to be hard. But I'm not hard. I've barely been able to live with myself for surviving something my family didn't—something that wasn't even my fault. There's no way in hell I would've been chill with myself for beating someone to death.

I storm toward our bikes. My handles are tangled in Tagoe's wheel from after we chased Peck here, jumping off our bikes to tackle him. "You guys can't follow me," I say, picking my bike up. "You get that, right?"

"Nah, we're with you, just—"

"Not happening," I interrupt. "I'm a ticking time bomb, and even if you're not blowing up when I do, you might get burned—maybe literally."

"You're not ditching us," Malcolm says. "Where you go, we go."

Tagoe nods, his head jerking to the right, like his body is betraying his instinct to follow me. He nods again, no twitch this time.

"You two are straight-up shadows," I say.

"That because we're black?" Malcolm asks.

"Because you're always following me," I say. "Loyal to the end."

The end.

That shuts us up. We get on our bikes and ride off the curb, the wheels bumping and bumping. This is the wrong day to have left my helmet behind.

Tagoe and Malcolm can't stay with me the entire day, I know that. But we're Plutos, bros from the same foster home, and we don't turn our backs on each other.

"Let's go home," I say.

And we out.

MATEO

1:06 a.m.

I'm back in my bedroom—so much for never returning here again—and I immediately feel better, like I just got an extra life in a video game where the final boss was kicking my ass. I'm not naive about dying. I know it's going to happen. But I don't have to rush into it. I'm buying myself more time. A longer life is all I've ever wanted, and I have the power to not shoot that dream in the foot by walking out that front door, especially this late at night.

I jump into bed with the kind of relief you only find when you're waking up for school and realize it's Saturday. I throw my blanket around my shoulders, hop back on my laptop, and—ignoring the email from Death-Cast with the time-stamped receipt of my call with Andrea—continue reading yesterday's *CountDowners* post from before I got the call.

The Decker was twenty-two-year-old Keith. His statuses didn't provide much context about his life, only that he'd been a loner who preferred runs with his golden retriever Turbo instead of social outings with his classmates. He was looking to find Turbo a new home because he was pretty sure his father would give ownership of Turbo to the first available person, which could be anyone because Turbo is so beautiful. Hell, *I* would've adopted him even though I'm severely allergic to dogs. But before Keith gave up his dog, he and Turbo were running through their favorite spots one last time and the feed stopped somewhere in Central Park.

I don't know how Keith died. I don't know if Turbo made it out alive or if he died with Keith. I don't know what would've been preferred for Keith or Turbo. I don't know. I could look into any muggings or murders in Central Park yesterday around 5:40 p.m., when the feed stopped, but for my sanity this is better left a mystery. Instead I open up my music folder and play Space Sounds.

A couple years ago some NASA team created this special instrument to record the sounds of different planets. I know, it sounded weird to me too, especially because of all the movies I've watched telling me about how there isn't sound in space. Except there is, it just exists in magnetic vibrations. NASA converted the sounds so the human ear could hear them, and even though I was hiding out in my room, I stumbled on something magical from the universe—something those who don't follow what's trending online would miss out on. Some of the planets sound ominous, like something you'd find in a science fiction movie set in some alien world—"alien world" as in world with aliens, not non-Earth world. Neptune sounds like a fast current, Saturn has this terrifying howling to it that I never listen to anymore, and the same goes for Uranus except there are harsh winds whistling that sound like spaceships firing lasers at each other. The sounds of the planets make for a great conversation starter if you have people to talk to, but if you don't, they make for great white noise when you're going to sleep.

I distract myself from my End Day by reading more *Count-Downers* feeds and by playing the Earth track, which always reminds me of soothing birdsong and that low sound whales make, but also feels a little bit off, something suspicious I can't put my finger on, a lot like Pluto, which is both seashell and snake hiss.

I switch to the Neptune track.

RUFUS

1:18 a.m.

We're riding to Pluto in the dead of night.

"Pluto" is the name we came up with for the foster home we're all staying at since our families died or turned their backs on us. Pluto got demoted from planet to dwarf planet, but we'd never treat each other as something lesser.

It's been four months that I've been without my people, but Tagoe and Malcolm have been getting cozy with each other a lot longer. Malcolm's parents died in a house fire caused by some unidentified arsonist, and whoever it was, Malcolm hopes he's burning in hell for taking away his parents when he was a thirteen-year-old troublemaker no one else wanted except the system, and barely even them. Tagoe's mom bounced when he was a kid, and his pops ran off three years ago when he couldn't keep up with the bills. A month later Tagoe found out his pops had committed suicide, and homeboy still hasn't shed a tear over the guy, never even asked how or where he died.

Even before I found out I was dying, I knew home, Pluto, wasn't gonna be home for me much longer. My eighteenth birthday is coming up—same for Tagoe and Malcolm, who both hit eighteen in November. I was college bound like Tagoe, and we'd figured Malcolm would crash with us as he gets his shit together. Who knows what's what now, and I hate that I already have an out to these problems. But right now, all that matters is we're still together. I got Malcolm and Tagoe by my side, like they've been from day one when I got to the home. Whether it was for family time or bitching sessions, they were always at my left and right.

I wasn't planning on stopping, but I pull over when I see the church I came to a month after the big accident—my first weekend out with Aimee. The building is massive, with off-white bricks and maroon steeples. I'd love to take a picture of the stained-glass windows, but the flash might not catch it right. Doesn't matter anyway. If a picture is Instagram worthy, I slap on the Moon filter for that classic black-and-white effect. The real problem is I don't think a photo of a church taken by my nonbelieving ass is the best last thing to leave behind for my seventy followers. (Hashtag not happening.)

"What's good, Roof?"

"This is the church where Aimee played piano for me," I say. Aimee is pretty Catholic, but she wasn't pushing any of that on me. We'd been talking about music, and I mentioned digging some of the classical stuff Olivia used to put on when she was studying, and Aimee wanted me to hear it live—and she wanted to be the one who played it for me. "I have to tell her I got the alert."

Tagoe twitches. I'm sure he's itching to remind me that Aimee said she needs space from me, but those kinds of requests get tossed out the window on End Days.

I climb off the bike, throwing down the kickstand. I don't go far from them, just closer to the entrance right as a priest is escorting a crying woman out the church. She's knocking her rings together, topaz, I think, like the kind my mom once pawned when she wanted to buy Olivia concert tickets for her thirteenth birthday. This woman has gotta be a Decker, or know one. The graveyard shift here is no joke. Malcolm and Tagoe are always mocking the churches that shun Death-Cast and their "unholy visions from Satan," but it's dope how some nuns and priests keep busy way past midnight for Deckers trying to repent, get baptized, and all that good stuff.

If there's a God guy out there like my mom believed, I hope he's got my back right now.

I call Aimee. It rings six times before going to voice mail. I call again and it's the same thing. I try again, and it only rings three times before going to voice mail. She's ignoring me.

I type out a text: Death-Cast called me. Maybe you can too.

Nah, I can't be a dick and send that.

I correct myself: Death-Cast called me. Can you call me back?

My phone goes off before a minute can pass, a regular ring and not that heart-stopping Death-Cast alert. It's Aimee.

"Hey."

"Are you serious?" Aimee asks.

If I weren't serious, she'd certainly kill me for crying wolf. Tagoe once played that game for attention and Aimee shut that down real fast.

"Yeah. I gotta see you."

"Where are you?" There's no edge to her, and she's not trying to hang up on me like she has on recent calls.

"I'm by the church you took me to, actually," I say. It's mad peaceful, like I could stay here all day and make it to tomorrow. "I'm with Malcolm and Tagoe."

"Why aren't you at Pluto? What are you guys doing out on a Monday night?"

I need more time before answering this. Maybe another eighty years, but I don't have that and I don't wanna man up to it right now. "We're headed back to Pluto now. Can you meet us there?"

"What? No. Stay at the church and I'll come to you."

"I'm not dying before I can make it back to you, trust—"

"You're not invincible, dumbass!" Aimee is crying now, and her voice is shaking like that time we got caught in the rain without jackets. "Ugh, god, I'm sorry, but you know how many Deckers make those promises and then pianos fall on their heads?"

"I'm gonna guess not many," I say. "Death by piano doesn't seem like a high probability."

"This is not funny, Rufus. I'm getting dressed, do not move. I'll be thirty minutes, tops."

I hope she's gonna be able to forgive me for everything, tonight included. I'll get to her before Peck can, and I'll tell my side. I'm sure Peck is gonna go home, clean himself up, and call Aimee off his brother's phone to tell her what a monster I am. He better not call the cops though, or I'll be spending my End Day behind bars, or maybe find myself on the wrong end of some officer's club. I don't wanna think about any of that, I just wanna get to Aimee and say goodbye to the Plutos as the friend they know I am, not the monster I was tonight.

"Meet me at home. Just . . . get to me. Bye, Aimee."

I hang up before she can protest. I get my bike, climbing on it as she calls nonstop.

"What's the plan?" Malcolm asks.

"We're going back to Pluto," I tell them. "You guys are gonna throw me a funeral."

I check the time: 1:30.

There's still time for the other Plutos to get the alert. I'm not wishing it on them, but maybe I won't have to die alone.

Or maybe that's how it has to be.

MATEO

1:32 a.m.

Scrolling through *CountDowners* is a very serious downer. But I can't look away because every registered Decker has a story they want to share. When someone puts their journey out there for you to watch, you pay attention—even if you know they'll die at the end.

If I'm not going outside, I can be online for others.

There are five tabs on the site—Popular, New, Local, Promoted, Random—and I browse through Local searches first, as usual, to make sure I don't recognize anyone. . . . No one; good.

It could've been nice to have some company today, I guess.

I randomly select a Decker. Username: Geoff_Nevada88. Geoff received his call four minutes after midnight and is already out in the world, heading to his favorite bar, where he hopes he doesn't get carded because he's a twenty-year-old who recently lost his fake ID. I'm sure he'll get through okay.

I pin his feed and will receive a chime next time he updates.

I switch to another feed. Username: WebMavenMarc. Marc is a former social media manager for a soda company, which he's mentioned twice in his profile, and he isn't sure if his daughter will reach him in time. It's almost as if this Decker is right in front of me, snapping his fingers in my face.

I have to visit Dad, even if he's unconscious. He has to know I made my way to him before I died.

I put down my laptop, ignoring the chimes from the couple accounts I've pinned, and go straight to Dad's bedroom. His bed was unmade the morning he left for work, but I've made it for him since then, making sure to tuck the comforter completely under the pillows, as he prefers it. I sit on his side of the bed—the right side, since my mother apparently always favored the left, and even with her gone he still lives his life in two sides, never writing her out—and I pick up the framed photo of Dad helping me blow out the candles of my *Toy Story* cake on my sixth birthday. Well, Dad did all the work. I was laughing at him. He says the gleeful look on my face is why he keeps this picture so close.

I know it's sort of strange, but Dad is just as much my best friend as Lidia is. I could never admit that out loud without someone making fun of me, I'm sure, but we've always had a great relationship. Not perfect, but I'm sure every two people out there—in my school, in this city, on the other side of the world—struggle with dumb and important things, and the closest pairs just find a way to get over them. Dad and I would never have one of those relationships where we had a falling-out and never talked to each other again, not like these Deckers on some *CountDowners* feeds who hate their fathers so much they either never visited them on their deathbeds or refused to make amends before they themselves died. I slip the photo out of the frame, fold it, and put it in my pocket—the creases won't bother Dad, I don't think—and get up to go to the hospital and say my goodbye and make sure this photo is by his side when he finally wakes up. I want to make sure he quickly finds some peace, like it's an ordinary morning, before someone tells him I'm gone.

I leave his room, pumped to go out and do this, when I see the stack of dishes in the sink. I should clean those up so Dad doesn't come home to dirty plates and mugs with impossible stains from all the hot chocolate I've been drinking.

I swear this isn't an excuse to not go outside.

Seriously.

RUFUS

1:41 a.m.

We used to beast through the streets on our bikes like we were racing without brakes, but not tonight. We look both ways constantly and stop for red lights, like now, even when the street is clear of cars. We're on the block with that Decker-friendly club, Clint's Graveyard. There's a crowd forming of twentysomething-year-olds and the line is straight chaos, which has gotta be keeping the paychecks coming for the bouncers dealing with all these Deckers and their friends trying to get crazy on the dance floor one last time before their time is up.

This brunette girl, mad pretty, is bawling when a guy advances on her with some tired-ass pickup line ("Maybe you'll live to see another day with some Vitamin Me in your system."), and her friend swings her purse at him until he backs up. Poor girl can't even get a break from assholes hitting on her when she's grieving herself.

It's a green light and we ride on, finally reaching Pluto minutes later. The foster home is a jacked-up duplex with the face of a battered building—bricks missing, indecipherable and colorful graffiti. There are bars on the ground floor windows, not because we're criminals or anything like that, but so no one busts in and steals from a bunch of kids who've already lost enough. We leave our bikes down at the bottom of the steps, racing up to the door and letting ourselves in. We go down the hall, not bothering to tiptoe across the tacky, chessboard-like tiled floor into the living room, and even though there's a bulletin board with information about sex, getting tested for HIV, abortion and adoption clinics, and other sheets of that nature, this place still feels like a home and not some institution.

There's the fireplace that doesn't work but still looks dope. The warm orange paint covering the walls, which had me ready for fall this summer. The oak table we'd gather around to play Cards Against Humanity and Taboo on weeknights after dinner. The TV where I'd watch this reality show *Hipster House* with Tagoe, even though Aimee hated all those hipsters so much she wished I watched cartoon porn instead. The couch where we'd take turns napping since it's more comfortable than our beds.

We go up to the second floor, where our bedroom is, this tight spot that wouldn't really be all that comfortable for one person, let alone three, but we make it work. There's a window we keep open on the nights Tagoe eats beans, even if it's mad loud outside.

"I gotta say it," Tagoe says, closing the door behind us. "You've come really far. Think about all you've done since coming here."

"There's so much more I could be doing." I sit on my bed and throw my head back on my pillow. "It's mad pressure to do all my living in one day." Might not even be a full day. I'll be lucky to get twelve hours.

"No one's expecting you to cure cancer or save endangered pandas," Malcolm says.

"Yo, Death-Cast is lucky they can't predict when an animal is gonna die," Tagoe says, and I suck my teeth and shake my head because he's speaking up for pandas when his best friend is dying. "What, it's true! You would be the most hated dude on the planet if you called up the last panda ever. Imagine the media, there'd be selfies and—"

"We get it," I interrupt. I'm not a panda so the media doesn't give a shit about me. "You guys gotta do me the biggest favor. Wake up Jenn Lori and Francis. Tell them I wanna have a funeral before heading out." Francis never really took a liking to me, but I got a home out of this arrangement and that's more than others get.

"You should stay here," Malcolm says. He opens up the only closet. "Maybe we can beat this. You can be the exception! We can lock you in here."

"I'll suffocate or the shelf with your heavy-ass clothes will collapse on my head." He should know better than to believe in exceptions and shit like that. I sit up. "I don't have a lot of time, guys." I shake a little, but I get it together. I can't let them see me freaking.

Tagoe twitches. "You gonna be okay by yourself?"

It takes a few seconds before I get what he's really asking me. "I'm not offing myself," I say.

I'm not trying to die.

They leave me alone in the room with laundry I'll never have to worry about washing and summer course work I'll never have to finish—or start. Bunched up in the corner of my bed is Aimee's blanket, this yellow thing with a pattern of colorful cranes, which I wrap around my shoulders. It belonged to Aimee as a kid, a relic from her mother's childhood. We started dating when she was still here at Pluto, and we'd rest underneath the blanket together and use it for the occasional living room picnic. Those were mad chill times. She didn't ask for the blanket back after we broke up, which I think was her way of keeping me around, even when she wanted distance. Like I still have a chance with her.

This room couldn't be more different from the bedroom I grew up in—beige walls instead of green; two extra beds, and roommates; half the size; no weights or video game posters—but it still feels like home, and it showed me how people matter more than stuff. Malcolm learned that lesson after firefighters put out the flames that burned his house, parents, and favorite things.

We keep it simple here.

Behind my bed, I have pictures thumb-tacked to the wall, all printed out by Aimee from my Instagram: Althea Park, where I always go to think; my sweaty white T-shirt hanging from my bike's handlebars, taken after my first marathon last summer; an abandoned stereo on Christopher Street, playing a song I'd never heard before and never heard again; Tagoe with a bloody nose from that time we tried creating a handshake for the Plutos and it all went wrong because of a stupid head-butt; two sneakers—one size eleven, the other size nine—from that time I bought new kicks but didn't make sure they matched before leaving the store; me and Aimee, my eyes uneven, kind of like when I'm high, which I wasn't (yet), but it's still a keeper because the streetlight threw a cool glow on her; footprints in the mud from when I chased Aimee around the park after a long week of rain; two shadows sitting beside each other, which Malcolm wanted no part of, but I took anyway; and tons more I gotta leave behind for my boys when I walk out of here.

Walking out of here . . .

I really don't wanna go.

MATEO

1:52 a.m.

I'm almost ready to go.

I did the dishes, swept dust and candy wrappers out from underneath the couch, mopped the living room floor, wiped the bathroom sink clean of my toothpaste smears, and even made my bed. I'm back in front of my laptop, faced with a greater challenge: the inscription for my headstone in no more than eight words. How do I sum up my life in eight words?

He Lived Where He Died: In His Bedroom.

What a Waste of a Life.

Children Take More Risks Than Him.

I have to do better. Everyone wanted so much more out of me, myself included. I have to honor this. It's my last day to do so.

Here Lies Mateo: He Lived for Everyone.

I hit *Submit.*

There's no going back. Yeah, I can edit, but that's not how promises work, and living for everyone is a promise to the world.

I know it's early in the day, but my chest squeezes because it's also getting late, for a Decker, at least. I can't do this alone, the leaving part. I'm really not dragging Lidia into my End Day. Once I get out of here—not if—I'll go see Lidia and Penny, but I'm not telling Lidia. I don't want her to consider me dead before I am, or ever bring her any sadness. Maybe I'll send her a postcard explaining everything while I'm out living.

What I need is a coach who can double as a friend for me, or a friend who can serve as a coach for me. And that's what this popular app often promoted on *CountDowners* provides.

The Last Friend app is designed for lonely Deckers and for any good soul who wants to keep a Decker company in their final hours. This isn't to be confused with Necro, which is intended for anyone who wants a one-night stand with a Decker—the ultimate no-strings-attached app. I've always been so disturbed by Necro, and not just because sex makes me nervous. But no, the Last Friend app was created so people can feel worthy and loved before they die. There are no user charges, unlike Necro, which goes for $7.99 a day, which disturbs me because I can't help but feel as if a human is worth more than eight bucks.

Anyway, just like any potential new friendship, the

relationships born from the Last Friend app can be pretty hit-or-miss. I was once following this *CountDowners* feed where this Decker met a Last Friend, and she was slow about updating, sometimes for hours, to the point where viewers in the chat room assumed she'd died. She was actually very much alive, just living her last day right, and after she died her Last Friend wrote a brief eulogy that taught me more about the girl than I'd learned in any of her updates. But it's not always sweet like that. A few months ago this Decker with a sad life unwittingly befriended the infamous Last Friend serial killer, and that was so tragic to read about, and one of the many reasons I struggle with trusting this world.

I think engaging with a Last Friend could do me some good. Then again, I don't know if it's sadder to die alone or in the company of someone who not only doesn't mean anything to you, but also probably doesn't care much for you either.

Time is wasting.

I have to take a shot and find the same bravery hundreds of thousands of Deckers before me have found. I check my bank account online, and what remains from my college funds has been automatically deposited into my account, which is only about two thousand dollars, but it's more than enough money to get through the day. I can visit the World Travel Arena downtown, where Deckers and guests can experience the cultures and environments of different countries and cities.

I download the Last Friend app on my phone. It's the fastest download ever, like it's some sentient being who understands the whole point of its existence is that time is running out for someone. The app has a blue interface with an animation of a gray clock as two silhouettes approach each other and high five. *LAST FRIEND* zooms into the center and a menu drops down.

- ☐ Dying Today
- ☐ Not Dying Today

I click *Dying Today.* A message pops up:

We here at Last Friend Inc. are collectively sorry for this loss of you. Our deepest sympathies extend to those who love you and those who will never meet you. We hope you find a new friend of value to spend your final hours with today. Please fill out the profile for best results.

Deeply sorry to lose you,
Last Friend Inc.

A blank profile pops up and I fill it out.

Name: Mateo Torrez
Age: 18

Gender: Male

Height: 5'10"

Weight: 164 lbs.

Ethnicity: Puerto Rican

Orientation: <skip>

Job: <skip>

Interests: Music; Wandering

Favorite Movies / TV Shows / Books: Timberwolves by Gabriel Reeds; "Plaid Is the New Black"; the Scorpius Hawthorne series

Who You Were in Life: I'm an only child and I've only ever really had my dad. But my dad has been in a coma for two weeks and will probably wake up after I'm gone. I want to make him proud and break out. I can't go on being the kid who keeps his head low, because all that did was rob me of being out there with you all—maybe I could've met some of you sooner.

Bucket List: I want to go to the hospital and say goodbye to my dad. And then my best friend, but I don't want to tell her I'm dying. After that, I don't know. I want to make a difference for others and find a different Mateo while I'm at it.

Final Thoughts: I'm going for it.

I submit my answers. The app prompts me to upload a photo. I scroll through my phone's album and there are a lot of photos of Penny and screenshots of songs I'd recommend to Lidia. There are others of me out in the living room with Dad. There's my junior year photo, which is lame. I stumble on one I took of myself wearing the Luigi hat I won in June for entering this Mario Kart contest online. I was supposed to send the contest host my picture to be featured on the website, but I didn't think the boy-goofing-around-in-the-Luigi-hat was very me so I never submitted it.

But I was wrong, go figure. This is exactly the person I always wanted to be—loose, fun, carefree. No one will look at this photo and think it was out of character, because none of these people know me, and their only expectations of me are to be the person I'm presenting myself as in my profile.

I upload the photo and a final message pops up: Be well, Mateo.

RUFUS

1:59 a.m.

My foster parents are waiting downstairs. They tried rushing in here the second they found out, but Malcolm played bodyguard because he knew I still needed a minute. I change into my cycling gear—my gym tights with blue basketball shorts over them so my package isn't poking out there like Spider-Man's, and my favorite gray fleece—because there's no other way I can imagine getting around this city on my End Day except on my bike. I grab my helmet because safety first. I take one last look at the room. I don't break down or nothing like that, seriously, even as I remember playing catch with my boys. I leave the light on as I step out and keep the door open so Malcolm and Tagoe don't get weird about going back in.

Malcolm gives me a little smile. His playing-it-cool game is weak 'cause I know he's been losing his head, they all are. I would too if the cards were reversed.

"You actually got Francis awake?" I ask.

"Yeah."

It's possible I'm gonna die at the hands of my foster father; if you're not his alarm clock, you shouldn't wake him up.

I follow Malcolm downstairs. Tagoe, Jenn Lori, and Francis are there, but they don't say anything. The first thing I wanna ask is if anyone has heard from Aimee, like if her aunt is holding her up, but that's not right.

I really hope she didn't change her mind about wanting to see me.

It's gonna be okay, I gotta focus on everyone who is here.

Francis is wide awake and wearing his favorite-slash-only bathrobe, like he's some kingpin whose business makes him stacks on stacks of money instead of a technician spending the little he makes on us. Good guy, but he looks mad wild because his hair is patchy since he cuts it himself to save a few bucks, which is crazy stupid because Tagoe is a haircut artist. I kid you not, Tagoe gives the best fades in the city and that bastard better open up his own barbershop one day and give up his screenwriting dreams. Francis is too white to rock a fade, though.

Jenn Lori dries her eyes with the collar of her old college T-shirt before putting her glasses back on. She's at the edge of her seat, like when we'd watch Tagoe's favorite slasher flicks, and just like then, she gets up, but not because of some gross spontaneous combustion. She hugs me and cries into my shoulder, and it's the first time anyone's hugged me since I got the alert and I don't want her to let go, but I have to keep it moving. Jenn stays by my side as I stare at the floor.

"One less mouth to feed, right?" No one laughs. I shrug. I don't know how to do this. No one gives you lessons on how to brace everyone for your death, especially when you're seventeen and healthy. We've all been through enough seriousness and I want them to laugh. "Rock, Paper, Scissors, anyone?"

I clap my fist against my palm, playing Scissors against no one. I do it again, this time playing Rock, still against no one. "Come on, guys." I go again and Malcolm plays Paper against my Scissors. It takes another minute, but we get several rounds going. Francis and Jenn Lori are easy to beat. I go up against Tagoe and Rock beats Scissors.

"Do-over," Malcolm says. "Tagoe switched from Paper to Rock last second."

"Man, of all days to cheat Roof, why today?" Tagoe shakes his head.

I give Tagoe a friendly bro push. "Because you're a dick."

The doorbell rings.

I dart to the door, heart racing like whoa, and open it. Aimee's face is so flushed I almost can't make out the huge birthmark on her cheek.

"Are you kidding me?" Aimee asks.

I shake my head. "I can show you the time stamp on my phone."

"Not about your End Day," Aimee says. *"This."* She steps to the side and points at the bottom of the stairs—at Peck and his wrecked face. The one I said I never wanted to see again as long as I lived.

MATEO

2:02 a.m.

I don't know how many Last Friend accounts are active in the world, but there are currently forty-two online in New York City alone, and staring down these users feels a lot like being in my high school auditorium on the first day of classes. There's all this pressure, and I don't know where to start—until I receive a message.

There's a bright blue envelope in my inbox, and it glows in pulses, waiting to be clicked open. There's no subject line, just some basic information: *Wendy Mae Greene. 19 years old. Female. Manhattan, New York (2 miles away)*. I click her profile. She isn't a Decker, just a girl who's up late looking to console one. In her bio she's a self-described "bookworm obsessed with all things Scorpius Hawthorne," and this common link is probably why she's reaching out. She also likes walking around, too, "especially in late May when the weather is perfect." I won't be around for late May, Wendy Mae. I wonder how long she's had this profile and if anyone's told her that speaking about the future like that might offend some Deckers, how it might be mistaken as showing off how much life she still has left to live. I move past it and click her photo. She seems nice—light skinned, brown eyes, brown hair, a nose piercing, and a big smile. I open the message.

Wendy Mae G. (2:02 a.m.): hi mateo. u have great taste in bks. bet ur wishing u had a death cloaking spell, huh??

I'm sure she means well, but between her bio and this message, she's hammering me with nails instead of giving me the pat on the back I was hoping for. I won't be rude, though.

Mateo T. (2:03 a.m.): Hey, Wendy Mae. Thanks, you have great taste in books too.

Wendy Mae G. (2:03 a.m.): scorpius hawthorne 4 life . . . how r u doing?

Mateo T. (2:03 a.m.): Not great. I don't want to leave my room, but I know I have to get out of here.

Wendy Mae G. (2:03 a.m.): what was the call like? were you scared?

Mateo T. (2:04 a.m.): I freaked out a little bit–a lot of bit, actually.

Wendy Mae G. (2:04 a.m.): lol. ur funny. n really cute. ur mom n dad must be losing their heads 2 rite?

Mateo T. (2:05 a.m.): I don't mean to be rude, but I have to go now. Have a nice night, Wendy Mae.

Wendy Mae G. (2:05 a.m.): wat did i say? y do u dead guys always stop talking 2 me?

Mateo T. (2:05 a.m.): It's no big deal, really. It's hard for my parents to lose their heads when my mom is out of the picture and my dad is in a coma.

Wendy Mae G. (2:05 a.m.): how was i supposed 2 kno that?

Mateo T. (2:05 a.m.): It's in my profile.

Wendy Mae G. (2:05 a.m.): fine, watevr. do u have an open house then? i'm supposed to lose my virginity to my bf but i want to practice first and maybe u can help me out.

I click out while she's typing another message and block her for good measure. I get her insecurities, I guess, and I feel bad for her and her boyfriend if she manages to cheat on him, but I'm not some miracle worker. I receive some more messages, these with subject lines:

Subject: 420?

Kevin and Kelly. 21 years old. Male.

Bronx, New York (4 miles away).

Decker? No.

Subject: My condolences, Mateo (great name)

Philly Buiser. 24 years old. Male.

Manhattan, New York (3 miles away).

Decker? No.

Subject: u selling a couch? good condition?

J. Marc. 26 years old. Male.

Manhattan, New York (1 mile away).

Decker? No.

Subject: Dying sucks, huh?

Elle R. 20 years old. Female.

Manhattan, New York (3 miles away).

Decker? Yes.

I ignore Kevin and Kelly's message; not interested in pot. I delete J. Marc's message because I'm not selling the couch Dad will need again for his weekend naps. I'm going to answer Philly's message—because it came first.

Philly B. (2:06 a.m.): Hey, Mateo. How's it going?

Mateo T. (2:08 a.m.): Hey, Philly. Is it too lame to say I'm hanging in there?

Philly B. (2:08 a.m.): Nah, I'm sure it's rough. Not looking forward to the day Death-Cast calls me. Are you sick or something? Pretty young to be dying.

Mateo T. (2:09 a.m.): I'm healthy, yeah. I'm terrified of how it's going to happen, but I'm nervous I'll somehow disappoint myself if I don't get out there. I definitely don't want to stink up the apartment by dying in here.

Philly B. (2:09 a.m.): I can help with that, Mateo.

Mateo T. (2:09 a.m.): Help with what?

Philly B. (2:09 a.m.): Making sure you don't die.

Mateo T. (2:09 a.m.): That's not a thing anyone can promise.

Philly B. (2:10 a.m.): I can. You seem like a cool guy who doesn't deserve to die so you should come over to my apartment. It'll have to be a secret, though, but I have the cure to death in my pants.

I block Philly and open up Elle's message. Maybe the third time will be the charm.

RUFUS

2:21 a.m.

Aimee gets in my face and pushes me against the fridge. She doesn't play when it comes to violence because her parents got real extra when they tag-team-robbed a convenience store, assaulting the owner and his twenty-year-old son. Shoving me around isn't gonna get her locked up like them, though.

"Look at him, Rufus. What the fuck were you thinking?"

I refuse to look at Peck, who's leaning against the kitchen counter. I already saw the damage I did when he walked in—one eye shut, a cut on his lip, spots of dried blood on his swollen forehead. Jenn Lori is right next to him, pressing ice against his forehead. I can't look at her either, she's so disappointed in me, End Day or not. Tagoe and Malcolm flank me, quiet too since she and Francis already gave them shit for hitting the streets with me way past bedtime to rough Peck up.

"Not feeling so brave now, right?" Peck asks.

"Shut up." Aimee whips around, slamming her phone against the counter, startling everyone. "Don't follow us." She pushes open the kitchen door and Francis is not-so-casually hanging out by the staircase, trying to stay in the know but also keep back so he doesn't have to shame or punish a Decker.

Aimee drags me into the living room by my wrist. "So, what? Death-Cast calls and so you're free to lay into whoever the fuck you want?"

I guess Peck didn't tell her I was beating his ass before I got the alert. "I . . ."

"What?"

"There's no point lying. I was coming for him."

Aimee takes a step back, like I'm some monster who might lash out at her next, which kills me.

"Look, Ames, I was freaking out. I already felt like I didn't have a future before Death-Cast dropped that grenade in my lap. My grades have always been shit, I'm almost eighteen, I lost you, and I was wilding out because I didn't know what I was gonna do. I felt like a straight-up nobody and Peck pretty much said the same damn thing."

"You're not a nobody," Aimee says, shaking a little as she comes toward me, no longer scared. She takes my hand and we sit on the couch where she first told me she was leaving Pluto because her aunt on her mom's side had enough dough to take her in. A minute later, she also broke up with me because she wanted a clean slate, some cheap-ass tip from her elementary school classmate—Peck. "We didn't make sense anymore. And there's no point lying, like you said, even on your last day." She holds my hand while she cries, which I was doubting she'd even do because she was so pissed when she got here. "I read our love wrong, but that doesn't mean I don't love you. You were there for me when I needed to act out and be angry, and you made me happy when I was tired of hating everything. Nobodies can't make someone feel all of that." She hugs me, resting her chin on my shoulder the same way she would relax on my chest whenever she was about to watch one of her historical documentaries.

I hold her because I don't have anything new to say. I wanna kiss her, but I don't need some fakeness from her. She's mad close though, and I pull back so I can see her face because maybe one last kiss might be real for her too. She's staring at me and I lean in—

Tagoe comes into the living room and covers his eyes. "Oh! Sorry."

I back up. "Nah, you good."

"We should do the funeral," Tagoe says. "But take your time. It's your day. Sorry, it's not your day, it's not like a birthday, it's the opposite." He twitches. "I'm gonna get everyone in here." He steps.

"I don't want to hog you," Aimee says. She doesn't let me

go, not until everyone comes in.

I needed that hug. I'm looking forward to hugging the Plutos for a final Pluto Solar System group hug after the funeral.

I stay seated in the center of the couch. I'm battling my lungs for my next breath, hard-core. Malcolm sits to my left, Aimee to my right, and Tagoe at my feet. Peck keeps his distance, playing around on Aimee's phone. I hate that he's on her phone, but I broke his so I gotta stay shut.

This is my first Decker funeral, since my family didn't care about throwing one for themselves because we all had each other and didn't need anyone else, not coworkers or old friends. Maybe if I'd gone to others I'd be ready for the way Jenn Lori speaks directly to me and not the other attendees. It makes me feel vulnerable and seen, and it gets me teary eyed, like when someone sings "Happy Birthday" to me—seriously, every year, it never fails.

Failed.

". . . You never cried even though you had every reason to, like you were trying to prove something. The others . . ." Jenn Lori doesn't turn to the Plutos, not even a little. She doesn't break eye contact, like we're in a staring contest. Respect. "They all cried, but your eyes were so sad, Rufus. You didn't look at any of us for a couple days. I was convinced if someone posed as me you wouldn't have known any better. Your hollowness was heavy until you found friends, and more."

I turn and Aimee won't take her eyes off me—same sad look she gave me when she broke up with me.

"I always felt good when you were all together," Francis says.

He's not talking about tonight, I know that. Dying sucks, I bet, but getting locked up in prison while life keeps going on without you has gotta be worse.

Francis keeps staring but doesn't say anything else. "We don't have all day." He waves Malcolm over. "Your turn."

Malcolm steps to the center of the room, his hunched back to the kitchen. He clears his throat, and it's harsh, like he's got something stuck in his pipes, and some spit flies out of his mouth. He's always been a mess, the kind of dude who will unintentionally embarrass you because he has bad table manners and no filter. But he can also tutor you in algebra and keep a secret, and that's the stuff I would talk about if I were giving his eulogy. "You were—you are our bro, Roof. This is bullshit. Total fucking bullshit." His head hangs low as he picks at the cuticles on his left hand. "They should take me instead."

"Don't say that. Seriously, shut up."

"I'm serious," he says. "I know no one's living forever, but you should live longer than others. You matter more than other people. That's life. I'm this big nothing who can't keep a job bagging groceries, and you're—"

"Dying!" I interrupt, standing. I'm heated and I punch

him mad hard in the arm. Not saying sorry either. "I'm dying and we can't trade lives. You're not a big nothing, but you can step your damn game up anyway."

Tagoe stands, massaging his neck, beating back a twitch. "Roof, I'll miss you shutting us up like this. You stop me from assassinating Malcolm whenever he eats off our plates and doesn't flush twice. I was ready to see your damn mug until we were old." Tagoe takes off his glasses, wiping his tears with the back of his hand, and closes it into a tight fist. He looks up, like he's waiting for some Death piñata to drop from the ceiling. "You're supposed to be a lifer."

No one says anything, they just cry harder. The sound of everyone grieving me before I'm gone gives me crazy chills. I wanna console them and stuff, but I can't snap out of my daze. I spent a lot of time feeling guilty for living after I lost my family, but now I can't beat this weird Decker guilt for dying, knowing I'm leaving this crew behind.

Aimee steps up to the center and we all know this is about to get mad real. Brutal. "Is it lame to say I think I'm stuck in a nightmare? I always thought everyone was being so dramatic when they said that: 'This feels like a nightmare.' Like, really, that's all you feel when tragedy happens? I don't know how I wanted them to feel, but I can say now they hit the nail on the head. There's another cliché for you, whatever. I want to wake up. And if I can't wake up, I want to go to sleep forever where there's a chance I dream everything beautiful about you, like how you looked at me for me and not because you wanted to gawk at this fuckery on my face."

Aimee touches her heart, choking on her next words. "It hurts so much, Rufus, to think you won't be around for me to call or hug and . . ." She stops looking at me; she's squinting at something behind me, and her hand drops. "Did someone call the police?"

I jump out of my seat and see the flashes of red and blue in front of the duplex. I'm in full-on panic mode that feels insanely brief and mad long, like eight forevers. There's only one person who isn't surprised or freaking out. I turn to Aimee and her eyes follow mine back to Peck.

"You didn't," Aimee says, charging toward him. She snatches her phone from him.

"He assaulted me!" Peck shouts. "I don't care if he's on his way out!"

"He's not expired meat, he's another human being!" Aimee shouts back.

Holy shit. I don't know how Peck did it because he hasn't made any calls here, but he got the cops on me at my own funeral. I hope Death-Cast calls that bastard in the next few minutes.

"Go out the back," Tagoe says, twitches running wild.

"You have to come with me, you guys were there."

"We'll slow them down," Malcolm says. "Talk them out of it."

There's a knock on the door.

Jenn Lori points at the kitchen. "Go."

I grab my helmet, walking backward toward the kitchen, taking in all the Plutos. My pops once said goodbyes are "the most possible impossible" 'cause you never wanna say them, but you'd be stupid not to when given the shot. I'm getting cheated out of mine because the wrong person showed up at my funeral.

I shake my head and run out the back, catching my breath. I rush through the backyard we all hated because of relentless mosquitoes and fruit flies, then hop the fence. I sneak back around to the front of the house to see if there's a chance I can grab my bike before having to book it on my feet. The cop car is parked outside, but both officers must be inside, maybe even in the backyard by now if Peck snitched. I grab my bike and run with it down the sidewalk, hopping onto the seat once I get enough momentum.

I don't know where I'm going, but I keep going.

I lived through my funeral, but I wish I was already dead.

MATEO

2:52 a.m.

The third time was not the charm. I can't even tell you if Elle is actually a Decker, but I blocked her without investigating because she spammed me with links to "funny snuff videos gone wrong." I closed the app afterward. Have to admit it, I feel a little vindicated in how I've lived my life because people can be the worst. It's hard to have a respectful conversation, let alone make a Last Friend.

I keep receiving pop-up notifications for new messages, but I ignore them because I'm on the tenth level of A Dark Vanishing, this brutal Xbox Infinity game that has me wanting to look up cheat codes. My hero, Cove, a level-seventeen sorcerer with fire for hair, can't advance through this poverty-stricken kingdom without an offering to the princess. So I walk (well, Cove walks) past all the hawkers trying to sell off their bronze pins and rusty locks and go straight for the pirates. I must've gotten lost in my head on the way to the harbor because Cove steps on a land mine and I don't have time to ghost-phase through the explosion—Cove's arm flies through a hut's window, his head rockets into the sky, and his legs burst completely.

My heart pounds all through the loading screen until Cove is suddenly back, good as new. Cove's got it good.

I won't be able to respawn later.

I'm wasting away in here and . . .

There are two bookcases in my room. The blue bookcase on the bottom holds my favorite books that I could never get myself to purge when I did my monthly book donations to the teen health clinic down the block. The white bookcase on top is stacked with books I always planned on reading.

. . . I grab the books as if I'll have time to read them all: I want to know how this boy deals with a life that's moved on without him after he's resurrected by a ritual. Or what it was like for the little girl who couldn't perform at the school talent show because her parents received the Death-Cast alert while she was dreaming of pianos. Or how this hero known as the People's Hope receives a message from these Death-Cast-like prophets telling him he's going to die six days before the final battle where he was the key to victory against the King of All Evil. I throw these books across the room and even kick some of my favorites off their shelves because the line between favorites and books that will never be favorites doesn't matter anymore.

I rush over to my speakers and almost hurl them against the wall, stopping myself at the last second. Books don't require electricity, but speakers do, and it can all end here. The speakers and piano taunt me, reminding me of all the times I rushed home from school to have as much private time as I could with my music before Dad returned from his managerial shifts at the crafts store. I would sing, but not too loudly so my neighbors couldn't overhear me.

I tear down a map from the wall. I have never traveled outside of New York and will never get on a plane to touch down in Egypt to see temples and pyramids or travel to Dad's hometown in Puerto Rico to visit the rainforest he frequented as a kid. I rip up the map, letting all the countries and cities and towns fall at my feet.

It's chaos in here. It's a lot like when the hero in some blockbuster fantasy film is standing in the rubble of his war-ravaged village, bombed because the villains couldn't find him. Except instead of demolished buildings and disintegrated bricks, there are books open face-first on the floor, their damaged spines poking up, while others are piled on one another. I can't put everything back together or I'll find myself alphabetizing all the books and taping the map back together. (I swear this isn't some excuse to not clean my room.)

I turn off the Xbox Infinity, where Cove has respawned, all limbs together as if he didn't just explode minutes ago.

Cove is standing at the start point, idly dangling his staff.

I have to make a move. I pick up my phone again, reopening the Last Friend app. I hope I step over the people who are dangerous like land mines.

RUFUS

2:59 a.m.

Wish Death-Cast called before I ruined my life tonight.

If Death-Cast hit me up last night, they would've knocked me out of that dream I was having where I was losing a marathon to some little kids on tricycles. If Death-Cast hit me up one week ago, I wouldn't have been up late reading all the notes Aimee wrote me when we were still a thing. If Death-Cast called two weeks ago, they would've interrupted that argument I was having with Malcolm and Tagoe about how Marvel heroes are better than DC heroes (and maybe I would've asked the herald to weigh in). If Death-Cast called one month ago, they would've killed the dead silence that came with me not wanting to talk with anyone after Aimee left. But nah, Death-Cast called tonight while I was pounding on Peck, which led to Aimee dragging him to the duplex to confront me, which led to Peck getting the cops involved and cutting my funeral short, which led to me being one hundred percent alone right now.

None of that would've happened if Death-Cast called one day sooner.

I hear police sirens and keep pedaling. I hope something else is happening.

I give it a few more minutes before I take a break, stopping between a McDonald's and a gas station. It's mad bright, maybe kneeling over here is stupid, but staying in plain sight might be a good hiding spot. I don't know, I'm not James Bond, I don't have some guidebook on how to hide from the bad guys.

Shit, *I'm* the bad guy.

I can't keep moving, though. My heart is racing, my legs are on fire, and I gotta catch my breath.

I sit on the curb outside the gas station. It smells like piss and cheap beer. There's graffiti of two silhouettes on the wall with the air pumps for bike tires. The silhouettes are both shaped like the dude on the men's bathroom sign. In orange spray paint it says: *The Last Friend App.*

I keep getting dicked out of proper goodbyes. No final hug with my family, no final hug with the Plutos. It's not even the goodbyes, man, it's not getting to thank everyone for all they did for me. The loyalty Malcolm showed me time and time again. The entertainment Tagoe delivered with his B-movie scripts, like *Canary Clown and the Carnival of Doom* and *Snake Taxi*—though *Substitute Doctor* was just so bad, even for a bad movie. Francis's character impressions had me dying so hard I'd beg him to shut up because my rib cage hurt. The afternoon Jenn Lori taught me to play solitaire so I could keep myself moving, but also have alone time. The really great chat I had with Francis when we were the last two awake, about how instead of complimenting an attractive anyone on their looks my pickup lines should be more personal because "anyone can have pretty eyes, but only the right kind of person can hum the alphabet and make it your new favorite beat." The way Aimee always kept it real, even just now when she set me free by telling me she wasn't in love with me.

I could've really gone for one last Pluto Solar System group hug. I can't go back now. Maybe I shouldn't have run. The charges probably went up for running, but I didn't have time to think.

I gotta make this up to the Plutos. They spoke nothing but truth during their eulogies. I've messed up a bit lately, but I'm good. Malcolm and Tagoe wouldn't have been my boys if I weren't, and Aimee wouldn't have been my girl if I were scum.

They can't be with me, but that doesn't mean I have to be alone.

I really don't wanna be alone.

I pick myself up and walk over to the wall with the graffiti and some oil-stained poster for something called

Make-A-Moment. I stare at the Last Friend silhouettes on the wall. Ever since my family died, I would've bet anything I was gonna die alone. Maybe I will, but just because I was left behind doesn't mean I shouldn't have a Last Friend. I know there's a good Rufus in me, the Rufus I used to be, and maybe a Last Friend can drag him out of me.

Apps really aren't my thing, but neither is beating in people's faces, so I'm already out of my element today. I enter the app store and I download Last Friend. The download is mad fast; probably a bitch on my data, but who cares.

I register as a Decker, set up my profile, upload an old photo off my Instagram, and I'm good to go.

Nothing like receiving seven messages in my first five minutes to make me feel a little less lonely—even though one guy is throwing some bullshit about having the cure to death in his pants and yo, I'll take death instead.

MATEO

3:14 a.m.

I adjust the settings on my profile so I'll only be visible to anyone between the ages of sixteen and eighteen; older men and women can no longer hit on me. I take it one step further and now only registered Deckers can connect with me so I don't have to deal with anyone looking to buy a couch or pot. This diminishes the online numbers significantly. I'm sure there are hundreds, maybe thousands, of teens who received the alert today, but there are only eighty-nine registered Deckers between the ages of sixteen and eighteen online right now. I receive a message from an eighteen-year-old girl named Zoe, but I ignore it when I see a profile for a seventeen-year-old named Rufus; I've always liked that name. I click on his profile.

Name: Rufus Emeterio

Age: 17.

Gender: Male.

Height: 5'10".

Weight: 169 lbs.

Ethnicity: Cuban-American.

Orientation: Bisexual.

Job: Professional Time Waster.

Interests: Cycling. Photography.

Favorite Movies / TV Shows / Books: <skip>

Who You Were in Life: I survived something I shouldn't have.

Bucket List: Do it up.

Final Thoughts: It's about time. I've made mistakes, but I'm gonna go out right.

I want more time, more lives, and this Rufus Emeterio has already accepted his fate. Maybe he's suicidal. Suicide can't be predicted specifically, but the death itself is still foreseen. If he is self-destructive, I shouldn't be around him—he might actually be the reason I'm about to clock out. But his photo clashes with that theory: he's smiling and he has welcoming eyes. I'll chat with him and, if I get a good vibe, he might be the kind of guy whose honesty will make me face myself.

I'm going to reach out. There's nothing risky about hello.

Mateo T. (3:17 a.m.): sorry you'll be lost, Rufus.

I'm not used to reaching out to strangers like this. There have been a few times in the past I considered setting up a profile to keep Deckers company, but I didn't think I could provide much for them. Now that I'm a Decker myself I understand the desperation to connect even more.

Rufus E. (3:19 a.m.): Hey, Mateo. Nice hat.

He not only responded, but he likes my Luigi hat from my profile picture. He's already connecting to the person I want to become.

Mateo T. (3:19 a.m.): Thanks. Think I'm going to leave the hat here at home. I don't want the attention.

Rufus E. (3:19 a.m.): Good call. A Luigi hat isn't exactly a baseball cap, right?

Mateo T. (3:19 a.m.): Exactly.

Rufus E. (3:20 a.m.): Wait. You haven't left your house yet?

Mateo T. (3:20 a.m.): Nope.

Rufus E. (3:20 a.m.): Did you just get the alert a few minutes ago?

Mateo T. (3:20 a.m.): Death-Cast called me a little after midnight.

Rufus E. (3:20 a.m.): What have you been doing all night?

Mateo T. (3:20 a.m.): Cleaning and playing video games.

Rufus E. (3:20 a.m.): Which game?

Rufus E. (3:21 a.m.): N/m the game doesn't matter. Don't you have stuff you wanna do? What are you waiting for?

Mateo T. (3:21 a.m.): I was talking to potential Last Friends and they were . . . not great, is the kindest way to put it.

Rufus E. (3:21 a.m.): Why do you need a Last Friend before starting your day?

Mateo T. (3:22 a.m.): Why do YOU need a Last Friend when you have friends?

Rufus E. (3:22 a.m.): I asked you first.

Mateo T. (3:22 a.m.): Fair. I think it's insane to leave the apartment knowing something or SOMEONE is going to kill me. Also because there are "Last Friends" out there claiming they have the cure to death in their pants.

Rufus E. (3:23 a.m.): I spoke to that dick too! Not his dick, exactly. But I reported and blocked him afterward. I promise I'm better than that guy. I guess that's not saying much. Do you wanna video-chat? I'll send you the invite.

An icon of a silhouette speaking into a phone flashes. I almost reject the call, too confused about the suddenness of this moment, but I answer before the call goes away, before Rufus goes away. The screen goes black for a second, and then a total stranger with the face Rufus has in his profile appears. He's sweating and looking down, but his eyes quickly find me and I feel exposed, maybe even a little threatened, like he's some scary childhood legend that can reach through the screen and drag me into a dark underworld. In my overactive imagination's defense, Rufus has already tried bullying me out of my own world and into the world beyond, so—

"Yo," Rufus says. "You see me?"

"Yeah, hey. I'm Mateo."

"Hey, Mateo. My bad for springing the video chat on you," Rufus says. "Kind of hard to trust someone you can't see, you get me?"

"No worries," I say. There's a glare, which is a little blinding wherever he is, but I can still make out his light brown face. I wonder why he's so sweaty.

"You wanted to know why I'd prefer a Last Friend over my real-life friends, right?"

"Yeah," I say. "Unless that's too personal."

"Nah, don't worry about that. I don't think 'too personal' should exist between Last Friends. Long story short: I was with my parents and sister when our car crashed into the Hudson River and I had to watch them die. Living with that guilt isn't something I want for my friends. I have to throw that out there and make sure that you're okay with this."

"With you leaving your friends behind?"

"No. The chance you might have to watch me die."

I'm being faced with the heaviest of chances today: I may have to watch him die, unless it's the other way around, and both possibilities make me want to throw up. It's not that I feel a deep connection or anything to him already, but the idea of watching anyone die makes me sick and sad and angry—and that's why he's asking. But not doing anything is hardly comforting, either. "Okay, yeah. I can do it."

"Can you? There's the whole you-not-leaving-your-house problem. Last Friend or not, I'm not spending the rest of my life holed up in someone's apartment—and I don't want you to either, but you gotta meet me halfway, Mateo," Rufus says. The way he says my name is a little more comforting than the way I imagined that creep Philly would say it; it's more like a conductor giving a pep talk before a sold-out performance. "Believe me, I know it can get ugly out here. There was a point where I didn't think any of this was worthwhile."

"Well, what changed?" I don't mean it to sound like a challenge, but it kind of is. I'm not leaving the safety of my apartment that easily. "You lost your family and then what?"

"I wasn't about this life," Rufus says, looking away. "And I would've been game with game over. But that's not what my parents and sis wanted for me. It's mad twisted, but surviving showed me it's better to be alive wishing I was dead than dying wishing I could live forever. If I can lose it all and change my attitude, you need to do the same before it's too late, dude. You gotta go for it."

Go for it. That's what I said in my profile. He's paid more attention than the others and cared about me the way a friend should.

"Okay," I say. "How do we do this? Is there a handshake

or something?" I'm really hoping my trust isn't betrayed the way it's been in the past.

"We can get a handshake going when we meet, but until then I promise to be the Mario to your Luigi, except I won't hog the spotlight. Where we should we meet? I'm by the drugstore south of—"

"I have one condition," I say. His eyes squint; he's probably nervous about the curveball I'm throwing his way. "You said I have to meet you halfway, but you need to pick me up from home. It's not a trap, I swear."

"Sounds like a trap," Rufus says. "I'm gonna find a different Last Friend."

"It's really not! I swear." I almost drop the phone. I've screwed everything up. "Seriously, I—"

"I'm kidding, dude," he says. "I'll send you my phone number and you can text me your address. Then we can come up with a plan."

I'm just as relieved as I was when Andrea from Death-Cast called me Timothy during the call, when I thought I'd actually lucked into more life. Except this time it's okay to fully relax—I think. "Will do," I say.

He doesn't say bye or anything, he just looks at me for a little longer, likely sizing me up, or maybe questioning whether or not I'm actually luring him into a trap.

"See you in a bit, Mateo. Try not to die before I get there."

"Try not to die getting here," I say. "Be safe, Rufus."

Rufus nods and ends the video chat. He sends me his phone number and I'm tempted to call it to make sure he's the one who picks up, and not some creep who's paying him to collect addresses of young vulnerable guys. But if I keep second-guessing Rufus, this Last Friend business won't work.

I am a little concerned about spending my End Day with someone who's accepted dying, someone who's made mistakes. I don't know him, obviously, and he might turn out to be insanely destructive—he is outside in the middle of the night on a day he's slated for death, after all. But no matter what choices we make—solo or together—our finish line remains the same. It doesn't matter how many times we look both ways. It doesn't matter if we don't go skydiving to play it safe, even though it means we'll never get to fly like my favorite superheroes do. It doesn't matter if we keep our heads low when passing a gang in a bad neighborhood.

No matter how we choose to live, we both die at the end.

PART TWO

The Last Friend

A ship in harbor is safe,

but that is not what ships are built for.

—John A. Shedd

ANDREA DONAHUE

3:30 a.m.

Death-Cast did not call Andrea Donahue because she isn't dying today. Andrea herself, one of Death-Cast's top reps since their inception seven years ago, has made her fair share of End Day calls. Tonight, between midnight and three, Andrea called sixty-seven Deckers; not her best number, but it's proven difficult to beat her record of ninety-two calls in one shift ever since she was put under inspection for rushing through calls.

Allegedly.

On her way out of the building, limping, with her cane, Andrea hopes HR won't review her call log tonight, even though she knows hope is a dangerous thing in this profession. Andrea mixed up several names, too eager to get from one Decker to the next. It'd be terrible timing to lose her job, with all the physical therapy she needs after her accident on top of her daughter's mounting tuition. Not to mention it's the only job she's ever been great at because of one major life hack she discovered that has sent others out the door and on to less distressing jobs.

Rule number one of one: Deckers are no longer people.

That's it. Abide by this one and only rule and you won't find yourself wasting hours with the company's counselors. Andrea knows there's nothing she can do for these Deckers. She can't fluff their pillows or serve them last meals or keep them alive. She won't waste her breath praying for them. She won't get invested in their life stories and cry for them. She simply tells them they're dying and moves on. The sooner she gets off the phone, the sooner she reaches the next Decker.

Andrea reminds herself every night how lucky these Deckers are to have her at their service. She doesn't just tell people they're dying. She gives them a chance to really live.

But she can't live for them. That's on them.

She's already done her part, and she does it well.

RUFUS

3:31 a.m.

I'm biking toward that Mateo kid's house. He better not be a serial killer or so help me . . . Nah, he's chill. It's obvious he spends way too much time in his head and is probably too antisocial for his own damn good. I mean, check this: I'm legit gonna pick him up from his house, like he's some prince stuck in a high tower in need of rescuing. I think once the awkwardness is out of the way he'll make for a solid partner-in-crime. If not, we can always part ways. It'll suck 'cause that's a waste of time we don't have, but it is what it is. If nothing else, having a Last Friend should make my friends feel a little better about me running wild around the city. It makes me feel a little better, at least.

MALCOLM ANTHONY

3:34 a.m.

Death-Cast did not call Malcolm Anthony tonight because he isn't dying today, but his future has been threatened. Malcom and his best friend Tagoe didn't offer the police any clues as to where they believe Rufus may be headed. Malcolm told the police Rufus is a Decker and absolutely not worth chasing, but the officers couldn't let Rufus go unpursued, not after his act of aggravated assault. So Malcolm came up with a genius, life-ruining idea: get himself arrested.

Malcolm argued with the police officer and resisted arrest, but the great flaw in his plan was being unable to communicate it to Tagoe, who jumped into the argument too with more aggression than Malcolm himself was using.

Both Malcolm and Tagoe are currently being taken to the police station.

"This is pointless," Tagoe says in the back of the cop car. He's no longer sucking his teeth or shouting about how he did nothing, the way he did when the handcuffs first went on, even though Malcolm and Aimee urged him to shut up. "They're not gonna find Rufus. He'll dust them on his—"

"Shut up." This time Malcolm isn't worried about extra charges coming Tagoe's way. Malcolm already knows Rufus managed to get away on his bike. The bike wasn't there when they were being escorted out of the house. And he knows Rufus *can* dust the police on his bike, but he doesn't want them keeping an eye out for boys on bikes and find him. If they want him, they're gonna have to work for it.

Malcolm can't give his friend an extra day, but he can find him extra time to live.

This is assuming Rufus is still alive.

Malcolm is game to take this hit for Rufus, and he knows he's not innocent himself, that's common sense. The Plutos snuck out earlier tonight with the intention of kicking Peck's ass, which Rufus did a fine job of all by himself. Malcolm has never even been in a fight before, even though many paint him to be a violent young man because he's six feet tall, black, and close to two hundred pounds. Just because he's built like a wrestler doesn't mean he's a criminal. And now Malcolm and Tagoe will be tagged as juvenile delinquents.

But they'll have their lives.

Malcolm stares out the window, wishing he could glimpse Rufus on his bike turning a corner, and finally he cries, these loud, stuttering sobs, not because he'll now have a criminal record, not because he's scared to go to the police station, not even because Rufus is dying, but because the biggest crime of all tonight was not being able to hug his best friend goodbye.

MATEO

3:42 a.m.

There's a knock at the front door and I stop pacing.

Different nerves hit me all at once: What if it's not Rufus, even though no one else should be knocking at my door this late at night? What if it is Rufus and he's got a gang of thieves with him or something? What if it's Dad, who didn't tell me he woke up so that he could surprise me—the sort of End Day miracle they make Lifetime movies about?

I approach the door slowly, nudge up the peephole's cover, and squint at Rufus, who's looking right at me, even though I know he can't actually make me out.

"It's Rufus," he says from the other side.

I hope it's only him out there as I slide the chain free from its track. I pull the door open, finding a very three-dimensional Rufus in front of me, not someone I'm looking at through video chat or a peephole. He's in a dark gray fleece and is wearing blue basketball shorts over these Adidas gym tights. He nods at me. There's no smile or anything, but it's friendly all the same. I lean forward, my heart pounding, and peek out into the hallway to see if he has some friends hiding against the walls, ready to jump me for the little I have. But the hallway is empty and now Rufus is smiling.

"I'm on *your* turf, dude," Rufus says. "If anyone should be suspicious, it's me. This better not be some fake sheltered-kid act, yo."

"It's no act," I promise. "I'm sorry, I'm just . . . on edge."

"We're in the same boat." He holds out his hand and I shake it. His palm is sweaty. "You ready to bounce? This is a trick question, obviously."

"I'm ready-ish," I answer. He's come straight to my door for my company today, to lead me outside my sanctuary so we can live until we don't. "Let me grab a couple of things."

I don't invite him in, nor does he invite himself inside. He holds the door open from the outside while I grab the notes for my neighbors and my keys. I turn off the lights and walk past Rufus, and he closes the door behind me. I lock up. Rufus heads toward the elevator while I go the opposite way.

"Where you going?"

"I don't want my neighbors to be surprised or worried when I'm not answering." I drop off one note in front of 4F. "Elliot cooked extra food for me because I was only eating waffles." I come back Rufus's way and leave the second note in front of 4A. "And Sean was going to take a look at our busted stove, but he doesn't have to worry about that now."

"That's chill of you," he says. "I didn't think to do that."

I approach the elevator and peek over my shoulder at Rufus, this stranger who's following me. I don't feel uneasy, but I am guarded. He talks like we've been friends for a while, but I'm still suspicious. Which is fair, since the only things I know about him are that his name is Rufus, he rides a bike, he survived a tragedy, and he wants to be the Mario to my Luigi. And that he's also dying today.

"Whoa, we're not taking the elevator," Rufus says. "Two Deckers riding an elevator on their End Day is either a death wish or the start to a bad joke."

"Good point," I say. The elevator is risky. Best-case scenario? We get stuck. Worst-case scenario? Obvious. Thankfully, I have Rufus here to be calculating for me; I guess Last Friends double as life coaches that way. "Let's take the stairs," I say, as if there's some other option to get outside, like a rope hanging from the hallway window or one of those aircraft emergency slides. I go down the four flights like a child being trusted with stairs for the first time, its parents a couple steps ahead—except no one is here to catch me should I fall, or should Rufus trip and tumble into me.

We get downstairs safely. My hand hovers over the lobby door. I can't do it. I'm ready to retreat back upstairs until Rufus moves past me and pushes open the door, and the wet late-summer air brings me some relief. I'm even hit with hope that I, and only I—sorry, Rufus—can beat death. It's a nice second away from reality.

"Go ahead," Rufus says. He's pressuring me, but that's the whole point of our dynamic. I don't want to disappoint either of us, especially myself.

I exit the lobby but stop once the door is behind me. I was last outside yesterday afternoon, when I was coming home from visiting Dad, an uneventful Labor Day. But being out here now is different. I check out the buildings I've grown up with but never paid any special attention to. There are lights on in my neighbors' apartments. I can even hear one couple moaning; the roaring audience laughter from a comedy special; someone else laughing from another window, possibly at the very loud comedy show or possibly because they're being tickled by a lover or laughing at a joke someone cared enough to text them at this late hour.

Rufus claps, snapping me out of my trance. "You get ten points." He goes to a railing and unlocks his steel-gray bike.

"Where are we going?" I ask, inching farther away from the door. "We should have a battle plan."

"Battle plans usually involve bullets and bombs," Rufus says. "Let's roll with game plan." He wheels his bike toward the street corner. "Bucket lists are pointless. You're not gonna get everything done. You gotta go with the flow."

"You sound like a pro at dying."

That was stupid. I know it before Rufus shakes his head.

"Yeah, well," Rufus says.

"I'm sorry. I just . . ." A panic attack is coming on; my chest is tightening, my face is burning up, my skin and scalp are itchy. "I can't wrap my head around the fact that I'm living a day where I might need a bucket list." I scratch my head and take a deep breath. "This isn't going to work. It's going to backfire on us. Hanging out together is a bad idea because it'll only double our chances of dying sooner. Like a Decker hot zone. What if we're walking down the block and I trip and bang my head against a fire hydrant and—" I shut up, cringing from the phantom pain you get when you think about falling face-first onto spiked fences or having your teeth punched out of your mouth.

"You can do your own thing, but we're done for whether we hang or not," Rufus says. "No point fearing it."

"Not that easy. We're not dying from natural causes. How can we try to live knowing some truck might run us down when we're crossing the street?"

"We'll look both ways, like we've been trained to do since we were kids."

"And if someone pulls out a gun?"

"We'll stay out of bad neighborhoods."

"And if a train kills us?"

"If we're on train tracks on our End Day, we're asking for it."

"What if—"

"Don't do this to yourself!" Rufus closes his eyes, rubbing them with his fist. I'm driving him crazy. "We can play this game all day, or we can stay out here and maybe, like, live. Don't do your last day wrong."

Rufus is right. I know he's right. No more arguing. "It's going to take me some time to get where you are with this. I don't become fearless just because I know my options are do something and die versus do nothing and still die." He doesn't remind me that we don't have a whole lot of time. "I have to say goodbye to my dad and my best friend." I walk toward the 110th Street subway station.

"We can do that," Rufus says. "I have nothing I'm gunning to do. I had my funeral and that didn't exactly go as planned. Not really expecting a do-over, though."

I'm not surprised someone so boldly living his End Day had a funeral. I'm sure he had more than two people to say goodbye to.

"What happened?" I say.

"Nonsense." Rufus doesn't elaborate.

I'm looking both ways, getting ready to cross the street, when I spot a dead bird in the road, its small shadow cast from a bodega's lit awning. The bird has been flattened; its severed head is a couple inches away. I think it was run down by a car and then split by a bike—hopefully not Rufus's. This bird definitely didn't receive an alert telling it that it would die tonight, or maybe yesterday, or the day before, though I like to imagine the driver that killed it at least saw the bird and honked their horn. But maybe that warning wouldn't have mattered.

Rufus sees the bird too. "That sucks."

"We need to get it out of the street." I look around for something to scoop it up with; I know I shouldn't touch it with my bare hands.

"Say what?"

"I don't have this dead-is-dead-so-just-walk-away attitude," I say.

"I definitely don't have this 'dead-is-dead-so-just-walk-away attitude' either," Rufus says, an edge to his voice.

I need to check myself. "I'm sorry. Again." I quit my hunt. "Here's the thing. When I was in third grade, I was playing outside in the rain when a baby bird fell out of its nest. I caught every second of it: the moment the bird leapt off the edge of the nest, spread its wings, and fell. The way its eyes darted around for help. Its leg broke on impact, and it couldn't drag itself to shelter, so the rain was pummeling it."

"That bird had some bad instincts, jumping out the tree like that," Rufus says.

The bird dared to leave home, at least. "I was scared it was going to freeze to death or drown in a puddle, so I ran out and sat down on the ground with the bird, sort of shielding it with my legs, like a tower." The cold wind got the best of us, and I had to take off from school the following Monday and Tuesday because I'd gotten really sick.

"What happened then?"

"I have no idea," I admit. "I remember I got a cold and missed school, but I must've blocked out what happened to the bird. I think about it every now and again because I know I didn't find a ladder and return it to its nest. Sucks to think I left it there to die in the rain." I've often thought that helping that bird was my first act of kindness, something I did because I wanted to help another, and not because my dad or some teacher expected me to do it. "I can do better for this bird, though."

Rufus looks at me, takes a deep breath, then turns his back and wheels his bike away from me. My chest tightens again, and it's very possible I have some health problems I'm going to discover and die from today, but I'm hit with relief when Rufus parks his bike along the sidewalk, throwing down the kickstand with his foot. "Let me find you something for the bird," he says. "Don't touch it."

I make sure no cars are coming from up the block.

Rufus returns with a discarded newspaper and hands it to me. "Best I can find."

"Thanks." I use the newspaper to scoop up the bird's body and its severed head. I walk toward the community garden opposite the subway station, set right in between the basketball court and the playground.

Rufus appears beside me on his bike, pedaling slowly.

"What are you doing with that?"

"Burying it." I enter the garden and find a corner behind a tree, away from the spot where community gardeners have been planting fruit trees and flowers and making the world glow a little more. I kneel and place the newspaper down, nervous the head is going to roll away. Rufus hasn't commented on it, but I feel the need to add, "I can't just leave the bird out there to be tossed into a trash can or flattened by cars over and over and over."

I like the idea of a bird that died so tragically ahead of its time resting amid life here in the garden. I even imagine that this tree was once a person, some Decker who was cremated and had asked to have their ashes packed into a biodegradable urn with a tree seed to give it life.

"It's a couple minutes after four," Rufus informs me.

"I'll be fast."

I take it he's not the bury-a-bird type. I know many people won't agree or understand this sentiment. After all, to most people, a bird is nothing compared to an actual human being, because actual human beings put on ties and go to work, they fall in love and get married, and they have kids and raise them. But birds do all of this too. They work—no ties, you got me there—and mate and nurture baby birds until they can fly. Some of them become pets who entertain children, children who learn to love and be kind to animals. Other birds are living until their time is up.

But this sentiment is a Mateo thing, meaning it's always made others think I'm weird. I don't share thoughts like these with just anyone, rarely even with Dad or Lidia.

Two fists can fit in this plot, and I'm shuffling the bird's body and head off the newspaper and into the hole right when a flash goes off behind me. No, the first thing I thought wasn't that an alien was beaming down warriors to take me out—okay, fine, it was. I turn to find Rufus aiming his phone's camera at me.

"Sorry," Rufus says. "Not every day you see someone burying a bird."

I scoop the soil over the bird, smoothing it flat before standing. "I hope someone is this kind to us when it's over."

RUFUS

4:09 a.m.

Yo, Mateo is *too good*. Definitely not suspicious of him anymore, it's not like he's got it in him to jump me. But I'm mad shocked to meet someone so . . . pure? I wouldn't say I've only ever surrounded myself with assholes, but Malcolm and Tagoe are never gonna bury a bird in their lives, let's be real fucking clear about that. Beating down that bastard Peck tonight proves we're not innocent. I'll bet you anything Mateo has no idea how to make a fist and couldn't imagine himself getting violent, not even when he was a kid and dumb shit was forgiven and written off because he was young.

There's no way I'm telling him about Peck. I'll take it to my grave today.

"We out to see who first?"

"My dad. We can take this subway." Mateo points. "It's only two stops downtown, but it's safer than walking."

Two stops downtown would be a quick five-minute bike ride for me, and I'm tempted to just meet him there, but my gut is telling me this Mateo kid will screw up and leave me hanging outside the train station. I carry my bike down the stairs by its handlebars and seat. I roll my bike around the corner while Mateo cautiously hangs back a bit, and I catch him peeking before following me, like when I went to that haunted house thing in Brooklyn with Olivia a few years ago—except I was a kid. I don't know what he's expecting to find, and I'm not asking either.

"You're good," I say. "Coast is clear."

Mateo creeps behind me, still suspicious of the empty corridor leading to the turnstiles. "I wonder how many other Deckers are hanging out with strangers right now. A lot are probably dead by now. Car accident or fire or shot or fallen down a manhole or . . ." He stops himself. Dude really knows how to paint a picture of tragedy. "What if they were on their way to say bye to someone close to them and then—" Mateo claps. "Gone. It's not fair. . . . I hope they weren't alone."

We get to the MetroCard vending machine. "Nope. Not fair. I don't think it matters who you're with when you die—someone's company isn't gonna keep you alive once Death-Cast hits you up." This has gotta be taboo for a Last Friend to say, but I'm not wrong. Still feel a little bad when it shuts Mateo up.

Deckers get some perks, like free unlimited passes for the

subway, you just gotta bother the teller with some form. But the "unlimited" part is bullshit because they expire at the end of your End Day. A few weeks ago the Plutos claimed we were dying so we could score free passes for our adventure to Coney Island, thinking the dude would give us a break and let us through. But nah, he had us waiting for confirmation from Death-Cast servers, which can take longer than waiting for an express train, so we just bounced. I buy an unlimited MetroCard, the non-Decker, I-still-got-tomorrows edition, and Mateo copies.

We swipe our way in to the platform. This could be our last ride for all we know.

Mateo points back at the booth. "Is it crazy to think the MTA won't need any station staffers in a few years because machines—maybe even robots—will take over their jobs? It's sort of happening already if you think about . . ."

The roar of the approaching train drowns Mateo out a little at the end there, but it's fine, I get what he's saying. The real victory here is catching a train instantly. Now we can safely rule out falling onto the exposed tracks, getting stuck while rats run by us, and straight chopped up and flattened by the train—damn, Mateo's grimness is already rubbing off on me.

Before the doors even open, I see one of those train takeovers going down, the ones where college kids host parties on trains to celebrate not getting the alert Mateo and I got. I guess dorm parties got old, so they're wilding out on the subway instead—and we're joining them, dammit. "Let's go," I tell Mateo when the doors open. "Hurry." I rush and wheel my bike in, asking someone to make room for us, and when I turn to make sure my back tire isn't keeping Mateo from getting in, I see he's not behind me at all.

Mateo is standing outside the car, shaking his head, and at the last second before the doors close he darts into the empty car ahead of mine, one that has sleeping passengers and isn't blasting a remixed version of "Celebration." (It's a classic anthem, but let's retire it already.)

Look, I don't know why Mateo bitched out, but it's not gonna ruin my vibe. It's a party car—I wasn't asking him to go bungee jumping or skydiving. It's far from daredevil territory.

"We Built This City" comes on, and a girl with two handheld stereos hops onto the bench seat to dance. Some dude is hitting on her, but her eyes are closed and she's just straight-up lost in her moment. In the corner some dude with a hood over his face is knocked out; either he's had a really good time or there's a dead Decker on this train.

Not funny.

I lean my bike against an empty bench seat—yeah, I'm that guy whose bike gets in everyone's way, but I'm also dying, so cut me some slack—and step over the sleeping guy's feet to peek into the next car. Mateo is staring into my car like some kid who's been grounded and forced to watch his friends play from his bedroom window. I gesture for him to come over, but he shakes his head and stares down at the floor, never looking up at me again.

Someone taps my shoulder. I turn and it's this gorgeous hazel-eyed black girl with an extra can of beer in her hand. "Want one?"

"Nah, I'm good." I shouldn't be getting buzzed.

"More for me. I'm Callie."

I miss that a little. "Kelly?"

She leans in to me, her breasts against my chest and her lips against my ear. "Callie!"

"Hey, Callie, I'm Rufus," I say back into her ear since she's already here. "What are you—"

"My stop is next," Callie interrupts. "Want to get off with me? You're cute and seem like a nice guy."

She's definitely my type, which means she's also Tagoe's type. (Malcolm's type is any girl who likes him back.) But since there isn't much I can offer her, besides what she's obviously suggesting, I gotta pass. Having sex with a college girl has gotta be on mad people's bucket lists—young people, married-dude people, boys, girls, you get it.

"I can't," I say. I gotta have Mateo's back, and I also have Aimee on the brain. I'm not trying to cheat that with something fake like this.

"Sure you can!"

"I really can't, and it sucks," I say. "I'm taking my friend to the hospital to see his dad."

"Forget you then." Callie turns her back on me, and she's talking to another guy within a minute, which is good on her since he actually follows her out of the train when we come to her stop. Maybe Callie and that guy will grow old together and tell their kids how they met at a subway party. But I bet you anything they'll just have sex tonight and he'll call her "Kelly" in the morning.

I take photos of the energy in the car: the guy who's managed to get the attention of the beautiful girl. Twins dancing together. The crushed beer cans and water bottles. And the freaking life of it all. I put my phone in my pocket, grab my bike, and wheel it through the doors between the cars—the ones the overhead announcements are constantly reminding us are for emergencies only. End Day or not, that announcement can suck it. The tunnel's air is chill, and the train's wheels screeching and screaming on the rails is a sound I won't miss. I enter the next car, but Mateo keeps staring at the floor.

I sit beside him and am about to go off on him, to tell him how I didn't take some older girl's invite to have sex on my last day to live ever because I'm a good Last Friend, but it's pretty damn obvious he doesn't need that guilt trip. "Yo, tell me more about these robots. The ones who are gonna take everyone's jobs."

Mateo stops looking at the floor for a sec, turning to see if I'm toying with him, and I'm clearly not, I'm mad chill on all this. He grins and rambles so hard: "It's going to take a while because evolution is never fast, but the robots are already here. You know that, right? There are robots that can cook dinner for you and unload the dishwasher. You can teach them secret handshakes, which is pretty mind-blowing, and they can solve a Rubik's Cube. I even saw a clip of a break-dancing robot a couple months ago. But don't you think these robots are one giant distraction while other robots receive job training at some underground robot headquarters? I mean, why pay someone twenty dollars an hour to give directions when our phones already do that, or even better, when a robot can do it for you? We're screwed." Mateo shuts up and is no longer grinning.

"Buzzkill, right?"

"Yeah," Mateo says.

"At least you won't have to ever worry about your boss firing you for a robot," I say.

"That's a pretty dark bright side," Mateo says.

"Dude, today is one huge dark bright side. Why'd you bail on the party car?"

"We have no business on that car," Mateo says. "What are we celebrating, dying? I'm not trying to dance with strangers while on my way to say goodbye to my dad and best friend, knowing damn well there's a chance I may not even reach them. That's just not my scene, and those aren't my people."

"It's just a party." The train stops. He doesn't respond. It's possible Mateo not being a daredevil will keep us alive longer, but I'm not banking on it being a memorable End Day.

AIMEE DUBOIS

4:17 a.m.

Death-Cast did not call Aimee DuBois because she isn't dying today. But she's losing Rufus—lost him already because of her boyfriend.

Aimee is speed-walking home, followed by Peck. "You're a monster. What kind of person tries to get someone arrested at their own funeral?"

"I got jumped by three guys!"

"Malcolm and Tagoe didn't touch you! And now they're going to jail."

Peck spits. "They ran their mouths, that's not on me."

"You have to leave me alone. I know you never liked Rufus, and he didn't give you any reason to, but he's still really important to me. I always wanted him in the picture and now he won't be. I had even less time with him because of you. If I can't see him, I don't want to see you either."

"You ending it with me?"

Aimee stops. She doesn't want to turn Peck's way because she hasn't considered this question yet. People make mistakes. Rufus made a mistake attacking Peck. Peck shouldn't have had his friends send the police after Rufus, but he wasn't wrong to have done so. Well, legally, no. Morally, hell yes.

"You keep putting him before me," Peck says. "I'm the one you've been coming to for all your problems. Not the guy who almost killed me. I'll let you think on that."

Aimee stares at Peck. He's a white teen with low-hanging jeans, baggy sweater, Caesar cut, and dried blood on his face because he's dating her.

Peck walks away and Aimee lets him.

She doesn't know where she stands with Peck in this world of gray.

She's not quite sure where she stands with herself either.

MATEO

4:26 a.m.

I'm failing to break out.

I couldn't surround myself with more strangers. They were harmless for the most part, the only red flag being how I don't want to be around people who get so drunk they pass out and eventually black out the nights they're lucky to be living. But I wasn't honest with Rufus, because, on a deep level, I do believe partying on the train is my kind of scene. It's just that the fear of disappointing others or making a fool of myself always wins.

I'm actually surprised Rufus is chaining his bike to a gate and following me into the hospital. We walk up to the front desk, and a red-eyed clerk smiles at me but doesn't actually ask how he can help me.

"Hi. I'd like to see my father. Mateo Torrez in Intensive Care." I pull out my ID and slide it across the glass counter to Jared, as the name tag pinned to his sky-blue scrubs reads.

"Visiting hours ended at nine, I'm afraid."

"I won't be long, I promise." I can't leave without saying goodbye.

"It's not happening tonight, kid," Jared says, the smile still there, except a little more unnerving. "Visiting hours resume at nine. Nine to nine. Catchy, right?"

"Okay," I say.

"He's dying," Rufus says.

"Your father is dying?" Jared asks me, the bizarre smile of someone working a four-in-the-morning shift finally gone.

"No." Rufus grabs my shoulder and squeezes. "*He* is dying. Do him a solid and let him upstairs to say goodbye to his father."

Jared doesn't look as if he particularly appreciates being spoken to this way, and I'm not a fan of it myself, but who knows where I would be without Rufus to speak up for me. I actually know where I'd be: outside this hospital, probably crying and holed up somewhere hoping I make it to nine. Hell, I'd probably still be at home playing video games or trying to talk myself into getting out of the apartment.

"Your father is in a coma," Jared says, looking up from his computer.

Rufus's eyes widen, like his mind has been blown. "Whoa. Did you know that?"

"I know that." Seriously, if it's not his first week on the job, Jared's got to be on some forty-hour shift. "I still want to say goodbye."

Jared gets his act together and stops questioning me. I get his initial resistance, rules are rules, but I'm happy when he doesn't drag this out any longer by asking me for proof. He takes photos of us, prints out visitor passes, and hands the passes to me. "Sorry about all this. And, you know . . ." His condolences, while hardly there, are way more appreciated than the ones I received from Andrea at Death-Cast.

We walk toward the elevator.

"Did you also wanna punch the smile off his face?" Rufus asks.

"Nope." It's the first time Rufus and I have spoken to each other since getting out of the train station. I press the visitor pass across my shirt, making sure it sticks with a couple pats. "But thanks for getting us in here. I would've never played the Decker card myself."

"No problem. We have zero time for could've-would've-should've," Rufus says.

I push the elevator button. "I'm sorry I didn't join in on the party car."

"I don't need an apology. If you're fine with your decision, that's on you." He walks away from the elevator and toward the staircase. "I'm not cool with us riding the elevator, though, so let's do this."

Right. Forgot. It's probably better to leave the elevators available to the nurses and doctors and patients at this time of night anyway.

I follow Rufus up the stairs, and it's only the second floor but I'm already out of breath. Really, maybe there's something physically wrong with me and maybe I'll die here on these steps before I can reach Dad or Lidia or Future Mateo. Rufus gets impatient and sprints up, sometimes even skipping two steps at a time.

On the fifth floor, Rufus calls down to me. "I hope you're serious about opening yourself up to new experiences, though. Doesn't have to be something like the party car."

"I'll feel ballsier once I've said my goodbyes," I say.

"Respect," Rufus says.

I trip up the steps, landing flat on the sixth floor. I take a deep breath as Rufus comes back down to help me up. "That was such a kid fall," I say.

Rufus shrugs. "Better forward than backward."

We continue to the eighth floor. The waiting area is straight ahead, with vending machines and a peach-colored couch between folding chairs. "Would you mind waiting out here? I sort of want one-on-one time with him."

"Respect," Rufus says again.

I push open the blue double doors and walk through. Intensive Care is quiet except for some light chatter and beeping machines. I watched this thirty-minute documentary on Netflix a couple years ago about how much hospitals have changed since Death-Cast came into the picture. Doctors work closely with Death-Cast, obviously, receiving instant updates about their terminal patients who've signed off on this agreement. When the alerts come in, nurses dial back on life support for their patients, prepping them for a "comfortable death" instead with last meals, phone calls to families, funeral arrangements, getting wills in order, priests for prayers and confessions, and whatever else they can reasonably supply.

Dad has been here for almost two weeks. He was brought in right after his first embolic stroke at work. I freaked out really hard, and before I went ahead and signed off on Dad's contact information being uploaded into the hospital's database, I spent the night of his admittance praying his cell phone wouldn't ring. Now, I'm finally free of the anxiety that Dr. Quintana might call to notify me my dad is going to die, and it's good to know Dad has at least another day in him; hopefully way more than one.

I show a nurse my visitor pass and bullet straight into Dad's room. He's very still, as machines are breathing for him. I'm close to breaking down because my dad might wake up to a world without me, and I won't be around to comfort him. But I don't break. I sit down beside him, sliding my hand under his, and rest my head on our hands. The last time I cried was the first night at the hospital—when things were looking really grim as we approached midnight. I swore he was minutes away from death.

I hate to admit it, but I'm a little frustrated Dad is not awake right now. He was there when my mother brought me into this life and when she left us, and he should be here for me now. Everything is going to change for him without me: no more dinners where instead of telling me about his day he would go on remembering the trials my mother put him through before she finally agreed to marry him, and how the love they shared was worth it while it lasted; he'll have to put away the invisible pad he would whip out whenever I said something stupid as a promise to embarrass me in front of my future children, even though I never really saw kids as part of my future; and he'll stop being a father, or at least won't have anyone to parent.

I release Dad's hand, grab a pen that's on his bedside chest of drawers, pull out our photo, and write on the back of it with an unsteady hand:

Thank you for everything, Dad.
I'll be brave, and I'll be okay.
I love you from here to there.
Mateo

I leave the photo on top of the chest.

Someone knocks on the door. I turn, expecting Rufus, but it's Dad's nurse, Elizabeth. Elizabeth has been taking care of Dad during the night shift, and she's always so patient with me whenever I call the hospital for updates. "Mateo?" She eyes me mournfully; she must know.

"Hi, Elizabeth."

"I'm sorry to interrupt. How are you feeling? Would you like me to call down to the cafeteria and see if they've put the Jell-O out yet?"

Yeah, she definitely knows.

"No, thank you." I focus on Dad again, how vulnerable and still he is. "How's he doing?"

"Stable. Nothing for you to worry about. He's in good hands, Mateo."

"I know."

I tap my fingers on Dad's chest of drawers, where his house keys, wallet, and clothes are. I know I have to say goodbye. Never mind that Rufus is out there waiting for me—Dad never would've wanted me spending my End Day in this room, even if he were awake. "You know about me, right?"

"Yes." Elizabeth covers Dad's skinny body with a new sheet.

"It isn't fair. I don't want to leave without hearing his voice."

Elizabeth is on the opposite side of the bed, her back to the window while mine is toward the door. "Can you tell me a little bit about him? I've been taking care of him for a couple weeks and all I know about his personal life is he wears mismatched socks and has a great son."

I hope Elizabeth isn't asking this because she doesn't think Dad will wake up to tell her himself. I don't want Dad dying soon after I do. He once told me that stories can make someone immortal as long as someone else is willing to listen. I want him to keep me alive the same way he did my mother.

"Dad loves creating lists. He wanted me to start a blog for his lists. He thought we'd become rich and famous, and that commenters would request special lists. He even believed he'd finally get on TV because of the lists. Appearing on TV has been a dream of his since he was a kid. I never had the heart to tell him his lists weren't that funny, but I liked seeing how his mind worked so I was happy whenever he gave me a new one to read. He was a really great storyteller. It sometimes feels like whiplash, like I was walking on the Coney Island beach with him where he proposed to my mother the first time—"

"The *first* time?"

Rufus. I turn and find him standing in the doorway.

"Sorry to eavesdrop. I was checking in on you."

"Don't worry about it. Come in," I say. "Elizabeth, this is Rufus, he's my . . . he's my Last Friend." I hope he's actually telling the truth, how he wanted to see how I was doing, and not that he's here to say goodbye and suggest we go our separate ways.

Rufus leans against the wall with folded arms. "So: this proposal?"

"My mother turned him down twice. He said she liked playing hard to get. Then she found out she was pregnant with me and he got down on one knee in the bathroom and she smiled and said yes."

I really like that moment.

I know I wasn't there, but the memory I've created in my head over the years is crystal clear. I don't know exactly what that bathroom looked like, since it was in their first, shoebox-sized apartment, but Dad always commented on how the walls were a muted gold, which I always took to mean aged yellow, and he said the floor tiles were checkered. And then there's my mother, who comes alive for me in his stories. In this particular one she's laughing and crying about making sure I'm not brought into this world a bastard, because of her family's traditions. It never would've mattered to me in the long run. The whole bastard thing is stupid.

"Sweetie, I wish I could wake him up for you. I really do."

Too bad life doesn't allow us to turn its gears, like a clock, when we need more time. "Can I have ten minutes alone? I think I know how I can say bye."

"Take your time, dude," Rufus says. It's surprising and generous.

"No," I say. "Give me ten minutes and come get me."

Rufus nods. "You got it."

Elizabeth rests a hand on my shoulder. "I'll be out by the front desk if you need anything."

Elizabeth and Rufus leave. The door closes behind them.

I hold Dad's hand. "It's time I tell you a story for once.

You were always asking me—begging me, sometimes—to tell you more about my life and how my day was, and I always shut down. But me talking is all we've got now, and I'm crossing my fingers and toes and unmentionables that you can hear me." I grip his hand, wishing he'd squeeze back.

"Dad, I . . ."

I was raised to be honest, but the truth can be complicated. It doesn't matter if the truth won't make a mess, sometimes the words don't come out until you're alone. Even that's not guaranteed. Sometimes the truth is a secret you're keeping from yourself because living a lie is easier.

I hum "Take This Waltz" by the late Leonard Cohen, one of those songs that never apply to me but help me lose myself anyway. I sing the lyrics I do remember, stumbling over some words and repeating others out of place, but it's a song Dad loved and I hope he hears me singing it since he can't.

RUFUS

4:46 a.m.

I'm sitting outside Mateo's father's room and I'm charged with telling Mateo it's time to go. Getting him out of his apartment was one thing, but I'm probably gonna have to knock the dude out and drag him out the hospital; someone would've had to do the same to get me away from my pops, coma or no coma.

That nurse, Elizabeth, looks at the clock and then at me before carrying a tray of stale-smelling food into another room.

Time for me to grab Mateo.

I get up from the floor and crack open the door to the room. Mateo is holding his father's hand and singing some song I've never heard before. I knock on the door and Mateo jumps, straight startled.

"Sorry, man. You good?"

Mateo stands and his face is flushed, like we got into a

snapping battle and I played him hard in front of mad people. "Yeah. I'm fine." That's a damn lie. "I should tidy up." It takes a minute before he lets go of his father's hand, almost like his father is holding him back, but Mateo manages to break free. He picks up a clipboard and drops it into a rack above his father's bed. "Dad usually leaves all his cleaning for Saturdays because he hates the idea of coming home from work on weekdays to more work. On the weekends we cleaned and earned our TV marathons." Mateo looks around and the rest of the room is pretty damn clean. I mean, I'm not eating off the floor, but that's a hospital thing.

"Did you get your goodbye in?"

Mateo nods. "Sort of." He walks toward the bathroom. "I'm going to make sure it's clean in there."

"I'm sure it is."

"I should make sure they have clean cups ready for when he wakes up."

"They're gonna take care of him."

"He might need a warmer sheet. He can't tell us if he's cold."

I walk over and hold Mateo by the shoulders, trying to still him 'cause he's shaking. "He doesn't want you here, okay?" Mateo's eyebrows squeeze together and his eyes get red. Sad-red, not pissed-red. "I didn't mean it like that. I say stupid things. He doesn't want you wasting away here. Look, you got a chance to say goodbye—I didn't get that with my fam. I took too much time trying to figure out what I was gonna say. I'm happy for you, but mad jealous, too. And if that isn't enough to get you out, I need you. I need a friend by my side."

Mateo looks around the room again, no doubt convincing himself he definitely does need to scrub the toilet this very second, or to make sure every single cup in this hospital is spotless so his father can't end up with a bad one, but I squeeze his shoulders and wake him out of all that. He heads over to the bed and kisses his father's forehead. "Goodbye, Dad."

Mateo walks backward, dragging his feet, and waves bye to his sleeping father. My heart is pounding, and I'm only a witness to this moment. Mateo must be about to explode. I place a hand on his shoulder and he flinches. "Sorry," he says at the doorway. "I really hope he wakes up today, just in time, you know."

I'm not betting on it, but I nod anyway.

We leave the room, and Mateo peeks in one last time before closing the door behind us.

MATEO

4:58 a.m.

I stop at the corner of the hospital.

It's not too late to run back to Dad's room and just live out my day there. But that's not fair, to put others in the hospital at risk of me, the ticking time bomb. I can't believe I'm back outside in a world that will kill me, accompanied by a Last Friend whose fate is screwed too.

There's no way this courage will hold.

"You good?" Rufus asks.

I nod. I really want to listen to some music right now, especially after singing in Dad's room. I cringe because Rufus caught me singing, but it's all right, it's all right. He didn't say anything, so maybe he didn't hear that much. The awkwardness of it all makes me even more antsy to listen to music, to hide away with something that has always been very solitary for me. Another of Dad's favorites is "Come What May," which my mother sang to him and womb-me during a shower they took together before her water broke. The line about loving someone until the end of time is haunting. The same could be said for my other favorite song, "One Song," from *Rent*. I'm extra wired, wanting to play it, especially as a Decker, since it's about wasted opportunities, empty lives, and time dying. My favorite lyric is "*One song before I go . . .*"

"Sorry if I pressured you to leave," Rufus adds. "You asked me to get you out of there, but I'm not sure you meant it."

"I'm glad you did," I admit. My dad would want this.

I look both ways before crossing the street. There are no cars, but there's a man on the corner up ahead tearing through trash bags, furiously, as if there's a garbage truck approaching to steal them all away. It's possible he's searching for something he accidentally threw out, but judging by the split leg of his jeans and the grime on his rust-colored vest, it's safe to guess he's homeless. The man retrieves a half-eaten orange, tucks it into his armpit, and continues going through the trash bags. He turns toward us as we approach the corner.

"Got a dollar? Any change?"

I keep my head low, same as Rufus, and walk past the man. He doesn't call after us or say anything else.

"I want to give him some money," I tell Rufus, even though it makes me really nervous to do so alone. I go through my pockets and find eighteen dollars. "Do you have some cash to give him, too?"

"Not to be a dick, but why?"

"Because he needs it," I say. "He's digging through trash for food."

"There's a chance he's not even homeless. I've been duped before," he says.

I stop. "I've been lied to before too." I've also made the mistake of ignoring others asking for help, and it's not fair. "I'm not saying we should give him our life savings, just a few bucks."

"When were you duped?"

"I was in fifth grade, walking to school. This guy asked for a dollar, and when I pulled out my five singles for lunch money, he punched me in the face and took it all." I'm embarrassed to admit that I was pretty inconsolable at school, crying so hard until Dad left work to visit me in the nurse's office to see how I was doing. He even walked me to school for two weeks afterward and begged me to be more careful with strangers, especially when money is involved. "I just don't think I should be the judge of who actually needs my help or not, like they should do a dance or sing me a song to prove they're worthy. Asking for help when you need it should be enough. And what's a dollar? We'll make a dollar again."

We won't actually make another dollar, but if Rufus was smart (or paranoid) like I was, he should have more than enough money in his bank account as well. I can't read Rufus's face, but he parks his bike, hits down on the kickstand. "Let's do this then." He reaches into his pocket and finds twenty dollars in cash. He walks ahead of me and I tail after him, my heart pounding, a little nervous this man might attack us. Rufus stops a foot away from the man and gestures to me, right when the man turns around and looks me square in the eye.

Rufus wants me to speak up.

"Sir, here's all we have on us." I take the twenty from Rufus and hold out the cash.

"Don't play with me." He looks around, like I'm setting him up. Accepting help shouldn't make someone suspicious.

"Not at all, sir." I step closer to him. Rufus stays by my side. "I know it's not a lot, and I'm sorry."

"This is . . ." The man comes at me and I swear I'm going to die of a heart attack, it's like my feet are cemented to a racetrack as a dozen cars speed toward me in colorful blurs, but he doesn't hit me. The man hugs me, the orange that was in his armpit dropping at our feet. It takes me a minute to find my nerves and muscles, but I hug him too, and everything about him, from his height to his thin body, reminds me of Dad. "Thank you. Thank you," he says. He releases me, and I don't know if his eyes are red because he's possibly without a bed and really tired, or if he's tearing up, but I don't pry because he doesn't have to prove himself to me. I wish I always had that attitude.

The man nods at Rufus and stuffs the cash in his pocket.

He doesn't ask for anything else; he doesn't hit me. He walks off, his shoulders a little straighter. I wish I'd gotten his name before he left, or at least introduced myself.

"Good call," Rufus says. "Hopefully karma takes care of you later for that one."

"This isn't about karma. I'm not trying to rack up I'm-a-Good-Person points." You shouldn't donate to charity, help the elderly cross the street, or rescue puppies in the hopes you'll be repaid later. I may not be able to cure cancer or end world hunger, but small kindnesses go a long way. Not that I'm saying any of this to Rufus, since all my classmates used to mock me for saying things like that, and no one should feel bad for trying to be good. "I think we made his day by not pretending he's invisible. Thanks for seeing him with me."

"I hope we helped the right person," Rufus says.

Much like Rufus can't expect me to be instantly brave, I can't expect him to be instantly generous.

I'm relieved Rufus didn't mention anything about us dying. It cheapens everything, doesn't it, if this man thinks we're only giving him everything we have on us because we may not have any use for it ten minutes from now.

Maybe he'll go on to trust others because he met us tonight. He definitely helped me out with that.

DELILAH GREY

5:00 a.m.

Death-Cast called Delilah Grey at 2:52 a.m. to tell her she's going to die today, but she's sure it's not true. Delilah isn't in some denial stage of grief. This has to be a cruel prank from her ex, a Death-Cast employee trying to scare her since she called off their yearlong engagement last night.

Toying with someone like this is incredibly illegal. This degree of fraud can have him thrown in jail for a minimum of twenty years and blacklisted from working pretty much anywhere ever again. Screwing around on the job at Death-Cast is, well, killer.

Delilah can't believe Victor would abuse his power like this.

She deletes the email with the time-stamp receipt of her call with the herald, Mickey, whom she cursed out before hanging up. She picks up her phone, tempted to call Victor. She shakes her head and places her phone back by the pillow on the side of the bed that was Victor's whenever he stayed over. Delilah refuses to give Victor the satisfaction of thinking she's paranoid, which she isn't. If he's waiting on her to log on to death-cast.com to see if her name is actually registered on the site as a Decker or to call him and threaten him with a lawsuit until he admits Mickey is a friend at work he recruited to scare her, he's going to be waiting a very long time—time she has plenty of.

Delilah is moving on with her day because just as she didn't second-guess her decision to call off the engagement, she will not second-guess that bullshit call.

She goes to the bathroom and brushes her teeth while admiring her hair in the mirror. Her hair is vibrant—*too* vibrant, according to her boss. In the past few weeks, Delilah needed a change, ignoring the voice in her head urging her to end things with Victor. Dyeing her hair was simpler. Fewer tears involved. When asked by the hairdresser what she wanted, Delilah asked for the aurora borealis treatment. The combination of pink, purple, green, and blue needs some touch-ups, but that can wait until next week after she catches up on assignments.

She returns to bed and opens her laptop. Breaking up with Victor last night before his shift pulled her away from her own work, a season premiere recap she's writing for *Infinite Weekly*, where she's been working as an editorial assistant since graduating from college this spring. She's not a *Hipster*

House fan, but those hipsters are more clickbait-y than the *Jersey Shore* crew, and someone has to write the pieces because the editors are busy covering the respected franchises. Delilah is well aware how lucky she is to be given the grunt work, and to have a job at all considering she's the new hire who missed several deadlines because she was preoccupied planning a wedding with someone she's only known for fourteen months.

Delilah turns on her TV to re-watch the painfully absurd premiere—a challenge in a crowded Brooklyn coffee shop where the hipsters have to cowrite short stories on a typewriter—and before she can switch to her DVR, a Fox 5 anchor shares something truly newsworthy, given her interests.

". . . and we've reached out to his agents for word. The twenty-five-year-old actor may have played the young antagonist of the blockbuster Scorpius Hawthorne films about the demonic boy wizard, but fans all over the world have been sharing nothing but love online for Howie Maldonado. Follow us on Twitter and Facebook for immediate updates on this developing story. . . ."

Delilah jumps out of bed, her heart pounding.

She isn't waiting around for this developing story.

Delilah will be the writer who reports the story.

MATEO

5:20 a.m.

I approach the ATM on the corner while Rufus watches my back. My dad thankfully had the common sense to send me to the bank after I turned eighteen so I could get a debit card. I withdraw four hundred dollars, the max limit at this ATM. My heart is pounding as I slide the cash into an envelope for Lidia, praying someone doesn't come out of nowhere and hold us up at gunpoint for the money—we know how that would end. I grab the receipt, memorizing how I have $2,076.27 left in my account as I tear up the slip. I don't need that much. I can get more cash for Lidia and Penny at another ATM or the bank, when it opens.

"It might be too early to go to Lidia's," I say. I fold up the envelope and put it in my pocket. "She'll know something is up. Maybe we can hang in her lobby?"

"Nah, dude. We're not sitting around in your bestie's lobby because you don't wanna burden her. It's five o'clock, let's eat. Potential Last Supper." Rufus leads the way. "My favorite diner is open twenty-four hours."

"Sounds good."

I've always been a superfan of mornings. I follow several Facebook pages about mornings in other cities ("Good Morning, San Francisco!") and countries ("Good Morning, India!"), and no matter the time of day, in my feed there are pictures of glowing buildings, breakfast, and people beginning their lives. There's newness that comes with the rising sun, and even though there's a chance I won't reach daytime or see sun rays filtering through trees in the park, I should look at today as one long morning. I have to wake up, I have to start my day.

The streets are really clear this early. I'm not anti-people, I just don't have the courage to sing in front of anyone. If I were alone right now, I'd probably play some depressing song and sing along. Dad taught me it's okay to give in to your emotions, but you should fight your way out of the bad ones, too. The days after his admittance, I was playing positive and soulful songs, like Billy Joel's "Just the Way You Are," so I wouldn't feel hopeless.

We reach Cannon Café. There's a triangular sign above the door with an illustrated logo of a cannon blasting a cheeseburger toward the café's name, with French fries exploding wayward like fireworks. Rufus chains his bike to a parking meter and I follow him inside the fairly empty café, immediately smelling scrambled eggs and French toast.

A tired-eyed host greets us, telling us we can sit wherever. Rufus passes me and goes all the way to the back, settling into a two-person booth beside the bathroom. The navy-blue leather seats are cracked in various places, and it reminds me of the couch I had as a kid where I would absentmindedly peel the fabric off until there was so much exposed cushion foam that Dad threw the couch out for our current one.

"This is my spot," Rufus says. "I come here once or twice a week. I get to say stuff like 'I'll have the usual.'"

"Why here? Is this your neighborhood?" I realize I have no idea where my Last Friend actually lives, or where he's from.

"Only for the past four months," Rufus says. "I ended up in foster care."

Not only do I not know much about Rufus, I haven't done anything for him. He's been all about the mission of shadowing me on my journey—getting me out of my home, going to and getting me out of the hospital, and soon coming with me to Lidia's. This Last Friendship has been very one-sided so far.

Rufus slides the menu my way. "There's a Decker discount on the back. Everything is free, if you can actually believe that."

This is a first. In all the *CountDowners* feeds I've read, the Deckers go to five-star restaurants expecting to be treated like kings with courtesy meals, but are only ever offered discounts. I like that Rufus returned here.

A waitress comes out from the back and greets us. Her blond hair is pulled back into a tight bun, and the button clipped to her yellow tie reads "Rae." "Good morning," she greets us, in a southern accent. She grabs the pen out from behind her ear, and I glimpse a curly tattoo above her elbow—I'll never grow into someone unafraid of needles. She twirls the pen between her fingers. "Late night for you two?"

"You could say that," Rufus answers.

"Feels more like a really early morning," I counter.

If Rae is actually interested in my distinction, she doesn't show it. "What can I get you two?"

Rufus looks at the menu.

"Don't you have a usual?" I ask him.

"Changing it up today. Last chance and all that." He puts the menu down and looks up at Rae. "What do you suggest?"

"What, did you get the alert or something?" Her laughter is short-lived. She turns to me and I lower my head until she crouches beside us. "No way." She drops her pen and notepad onto the table. "Are you boys okay? Sick? You're not pranking me for a free meal, are you?"

Rufus shakes his head. "Nah, not kidding. I come here a lot and wanted to roll through one last time."

"Are you seriously thinking about food right now?"

Rufus leans over and reads her pin. "Rae. What should I try?"

Rae hides behind her hand, shakes her shoulders, and mutters, "I don't know. Don't you just want the Everything Special? It has fries, sliders, eggs, sirloin, pasta . . . I mean, it has everything you could want that we have in the kitchen."

"No way I'm gonna eat all that. What's your favorite meal here?" Rufus asks. "Please don't say fish."

"I like the grilled chicken salad, but that's because I eat like a bird."

"I'll have that," Rufus decides. He looks at me. "What do you want, Mateo?"

I don't even bother looking at the menu. "I'll have whatever your usual is." Like him, I'm hoping it's not fish.

"You don't even know what it is."

"As long as it's not chicken tenders it'll be something new for me."

Rufus nods. He points to a couple items on the menu and Rae tells us she'll return shortly, then rushes away so quickly she leaves behind her pen and notepad. We overhear Rae telling the chef to make our order priority number one because "there are Deckers at the table." Not sure who our competition is—the guy in the back already drinking his coffee while he reads his newspaper? But I do appreciate Rae's heart, and I wonder if Andrea at Death-Cast was once like her before the job killed her compassion.

"Can I ask you something?" I say to Rufus.

"Don't waste your breath on questions like that. Just come out and say whatever you want," he says.

He's coming on a little strong, but good call.

"Why did you tell Rae we're dying? Doesn't that screw with her day?"

"I guess. But dying is screwing with my day and there isn't anything I can do about it," Rufus says.

"I'm not telling Lidia I'm dying," I say.

"That makes no sense. Don't be a monster. You have a chance to say goodbye, you should do it."

"I don't want to ruin Lidia's day. She's a single mom and she's already had a rough time since her boyfriend died." Maybe I'm not actually so selfless—maybe not telling her is really selfish, but I can't bring myself to do it, because how do you tell your best friend you won't be around tomorrow? How do you convince her to let you leave so you have a chance of living before you die?

I push back against my seat, pretty disgusted with myself.

"If that's your call, I back it. I don't know if she'll resent you or not, you know her best. But look, we gotta stop caring about how others will react to our deaths and stop second-guessing ourselves."

"What if by not second-guessing our actions we end ourselves?" I ask. "Don't you have little freak-outs wondering if life was better before Death-Cast?"

This question is suffocating.

"Was it better?" Rufus asks. "Maybe. Yes. No. The answer doesn't matter or change anything. Just let it go, Mateo."

He's right. I am doing this to myself. I'm holding myself back. I've spent years living safely to secure a longer life, and look where that's gotten me. I'm at the finish line, but I never ran the race.

Rae returns with drinks, hands a grilled chicken salad to Rufus, and places sweet potato fries and French toast in front of me. "If there's anything else I can get you boys please just shout for me. Even if I'm in the back or with another customer, I'm yours." We thank her but I can tell she's hesitant about walking away, almost as if she wants to scoot down next to one of us and just talk some more. But she collects herself and walks away.

Rufus taps my plate with his fork. "How's my usual looking for you?"

"I haven't had French toast in years. My dad really got into making BLTs on toasted tortillas every morning instead." I kind of forgot French toast was even a thing, but that cinnamon smell restores many memories of eating breakfast across from Dad at our rickety table while we listened to the news or brainstormed lists he should write. "This is pretty perfect. Do you want some?"

Rufus nods, but doesn't reach over to my plate. His mind

is elsewhere as he plays around with his salad, seemingly disappointed and only eating the chicken. He drops his fork and grabs the notepad and pen Rae left behind. He sketches a circle, bold. "I wanted to travel the world taking photos."

Rufus is drawing the world, outlining the countries he'll never get to visit.

"Like a photojournalist?" I ask.

"Nah. I wanted to do my own thing."

"We should go to the Travel Arena," I say. "It's the best way to travel the world in a single day. CountDowners speak highly of it."

"I never read that stuff," Rufus says.

"I read it daily," I admit. "It's comforting seeing other people breaking out."

Rufus glances up from his drawing, shaking his head. "Your Last Friend is gonna make sure you go out with a bang. Not a bad bang, or a you-know-what bang, but a good bang. That made no sense."

"I get it." I think.

"What did you see yourself doing? Like, as a job?" Rufus asks.

"An architect. I wanted to build homes and offices and stages and parks," I say. I don't tell him how I never wanted to work in any of those offices, or that I've also dreamt of performing on a stage I've built. "I played with Legos a lot as a kid."

"Same. My spaceships always came apart. Those smiling block-headed pilots never stood a chance." Rufus reaches over and carves himself a piece of French toast and then chews it, savoring the bite with his head down and eyes closed. It's hard watching someone swallow their favorite food one last time.

I have to get it together.

Things usually get worse before they get better, but today has to be the flip side.

Once our plates are clear, Rufus stands and gets Rae's attention. "Could we get the check when you have a sec?"

"It's on us," Rae says.

"Please let us pay. It would mean a lot to me," I say. I hope she doesn't see it as a guilt card.

"Seconded," Rufus says. Rufus may not be able to return here again, but we want to make sure they remain open for as long as possible for others, and money is how they pay the bills.

Rae nods vigorously, and she hands us a check. I hand her my debit card, and when she comes back, I tip her triple the inexpensive meal's cost.

I have less than two thousand dollars after this debit charge. I may not be able to restart anyone's life with this money, but every bit helps.

Rufus puts his drawing of the world inside his pocket. "Ready to go?"

I remain seated.

“Getting up means leaving,” I say.

“Yeah,” Rufus says.

“Leaving means dying,” I say.

“Nah. Leaving means living before you die. Let’s bounce.”

I stand, thanking Rae and the busboy and the host as we leave.

Today is one long morning. But I have to be the one who wakes up and gets out of bed. I look ahead at the empty streets, and I start walking toward Rufus and his bike, walking toward death with every minute we lose, walking against a world that’s against us.

RUFUS

5:53 a.m.

I can't front, Mateo is cool and neurotic and fine company, but it would've been really dope to have one last sit-down at Cannon's with the Plutos, talking about all the good and bad things that have gone down. But it's too risky. I know what's good with me and I'm not risking getting them hurt.

They could hit me back with a text, though.

I unchain my bike and wheel it out onto the street. I toss the helmet to Mateo, who just barely catches it. "So Lidia is right off where again?"

"Why are you giving me this?" Mateo asks.

"So you don't crack your head open if you fall off the bike." I sit on the bike. "It would suck if your Last Friend killed you."

"This isn't a tandem bike," he says.

"There are pegs," I say. Tagoe would ride on the back pegs all the time, trusting me to not crash into any cars and send him flipping off.

"You want me to stand on the back of your bike while we ride in darkness?" Mateo asks.

"While wearing a helmet," I say. Holy shit, I really thought he was ready to take chances.

"No. This bike is going to be the death of us."

This day is really doing a number on him. "No it won't. Trust me. I've ridden this bike every day for almost two years. Hop on, Mateo."

He's mad hesitant, that's obvious, but he forces the helmet onto his head. There's extra pressure to be cautious because I'd hate for an "I told you so!" in the afterlife. Mateo holds on to my shoulders, pressing down on them as he gets on the pegs. He's stepping his game up, I'm proud of him. It's like pushing a bird out of its nest—maybe even shoving because it should've flown out years ago.

A grocery store down the block is opening its roll-up doors for business as the moon hangs high above this bank up ahead. I press down on a pedal when Mateo hops off.

"Nope. I'm walking. And I think you should too." He unbuckles the helmet, takes it off his head, and hands it to me. "Sorry. I just have a bad feeling and I have to trust my gut."

I should throw on the helmet and ride away. Let Mateo go to Lidia, and I can do my thing, whatever that is. But instead of parting ways, I hang my helmet off the handlebars and swing my leg over the seat. "We should get walking then. I don't know how much life we have left but I don't want to miss it."

MATEO

6:14 a.m.

I'm already the worst Last Friend ever. It's time to be the worst best friend.

"This is going to suck," I say.

"Because you're not outing your death?"

"I'm not dead yet." I turn the corner. Lidia's apartment is a couple blocks away. "And no." The sky is finally lightening up, the orange haze of my final sunrise ready to take over. "Lidia was destroyed when we found out her boyfriend-future-husband-person was dying. He never got to meet Penny."

"I take it Penny is their daughter," Rufus says.

"Yeah. She was born a week after Christian died."

"How'd that go? The call?" Rufus asks. "If that's too personal you don't have to tell me. My family getting their call was a nightmare and I'm not a big fan of talking about that either."

I'm about to trust him with this story as long as he promises not to tell anyone, especially not Lidia, when I realize Rufus will die with this story. Short of him gossiping in some afterlife, I'm safe to tell him anything and everything. "Christian was traveling to outer Pennsylvania to sell these weird daggers and swords he inherited from his grandfather to this collector."

"Weird daggers and swords tend to sell for mad bank," Rufus says.

"Lidia didn't want him to go because she was having all these hysteria freak-outs, but Christian swore the money would be worth it in the long run. They could buy a better crib, diapers and formula for the next couple months, and clothes. He took off, stayed overnight in Pennsylvania, and woke up around one-something to the alert." My chest tightens reliving this, all the tears and screams. I stop and rest against the wall. "Christian tried reaching Lidia, but she slept through everything. He texted her every minute he could. He'd hitchhiked there with a Decker truck driver, and they both died trying to get back to their families in the city."

"Holy shit," Rufus says.

There was no consoling Lidia. She obsessively read Christian's final, frantic texts and hated herself for not waking up to any calls. There was a chance for her to see him one last time through The Veil—a video chat app that drains batteries quickly, but also creates a stronger personal hot spot for anyone who's somewhere with weak service, like a Decker on a highway headed home—and she missed those invites, too.

I don't know if it's true, but the way Lidia spoke about Penny in the beginning sounded like she resented her for wearing her out so much toward the end of her pregnancy that she slept through her boyfriend's final hours. But I know she was grieving and doesn't feel that way now.

Since then, Lidia dropped out of high school to take care of Penny full-time in a small apartment with her grandmother. She's not very tight with her own parents, and Christian's parents live in Florida. Her life is challenging enough without throwing a goodbye into things. I just want to see my best friend one last time.

"That's brutal," Rufus says.

"It was." Coming from him, it means a lot. "Let me call her." I walk a few feet away, giving myself some privacy.

I hit *Call.*

I can't believe I won't be there for Penny if something fatal strikes Lidia, but I'm also pretty relieved I'll never have to live through Lidia receiving the call.

"Mateo?" Lidia groggily answers.

"Yeah. Were you sleeping? Sorry, I thought Penny would be awake by now."

"Oh, she is. I'm being Mom of the Year by hiding under my pillow while she talks to herself in the crib. Why are you awake at ass o'clock?"

"I . . . wanted to go see my dad." I'm not lying, after all. "Can I come over for a bit? I'm in the area."

"Yes please!"

"Cool. See you in a bit."

I hail Rufus over and we walk to her apartment. It's in the kind of projects where the superintendent sits on the stoop reading a newspaper when there's clearly more work that can be done—like mopping and sweeping the floor, fixing the blinking lamp in the hallway, and setting up mouse traps. But this doesn't matter to Lidia. The breeze she gets on rainy evenings charms her, and she's taken a liking to her neighbor's cat, Chloe, that wanders the halls and is scared of mice. It's home, you know.

"I'm going up alone," I tell Rufus. "You'll be okay down here?"

"I'll be fine. I should call my friends anyway. They haven't responded to anything since I left."

"I won't be long," I say. And he doesn't tell me to take my time.

I run up the stairs, nearly falling face-first on the edge of a step before I catch myself on the railing, hovering an inch away from what could've been my death. I can't rush toward Lidia's company on my End Day. That urgency can—and almost just did—kill me. I reach the third floor and knock on her door. Penny is screaming from inside.

"IT'S OPEN!"

I walk in, and it smells like milk and clean clothes. There's a laundry basket right by the door, clothes spilling out. Empty formula bottles are also on the floor. And inside the playpen is Penny, who doesn't have her Colombian mother's light brown skin tone, but is instead very pale like Christian was, except right now she's red from screaming. Lidia is in the kitchen, warming up a bottle in a cup of hot water.

"You are a godsend," Lidia says. "I would hug you, but I haven't brushed my teeth since Sunday."

"You should go do that."

"Hey, nice shirt!" Lidia fastens a top onto the bottle and tosses it to me, right when Penny screams louder. "Just give it to her. She gets pissed if she doesn't hold her own bottle." Lidia ties her messy hair back with a rubber band and speed-walks toward the bathroom. "Oh my god, I get to pee by myself. I can't wait."

I kneel before Penny and offer her the bottle. She has attitude in her dark brown eyes, but when she grabs the bottle from me and sits back down on a stuffed bear, she smiles and flashes me her four baby teeth before getting to work on her bottle. All the baby books say Penny should be done with formula already, but Penny resists the real stuff. We have that in common.

Lidia comes out of the bathroom with a toothbrush hanging from her mouth as she puts batteries into a plastic toy butterfly. She's asking me something, but toothpaste-y saliva drips down her chin, and she rushes to the kitchen sink and spits. "Sorry. Gross. Do you want some breakfast? You're so damn skinny. Gross, I sound like your mother." She shakes her head. "Oh god, you know what I mean. I sound like I'm mothering you."

"No worries, Lidia. And I ate already, but thanks." I poke Penny's feet while she drinks, and she lowers her bottle to laugh. There's some gibberish I'm sure makes perfect sense to her, and then she returns to her bottle.

"Guess who got the alert?" Lidia asks, waving her phone.

I freeze while holding Penny's foot. There's no way Lidia knows I'm dying and there's no way she'd be this casual about letting me know she is. "Who?"

"Howie Maldonado!" Lidia checks her phone. "His fans are devastated."

"I'm sure." I share an End Day with my favorite fictional villain. I don't know what to make of that.

"How's your dad doing?" Lidia asks.

"Stable. I keep hoping for one of those TV miracles where he hears my voice and snaps awake, but that obviously didn't happen. Nothing we can do but wait." It's crunching my insides talking about this. I sit beside the playpen and pick up some stuffed animals—a smiling sheep, a yellow owl—and bounce them toward Penny before tickling her. I'll never have any moments like this with my own kids.

"I'm sorry to hear that. He'll pull through. Your dad is badass. I keep telling myself he's just taking a nap from all that badass-ness."

"Probably. Penny's done with her bottle. I can burp her."

"Godsend, Mateo. Godsend."

I wipe Penny's face clean, pick her up, and pat her back until I get that burp and laugh out of her. I do my signature Dinosaur Walk, where I stomp around like a T. rex with Penny in my arms, which always seems to relax her. Lidia walks over and turns on the TV.

"Yes, it's six-thirty. Time for cartoons, aka the only time I have to clean up the previous day's messes before it all goes to hell again." Lidia smiles at Penny, slides toward us, and kisses her on the nose. "What Mommy meant to say is what a treasure her little Penny is." Under her breath and behind a smile she adds, "A treasure that leaves nothing buried around."

I laugh and put Penny down. Lidia gives Penny the plastic butterfly and collects clothes from the floor. "What can I do to help?" I say.

"You can never change, for starters. Then you can throw all her toys back in the chest, but leave the sheep alone or she'll freak out. And in return I will love you forever and ever. I'm going to put her clothes in her drawers. Give me a minute or ten." Lidia leaves with the laundry basket.

"Take your time."

"Godsend!"

I love Lidia in all her forms. Before Penny, she wanted to graduate high school with top honors and go to college to pursue politics and architecture and music history. She wanted to travel to Buenos Aires and Spain, Germany and Colombia, but then she met Christian and got pregnant and found happiness in her new world.

Lidia used to be the girl who got her hair straightened after school every Thursday, was always glowing without makeup, and loved photo-bombing strangers' photos with goofy faces. Now her hair is what she calls "somewhat cute, somewhat lion's mane," and she will never approve any photo to go up online because she thinks she looks too burned out. I think my best friend glows even brighter than before because she's been through a change, an evolution that many can't handle. And she's done it solo.

When I'm done throwing all the toys back into their chest, I sit down with Penny on the floor, watching as she blows raspberries whenever the cartoon characters ask her questions. This is Penny's beginning. And one day she'll find herself on the terrible end of a Death-Cast call and it sucks how we're all being raised to die. Yes, we live, or we're given the chance to, at least, but sometimes living is hard and complicated because of fear.

"Penny, I hope you figure out how to become immortal so you can rule this place for as long as you like."

Here's my vision of Utopia: a world without violence and

tragedies, where everyone lives forever, or until they've led fulfilling and happy lives and decide themselves that they want to check out whatever's next for us.

Penny responds with gibberish.

Lidia comes out of the other room. "Why are you wishing Penny immortality and world domination while she's learning how to say 'one' in Spanish?"

"Because I want her to live forever, obviously." I smile. "And make minions of everyone else."

Lidia's eyebrows rise. She leans over, picks up Penny, and holds her out to me. "Penny for your thoughts?" We both cringe. "That is *never* going to be funny, is it? I just *keep* going for it, hoping that the next time will be *it*, but no."

"Maybe next time," I say.

"Honestly, you don't even have to give me your thoughts. If you want Penny you can have her for free." She flips Penny around and kisses her eyes and tickles her armpit. "Mommy meant to say that you're priceless, little Penny." Then she mutters, "The priciest priceless little Penny ever." She sets Penny back down in front of the TV and continues cleaning.

The relationship I have with Lidia isn't the kind you see in movies or maybe have with your own friends. We love each other to death, but we don't go around talking about it. It's understood between us. And words can sometimes be awkward, even when you've known someone for eight years.

But today I have to say more.

I prop up a framed picture of Lidia and Christian that was tipped over. "Christian has got to be crazy proud of you, you know. You're Penny's shot at happiness in a world that makes cheap promises and has no guarantees and doesn't always reward those who never did wrong. It's like, the world will just as easily screw with a good person as it will a not-so-good one, but you devote your days to someone else selflessly anyway. Not everyone is programmed like you."

Lidia stops sweeping. "Mateo, where is this random flattery coming from? What's going on?"

I carry a bottle of juice over to the sink. "Everything's okay." And everything will be okay. She'll be okay. "I should probably head out in a bit. I'm tired."

I'm not lying.

Lidia's eyes twitch. "Before you go, could you help me with a couple more chores?"

We move silently through the living room. She scrubs oatmeal off a pillow, and I dust her air conditioner. She collects cups, and I arrange all of Penny's shoes at the door. She folds laundry, peeking over at me, while I break down some diaper boxes. "Could you take out the garbage?" she asks, her voice cracking a little. "Then I need help assembling that little baby bookcase you and your dad got Penny."

"Okay."

I think she's catching on.

I place the envelope of cash on the kitchen counter when she leaves the room.

Even as I grab the trash bag out of the bin, I know I won't be able to return. I step out into the hallway and throw the bag down the chute. If I go back in, I'll never leave. And if I don't leave, I'll die in that apartment, possibly in front of Penny, and that's not how I want to be remembered—Rufus's approach is really smart and thoughtful.

I pull out my phone and block Lidia's number so she can't call or text me to come back.

I feel nauseous and a little dizzy, slowly making my way back downstairs, hoping Lidia understands, and hating myself so much I race down the stairs faster and faster. . . .

RUFUS

6:48 a.m.

Who put down ten dollars I'd find myself on Instagram on my End Day? Because you're now ten dollars richer.

The Plutos still haven't responded to a single text or phone call. I'm not freaking out too hard because they're not Deckers, but damn, could someone at least let me know if the cops are still on my ass or not? My money's on everyone being passed out. I'd nap too if you put a bed in front of me. A chair with armrests would work as well. Definitely not this lobby bench that could seat two people max. I'm not about to rest fetus-position style, that's not me.

I'm scrolling through Instagram, expecting to find a new post from Malcolm's account (@manthony012), but there's been nothing since nine hours ago when he uploaded that unfiltered photo of a Coca-Cola bottle with his name on it. He's Team Pepsi in the world war of Pepsi versus Coke, but he was so happy seeing his name in that bodega fridge that he couldn't resist. The caffeine only got him more hype before the fight.

I shouldn't call that thing with Peck a fight. Peck couldn't even get a swing on me with the way I pinned him.

I'm texting Aimee an apology, even though I only half-mean it because her little shit boyfriend unleashed the cops on me at my own damn funeral, when Mateo comes running down the stairs at a dangerous speed. He's bulleting to the front door and I catch up with him. His eyes are red and he's breathing hard, like he's fighting back a serious cry.

"You good?" He's not, that was stupid to ask.

"No." Mateo pushes the lobby door open. "Let's go before Lidia chases me down."

I'm eager to get a move on too, believe me, but his silent mode isn't gonna fly with me. I wheel my bike alongside him. "Come on, get whatever it is off your chest. Don't carry this around all day."

"I don't *have* all day!" Mateo shouts, like someone finally pissed off he's dying at eighteen. Turns out there's some fire in him. He stops at the curb and sits down, straight reckless, probably waiting for a car to knock him out of his misery.

Down goes my bike's kickstand, up goes Mateo as I slide my arms under his and pick him up. We move away from the curb and lean against the wall and he's shaking, like he really doesn't wanna be out here, and when he slides down to the ground, I go with him. Mateo takes off his glasses and rests his forehead on his knees.

"Look, I'm not gonna hit you with some impassioned speech. I don't have one in me and that's not what I'm about." I gotta do better than that. "But I know that frustration you're feeling, dude. You have options, thankfully. If you wanna go back to your dad or best friend, I'm not stopping you. If you wanna ditch me, I'm not chasing you. It's your last day, live it however the hell you want. If you want help living it, I got you."

Mateo lifts his head and squints at me. "Sounded pretty impassioned to me."

"Yeah. My bad." I like him better with his glasses, but no-glasses is a good look on him, too. "What do you wanna do?" If he ditches, I'll respect it, and I'll figure out my next move. I gotta see what's what with the Plutos, but I can't sneak back there, I don't know if there are eyes on the place.

"I want to keep moving forward," Mateo says.

"Good call."

He puts his glasses back on, and, I don't know, if you wanna put together some analogy on how he's seeing the world with new eyes or something, be my guest. I'm just relieved I'm not taking this day on alone.

"I'm sorry for yelling," Mateo says. "I still think not saying goodbye is the right move, but it's something I'll regret all day."

"I didn't get to say my piece to my friends either," I say.

"What happened at your funeral?"

All my talk about honesty and getting stuff off your chest, and I'm not being straight with him. "It got interrupted. I haven't been able to reach my friends again since then. I'm hoping they'll hit me up before . . ." I crack my knuckles as cars go by. "I want them to know I'm okay. No mystery over if I'm dead yet or not. But I can't keep texting them until *whatever* happens finally goes down."

"Set up a *CountDowners* profile," Mateo suggests. "I've followed enough stories online and I can help you navigate it."

I bet he can. Going by that logic, I've watched enough porn to make me a sex god. "Nah, that stuff isn't me. I never even got on board with Tumblr or Twitter. Just Instagram. The photography stuff is still pretty new, just a few months. Instagram is dope."

"Can I see your account?"

"Sure."

I hand him my phone.

My profile is public because I don't care if some stranger stumbles onto it. But it's crazy different watching a stranger scroll through my photos. I feel exposed, like I'm stepping out of the shower and someone is watching me wrap a towel around my boys. My earlier photos are pretty amateur-hour because of bad lighting, but there's no edit button and that's probably for the best.

"Why are they all in black and white?" Mateo asks.

"I got the account a few days after I moved in to the foster home. My boy Malcolm took this one photo of me, look . . ." I scoot closer to him and scroll down to my first wave of photos, self-conscious about my dirty fingernail for half a second before no longer giving a shit. I click the photo of me sitting on my bed at Pluto with my face in my hands. Malcolm is the credited photographer. "It was my third or fourth night there. We were playing board games and I was freaking out in my head because I was feeling guilty for having a decent time—nah, kill that. I was having mad fun, that's what made it worse. I walked away without a word and Malcolm hunted me down because I was taking too long and he captured my breakdown."

"Why?" Mateo asks.

"He said he liked tracking a person's growth and not just physically. He's hard on himself, but he's smart as hell." But for real, I kicked Malcolm in his giant knee when he first showed me that photo weeks later. Creep. "I keep my photos in black and white because my life lost color after they died."

"And you're living your life but not forgetting theirs?" Mateo asks.

"Exactly."

"I thought people got on Instagram just to be on Instagram."

I shrug. "Old school."

"Your photos look old school," Mateo says. He shifts, looking at me with wide eyes. He smiles at me for the first time and yo, this is not the face you see on a Decker. "You don't need the *CountDowners* app, you can post everything here. You can create a hashtag or whatever, too. But I think you should post your life in color. . . . Let that be how the Plutos remember you." The smile goes away because that's the nature of today. "Forget it. That's stupid."

"It's not stupid," I say. "I actually really like this. The Plutos can revisit the times I lived with them in black and white, like a cooler history book, and my End Day will have its own unfiltered contrast. Can you take a pic of me sitting here? In case it's my last post, I want everyone to see me alive."

Mateo smiles again, like he's the one posing for the photo. He gets up and points the camera my way.

I don't pose. I just sit here with my back against the wall, in the spot where I convinced my Last Friend to keep adventuring and where he gave me the idea to add some life to my profile. I don't even smile. I've never been a smiler and starting now feels off. I don't want them to see a stranger.

"Got it," Mateo says. He hands me the phone. "I can take another if you hate it."

I don't care about photo approval, I'm not that into myself. The photo is surprisingly dope though. Mateo caught me looking sad and proud all at once, like my parents looked the day Olivia graduated high school. And the front wheel of my bike makes a cameo too. "Thanks, dude."

I upload the picture, unfiltered. I consider captioning it with #EndDay, but I don't need fake sympathetic "oh no, R.I.P!!!!" comments or trolls telling me to "Rest in Pieces!!!!" The people who matter the most to me know.

And I hope they remember me as I was and not as the guy who punched in someone's face earlier for no real good reason.

PATRICK "PECK" GAVIN

7:08 a.m.

Death-Cast did not call Patrick "Peck" Gavin because he's not dying today, though he was expecting the alert before his attacker received the call himself.

He's home now, pressing a frozen hamburger patty against his bruises. It smells, but the migraine is fading away.

Peck shouldn't have left Aimee in the street, but she didn't want to see him and he's not exactly happy with her either. He used his old phone and called Aimee up, but the arguing only lasted so long before she began passing out from exhaustion, and it was so hard not to hang up on her when she said she wanted to make an effort to see Rufus again, to be with him on his End Day.

Peck used to operate by a code with people like Rufus.

A code that goes into play when someone tries to walk all over you.

Peck has a lot to sleep on. But things aren't looking good for Rufus if he's still around when Peck wakes up.

RUFUS

7:12 a.m.

My phone vibrates and I'm counting on it being the Plutos, but that hope gets squashed once a chime follows. Mateo checks his phone and gets the same notification—another message we both got today: Make-A-Moment location nearby: 1.2 miles.

I suck my teeth. "What the hell is this?"

"You never heard of it?" Mateo asks. "They launched last fall."

"Nope." I keep it moving down the block, half-listening, half-wondering why the Plutos haven't hit me back yet.

"It's sort of like the Make-A-Wish Foundation," Mateo says. "But any Decker can go, it's not just for kids. They have these low-grade virtual reality stations designed to give you the same thrills as crazy experiences like skydiving and racecar driving and other extreme risks Deckers can't safely experience on their End Day."

"So it's a straight rip-off, watered-down version of the Make-A-Wish Foundation?"

"I don't think it's all that bad," Mateo says.

I check my phone again to see if I've missed any messages. As I step off the curb Mateo's arm bangs into my chest.

I look right. He looks right. I look left. He looks left.

There are no cars. The street is dead quiet.

"I know how to cross the street," I say. "I've sort of been walking my entire life."

"You were on your phone," Mateo says.

"I knew no cars were coming," I say. Crossing the street is pretty instinctive at this point. If there are no cars, you go. If there are cars coming toward you, you don't go—or you go really quickly.

"I'm sorry," Mateo says. "I want this day to last."

He's on edge, I know. But he needs to step off at some point.

"I get it. But walking? I got this."

I look both ways again before crossing the empty street. If anyone should be nervous, it's the guy who watched his family drown in a sinking car. I didn't exactly beat my grief to the point where I would've ever seen myself comfortably getting in a car over the next few years, but then there's Malcolm, who digs fireplaces even though he lost his parents to a house fire. I don't have that in me. But I'm also not looking right to left, left to right, like Mateo is until we make it to the opposite curb, like there's a ninety-nine percent chance a car will pop out of nowhere and run us down in point-five seconds.

Mateo's phone rings.

"Make-A-Moment people making house calls?" I ask.

Mateo shakes his head. "Lidia is calling from her grandmother's phone. Should I . . ." He puts his phone back in his pocket and doesn't answer.

"Well played on her end," I say. "At least she's reaching out. Haven't heard shit from my friends."

"Keep trying."

Why not? I park my bike against the wall and FaceTime Malcolm and Tagoe. Both are no-gos. I FaceTime Aimee, and right when I'm about to hang up and send all the Plutos a picture of me flipping them off, Aimee answers, breathing quickly, her eyes strained, her hair sticking to her forehead. She's home.

"I was knocked out!" Aimee shakes her head. "What time is . . . You're alive. You . . ." She loses my eyes for a second; she's staring at one half of Mateo's face. She leans over like the phone's camera is a window she can stick her head out of for a closer look. It's like when I was thirteen and flipping through magazines, I'd scout for pictures of girls in skirts and dudes in shorts and would tilt the page to see what was underneath. "Who's that?"

"This is Mateo," I say. "He's my Last Friend." Mateo

waves. "And this is my friend Aimee." I don't add that she's the girl who body-slammed my heart, because I'm not trying to make everyone uncomfortable here. "I've been calling you."

"I'm sorry. Everything got crazy after you left," Aimee says, rubbing her eyes with her fist. "I got home a couple hours ago and my phone was dead and I set it to charge but fell asleep before it came back on."

"What the hell happened?"

"Malcolm and Tagoe got arrested," Aimee says. "They wouldn't stop mouthing off and Peck threw them under the bus since they were with you."

I storm away from Mateo, telling him to stay put. He looks pretty frightened; so much for taking any suspicion of me being a shitty person to the grave. "Are they okay? Which station?"

"I don't know, Roof, but you shouldn't go looking around for them unless you want to spend your last day in a holding cell where who-knows-what will happen to you."

"This is bullshit. They didn't do anything!" I raise my fist to punch in this car window, but that's not me, I swear it's not, I don't go around hitting things and hitting people. I slipped up with Peck, that's that. "And what's good with Peck?"

"He followed me home, but I didn't want to talk to him."

"You ended things with him, right?"

She doesn't answer.

If we were chatting on the phone instead of over video, I wouldn't have to be disappointed by the face she's giving me. I could pretend she's nodding her head, getting ready to break up with him if she hadn't already. But that's not what I'm seeing.

"It's complicated," Aimee says.

"You know, Ames, it didn't seem complicated or confusing when you broke up with me. That legit sucks, but there isn't a bigger kick to the nuts than you turning your back on the Plutos for the punk-ass kid who got them locked up. We're supposed to be tight and I'm gonna be out the picture soon enough and you're actually gonna tell me to my face that you're keeping that motherfucker in your life?" Screw body-slamming *my* heart, this girl ripped *her own* out mad long ago. "They were innocent."

"Rufus, they weren't totally innocent, you know that, right?"

"Yeah, bye. I gotta get back to my real friend."

Aimee begs me not to hang up and I hang the hell up anyway. I can't believe my boys are in jail for my stupidity and I can't believe she didn't tell me sooner.

I turn around to tell Mateo everything but he's gone.

AIMEE DUBOIS

7:18 a.m.

Aimee gives up calling Rufus. There are three possible explanations for why Rufus isn't picking up, ranked from greatest hope to biggest fear:

1. He's ignoring her but will call her back.
2. He's blocked her number and has no interest in reaching out.
3. He's dead.

Aimee goes on Rufus's Instagram, leaving comments on his pictures asking him to call her back. She charges her phone, raises the volume, and changes into an old T-shirt of Rufus's and her shorts.

Aimee has really gotten into exercise ever since becoming a Pluto. When she originally snuck into her foster parents' room, looking for something to steal from Francis, who gave her the weakest welcome, she spotted Jenn Lori's bedside dumbbells and gave lifting a shot. Her own parents, locked up for robbing a family-owned movie theater, inspired her kleptomaniac urges, but Aimee discovered working on herself made her feel more powerful than stealing from others.

Aimee already misses going on runs with Rufus while he rides his bike.

And she'll always think back to the time when she taught him to do a proper push-up.

And she has no idea what comes next.

MATEO

7:22 a.m.

I keep running down the block, far away from Rufus.

I'm Last Friend–less, but maybe dying alone is an okay End Day for someone who lived his life pretty alone.

I don't know what Rufus was involved in that led to his friends being arrested. Maybe he was hoping to use me as some alibi. But now I'm gone.

I stop to catch my breath. I sit on the stoop of this daycare and press my palm against my aching rib cage.

Maybe I should go back home and play some video games. Write more letters. I even wish I was still in high school and attending one of Mr. Kalampoukas's classes because he always made me feel seen. Though sharing a chemistry lab with kids who were always texting while mixing chemicals was terrifying, even last fall when it wasn't my End Day.

"MATEO!"

Rufus is riding his bike down the block, his helmet

swinging from the handlebars. I get up and keep moving, but it's no use. Rufus pulls up next to me, swinging his left leg behind the seat, and then hops off his bike. The bike falls to the ground as Rufus catches me by my arm. He looks me in the eyes, and when I realize he isn't pissed, but instead frightened, I'm absolutely certain he isn't how I end.

"Are you crazy?" Rufus asks. "We're not supposed to split up."

"And you're not supposed to be a total stranger," I say. We've been together for several hours now. I sat down with him at his favorite diner, where he told me who he wanted to be if he had years ahead of him. "But you're apparently running from the cops and you never mentioned that once."

"I don't know if the cops are actually looking for me," Rufus says. "They gotta know I'm a Decker, and it's not like I robbed a bank, so they're not gonna send the entire force looking for me."

"What *did* you do?"

Rufus lets go of me and looks around. "Let's go somewhere and talk. I'll give you the full story. The accident that killed my family and the stupid thing I did last night. No more secrets."

"Follow me."

I'm choosing the place. I mostly trust him, but until I know everything, I don't want to be completely alone with him again.

We walk in silence into Central Park, passing early risers as we do. There are enough cyclists and joggers around that I feel comfortable, especially since Rufus is keeping his distance by staying on the grass, where a young golden retriever is chasing its owner around. The dog reminds me of the *CountDowners* story I was following when I received my alert, though I'm sure this dog and that one aren't one and the same.

I maintain the silence at first because I wanted us to settle in before Rufus explains himself, but the deeper we go into the park, the quieter I get because of pure wonder, especially as we stumble onto a bronze sculpture of characters from *Alice in Wonderland*. Dark green leaves crush under my feet as I approach Alice and the White Rabbit and the Mad Hatter.

"How long has this been here?" I'm embarrassed to ask. I'm sure it's not new.

"I don't know. Probably forever," Rufus says. "You never seen it?"

"No." I look up at Alice, who's sitting on a gigantic mushroom.

"Wow. You're like a tourist in your own city," Rufus says.

"Except tourists know more about my own city than I do," I say. This is a completely unexpected find. Dad and I prefer Althea Park, but we've spent a lot of time in Central Park too. He loves Shakespeare in the Park. Plays aren't really my thing, but I went with him to one, and it was fun for me because the theater reminded me of coliseums in my favorite fantasy novels and gladiator matches in Rome from movies. I wish I'd discovered this piece of Wonderland as a kid so I could've climbed on top of the mushrooms with Alice and imagined adventures of my own.

"You found it today," Rufus says. "That's a win."

"You're right." I'm still stunned this has been here all along, because when you think of parks, you think of trees and fountains and ponds and playgrounds. It's sort of beautiful how a park can surprise me, and it gives me hope that I can surprise the world too.

But not all surprises are welcome.

I sit down on the mushroom beside the White Rabbit. Rufus sits next to the Mad Hatter. His silence is an awkward one, like those times in history class when we reviewed monumental events from the BDC days. My teacher, Mr. Poland, would tell us "how good we got it" for having Death-Cast's services. He'd assign us reports where we reimagined periods of significant deaths—the plague, the world wars, 9/11, et cetera—and how people would've behaved had Death-Cast been around to deliver the warning. The assignments, quite honestly, made me feel guilty for growing up in a time with a life-changing advancement, sort of like how we have medicine to cure common diseases that killed others in the past.

"You didn't murder anyone, right?" I finally ask. There's only one answer here that will get me to stay. The other will get me to call the police so he can be detained before killing anyone else.

"Of course not."

I've set the bar so high it should be easy enough for him to stay under. "Then what?"

"I jumped someone," Rufus says. He's staring straight ahead at his bike, parked by the pathway. "Aimee's new boyfriend. He was mouthing off about me and I was pissed because it felt like my life was ending in a lot of ways. I felt unwanted, frustrated, lost, and I needed to take it out on someone. But that's not me. It was a glitch."

I believe him. He's not monstrous. Monsters don't come to your home to help you live; they trap you in your bed and eat you alive. "People make mistakes," I say.

"And my friends are the ones being punished," Rufus says. "Their last memory of me will be running out the back door from my own funeral because the cops were coming for me. I left them behind. . . . I've spent the past four months feeling abandoned by my family dying, and in a split second I did the same damn thing to my new family."

"You don't have to tell me more about the accident if you don't want," I say. He feels guilty enough as it is, and just like I wouldn't ever push a homeless person into sharing their story so I can determine whether or not they deserve my charity, I don't need Rufus to jump through any more hoops to keep my trust.

"I don't wanna talk about it," Rufus says. "But I have to."

RUFUS

7:53 a.m.

I'm lucky to have a Last Friend, especially with my boys locked up and my ex-girlfriend on block. I get to talk about my family and keep them alive.

The sky is getting cloudy, and some strong breezes come our way, but no drops of rain yet.

"My parents woke up to the Death-Cast alert on May tenth." I'm gutted already. "Olivia and I were playing cards when we heard the phone ring, so we rushed to their bedroom. Mom was on the phone and keeping it together while Dad was across the room cursing them out in Spanish and crying. First time I ever saw him cry." That was brutal. It's not like he was mad macho, but I always felt like crying was some little bitch move, which is freaking stupid.

"Then the Death-Cast herald asked to speak with my pops and Mom lost it. It was that this-must-be-a-nightmare shit. Nothing scarier than watching your parents freaking out. I was panicking but I knew I would have Olivia." I wasn't supposed to be alone. "Then Death-Cast asked to speak with Olivia and my pops hung up the phone and threw it across the room." I guess throwing phones is in our genes.

Mateo is about to ask something, but stops.

"Say it."

"Never mind," Mateo says. "It's not important. Well, I was wondering if you were nervous about being end-listed that day and not knowing. Did you check the online database?"

I nod. Death-cast.com is helpful that way. Typing my social security number and not finding my name in the database that evening was a weird sort of relief. "It didn't seem right how my family was dying without me. Shit, I make it sound like I was getting left behind from a family vacation, but their End Day was spent with me already missing them. And Olivia could barely look at me."

I get it. It wasn't my fault I got to keep living, and it wasn't her fault she was dying.

"Were you two close?"

"Mad close. She was a year older. My parents were saving up money so Olivia and I could attend Antioch University in California this fall. She had a partial scholarship but hung back here at the community college so we wouldn't be separated until I could go with her." My breaths are tight, like when I was laying into Peck earlier. My parents tried convincing Olivia to take off to Los Angeles without me and not settle at a school in a city she was hating on, but she refused. Every morning, afternoon, evening, I always think she'd still be alive if she'd listened to our parents. She just wanted to reboot our lives together. "Olivia is the first person I came out to."

"Oh."

I don't know if he's playing it off like he doesn't know this from my Last Friend profile or if he's impacted by this piece of history between me and my sister or if he overlooked this on my profile and is some ass who cares about who other people kiss. I hope not. We're friends now, hands down, and it's not forced. I met this kid a few hours ago because some creative designer somewhere developed an app to forge connections. I'd hate to disconnect.

"*Oh* what?"

"Nothing. Honestly."

"Can I ask you something?" Let's get this over with.

"Did you ever come out to your parents?" Mateo asks.

Avoiding a question with another question. Classic. "On our last day together, yeah. I couldn't put it off any longer." My parents had never hugged me like they did on their End Day. I'm really proud I spoke up to get that moment out of them. "My mom got really sad because she'd never get a chance to meet her future daughter- or son-in-law. I was still a little uncomfortable, so I just laughed and asked Olivia if there was anything she wanted us all to do, hoping she'd hate me a little less. My parents wanted to ditch me."

"They were just looking out for you, right?"

"Yeah, but I wanted every possible minute with them, even if it meant being left with the memory of watching them all die in front of me," I say. "I didn't know any better." That idiocy died too.

"Then what happened?" Mateo asks.

"You don't have to have the details," I say. "You might be better off without them."

"If you have to carry this around, I will too."

"You asked for it."

I tell him everything: how Olivia wanted to go up one last time to this cabin near Albany where we always went for her birthday. The roads were slippery on our way upstate and our car flew into the Hudson River. I'd sat shotgun because I thought it bettered our chances of surviving a head-on car crash if both of my parents weren't in the front. It didn't matter. "Same song, different verse," I tell Mateo before going on about the screeching tires, the way we busted through the road's safety rail and tumbled into the river. . . .

"I sometimes forget their voices," I say. It's only been four months, but that's fact. "They blend with the voices of people around me, but I could recognize their screams anywhere." I'm getting goose bumps up my arms thinking about it.

"You don't have to go on, Rufus. I'm sorry, I shouldn't

have encouraged you to keep talking about it."

Mateo knows how this ends, but there's more to it. I stop because he has the basics and I'm crying a little and need to keep my shit together so he doesn't freak out. He places a hand on my shoulder and pats my back, and it reminds me of all the other seniors who tried comforting me over texts and Facebook but didn't know what to say or do because they'd never lost someone the way I had.

"You're okay," he adds. "Let's talk about something else, like . . ." Mateo scans the area around us. "Birds and beat-up buildings and—"

I straighten up. "That was pretty much it anyway. I ended up with Malcolm, Tagoe, and Aimee. We became the Plutos and that was exactly the kind of company I needed—we were all lost and okay with not being found for a while." I dry my eyes with my fist and shift toward Mateo. "And now you're stuck with me until the end. Don't run away again or you might get kidnapped and find yourself the inspiration for some shitty thriller movie."

"I'm not going anywhere," Mateo says. He has a kind smile. "What's next?"

"Game for whatever."

"Should we go make a moment?"

"I thought we were already making moments, but why not."

MATEO

8:32 a.m.

On the way to the Make-A-Moment station, Rufus stops in front of a sporting goods store. In the window there are posters of a man cycling, a woman in ski gear, and a man and woman running side by side, with celebrity smiles and zero sweat.

Rufus points at the woman in ski gear. "I always sent Olivia photos of people skiing. We went skiing every year, up at Windham. You're gonna think we were stupid for always going back. My pops broke his nose on the first trip by smashing it against a rock; we were really shocked he didn't die, even though Death-Cast hadn't called. My mom sprained her ankle on the next trip. Two years ago I got a concussion after skiing downhill. I suck at braking and almost ran down some kid, so I switched left at the last second and slammed into a tree like some fucking cartoon character."

"You're right," I say. "I have no idea why you kept going back."

"Olivia put her foot down after I was admitted to the hospital. But we continued driving up to Windham whenever we could because we loved the mountains, the snow, and playing games by our fireplace in the cabin." Rufus keeps it moving. "I'm hoping this spot is as safe and fun as that was."

A few minutes later we reach the Make-A-Moment station. Rufus stops and takes a picture of the entrance and its blue banner hanging above the door: No-Risk Thrills! He uploads it to Instagram in full color. "Look." He hands me his phone. It's open to the comments on his previous picture. "People are asking why I'm awake so early."

There are a couple comments from Aimee, begging him to pick up his phone. "What happened with Aimee?"

He shakes his head. "I'm done with her. Her boy is the reason Malcolm and Tagoe are in jail for something I did, and she's still dating him. She's not loyal."

"It's not because of any feelings you have for her?"

"No," Rufus says. He chains his bike to a parking meter.

It doesn't matter if he's telling the truth or not.

I drop it and we head inside.

I didn't expect this place to look like a travel agency. The wall behind the counter is half sunset orange, half midnight blue, and there are framed photos of people doing different activities, like rock climbing and surfing. It's easy on the eyes, I guess. Behind the counter is a young black woman in her twenties writing in a notebook that she puts away once she sees us. She's in a yellow polo shirt and her name tag reads "Deirdre." I've seen this name before, maybe in a fantasy novel.

"Welcome to Make-A-Moment," Deirdre says, not too cheery, not too distant. The right amount of solemn. She doesn't even ask us if we're Deckers. She slides a binder toward us. "There's currently a half-hour wait for the hot air balloon rides and swimming with sharks."

"Who the hell . . . ?" Rufus turns to me, then back to Deirdre. "Is swimming with sharks something people really feel like they're missing out on?"

"It's a popular attraction," Deirdre says. "Wouldn't you swim with sharks if you knew they couldn't bite you?"

Rufus sucks his teeth. "I don't mess with big bodies of water like that."

Deirdre nods as if she understands all of Rufus's history. "No prob. I'm here if you have any questions."

Rufus and I take a seat and flip through the binder. In addition to hot air balloon rides and swimming with sharks, the station offers skydiving, racecar driving, a parkour course, zip-lining, horseback riding, BASE jumping, white-water rafting, hang gliding, ice/rock climbing, downhill mountain biking, windsurfing, and tons more. I wonder if this business will ever expand to fictional thrills, like running away from dragons, fighting a Cyclops, and magic carpet rides.

We won't be around to know.

I shake it off. "You want to try mountain biking?" I ask. He loves biking and there's no water involved.

"Nah. I wanna do something new. How do you feel about skydiving?"

"Dangerous," I say. "But tell my story if this goes south." I wouldn't be surprised if I managed to die in a place that promises risk-free thrills.

"You got it."

Deirdre gives us a six-page-long waiver, which isn't uncommon for businesses serving Deckers, but it's also definitely not uncommon that we skim the form, because it's not as if we're going to be around to sue them if something does go wrong. There are so many freak accidents that can happen at any point. Every new minute we're alive is a miracle.

Rufus's signature is messy. I can make out only the first two letters before the remaining letters get lost in curves that look like a sales chart for a business that is rising and failing regularly. "Okay. I've signed away my right to bitch if I die."

Deirdre doesn't laugh. We pay two hundred and forty dollars each, the kind of price you can get away with charging people whose savings accounts would go to waste otherwise. "Follow me."

The long hallway reminds me of the storage center where Dad worked, except inside the lockers there weren't happy screams and laughter. At least none that I ever heard of. (Kidding.) These rooms are like karaoke rooms except some are twice, even three times as big. I peek in each window as we go down the hall, zigzagging like a pinball, finding Deckers with goggles in every room. Some are sitting inside racecars that are shaking, but not speeding down the racetracks. One Decker is "rock climbing" while an employee in the room texts away. A couple are kissing in a hot air balloon that is hovering six feet, but not in the sky. A crying man without goggles is holding the back of a laughing girl on top of a horse, and I can't tell which one of them is the Decker, or if it's both, but it makes me so sad that I stop looking into the rooms.

Our room isn't very large, but there are huge vents, safety mats leaning against the wall, and an instructor who's dressed like an aviator, with her curly brown hair pulled back in a ponytail. We dress up in matching gear and harnesses, the three of us looking like X-Men cosplayers, and Rufus asks the young woman, Madeline, to take a photo of us. I don't know if I should wrap my arm around him, so I follow his lead, placing my hands on my waist.

"Is this good?" Madeline asks, holding the phone out to us.

We look like we mean serious business, like we refuse to die until we save the world from all its ugliness.

"Dope," Rufus says.

"I can take more photos while you're diving!"

"That'd be cool."

Madeline breaks it down for us on how this works. We'll put on the goggles, the virtual experience will begin, and the room itself will play its own role in making this feel as real as possible. Madeline locks our harnesses to suspending hooks, and we climb a ladder up to a plank that looks like a diving board except we're only about six feet above the floor.

"When you're ready, press the button on your goggles and jump," Madeline says, dragging the mats under us. "You'll be fine." She turns on the high-powered vents, and the room becomes loud with wind.

"Ready?" Rufus mouths to me, dropping his goggles over his eyes.

I do the same with my goggles and nod. I click the green button by the lens. The virtual reality kicks in. We're inside a plane with an open door, and a three-dimensional man is giving me the thumbs-up to jump into the open blue sky. I'm scared to jump, not out of the plane, but into the actual open space before me. My harness might break, even though I feel one hundred percent secure.

Rufus shouts for a few seconds, descending a couple feet away from me, and goes quiet.

I lift my goggles away from my eyes, hoping I don't find Rufus on the floor with a twisted neck, but he's hovering in the air, being blown side to side by wind from the vents. I shouldn't be seeing Rufus like this, but I had to know he was okay, even if it ruins the experience a little bit. I still want that same exhilaration Rufus experienced, so I put the goggles back on, count down from three, and jump. I'm weightless as I hug my arms to my chest, like I'm speeding down a tunnel slide instead of free-falling through cloud after cloud, which I suppose I'm not actually doing either. I stretch my arms out, trying to touch the wisps at the edge of multiple clouds, as if I can actually grab one and roll it around in my hands like a snowball.

A couple minutes later, the magic wears off. I see the green field we're approaching and I know I should be relieved I'm almost there, I'm almost safe again, but there was never any true danger in the first place. It's not exciting. It's too safe.

It's exactly what I signed up for.

Virtual Mateo lands right as I do, my feet digging into the mat. I force a smile for Rufus, who smiles back at me. We thank Madeline for her help, take off the aviator gear, and let ourselves out.

"That was fun, right?" I say.

"We should've waited to swim with sharks," Rufus says as we pass Deirdre and leave.

"Thank you, Deirdre," I say.

"Congratulations on making a moment," Deirdre says, waving. It's odd to be praised for living, but I guess she can't exactly encourage us to come again.

I nod at her and follow Rufus out. "I thought you had fun! You cheered."

He's removing the chain from the bike no one stole, unfortunately. "For the main jump, yeah. It got wack after that. Did you actually like that? No judgment except yes judgment."

"I felt the same as you."

"It was your idea," Rufus says, walking his bike down the block. "You don't get any more ideas today."

"Sorry."

"I'm kidding, dude. It was interesting, but low casualties are the one thing this place has going for it, and that sort of risk-free fun isn't really fun at all. We should've read reviews before dropping bank on it."

"There aren't that many reviews online," I say. When your service is exclusive for Deckers, not many reviews are to be expected. I mean, I can't imagine any Decker who would spend precious time praising or bad-mouthing the foundation. "And I really am sorry. Not because we wasted money, but because we wasted time."

Rufus stops and pulls out his phone. "It wasn't a waste of time." He shows me the photo of us in our gear and uploads it to Instagram. He tags it #LastFriend. "I might get ten likes out of this."

LIDIA VARGAS

9:14 a.m.

Death-Cast did not call Lidia Vargas because she isn't dying today. But if she were, she would've told all her loved ones, unlike her best friend, who didn't come out and tell her he's dying.

Lidia figured it out. The clues were laid out for her to backtrack and piece everything together: Mateo coming over super early; the kind but out-of-the-blue words he'd said about her being an awesome mother; the envelope with four hundred dollars on her kitchen counter; blocking her number, which she'd taught him how to do.

In the first few minutes after Mateo pulled his disappearing act, Lidia freaked out, called her abuelita, and begged her to come home from the pharmacy where she works. Instead of fielding all of Abuelita's questions, she took her phone and called Mateo, but he still didn't respond. She's praying it's because he has Abuelita's number stored in his contacts list, and not because he's gone.

She's not thinking that way. Mateo won't live a long life, which is bullshit because he's the greatest soul in this universe, but he'll live a long day. He can die at 11:59 p.m., but not a minute before.

Penny is crying and Abuelita can't figure out what's wrong. Lidia knows all of Penny's cries and how to calm her down. If Penny has a fever, Lidia sits Penny in her lap, singing into her ear. If Penny falls, Lidia scoops her up and hands her a toy with blinking lights or one that jingles; some toys do both, unfortunately. If Penny is hungry or needs a new diaper, the next steps are easy. Penny misses her uncle Mateo. But Lidia can't FaceTime Mateo to say hi over and over because, again, he blocked her number.

Lidia logs on to Facebook. She used to use this account to keep up with friends from high school, but now she uploads photos of Penny for Christian's family without having to text his parents, grandparents, aunts and uncles, or that one cousin who's always asking for dating advice.

Lidia visits Mateo's page, which is a wasteland of nineteen mutual friends, two gorgeous pictures of sunrises in Brooklyn from a "Good Morning, New York!" fan page, an article about some instrument NASA created that allows you to hear what outer space sounds like, and a status from months ago that didn't receive nearly enough love about being accepted to his online college of choice. Mateo has never been good about sharing his own stuff, obviously, but you can always count on him to comment on your photo or show love to your status. If it matters to you, it matters to him.

Lidia hates that Mateo is out there by himself. This isn't the early 2000s, when people were dying without warning. Death-Cast is here to prepare Deckers and their loved ones, not for the Decker to turn their back on their loved ones. She wishes Mateo had let her into his life, every last minute of it.

She goes through Mateo's photos, starting from the most recent: Mateo and Penny napping on the same couch Lidia is sitting on now; Mateo carrying Penny through the reptile room at the zoo, where they were both scared of snakes escaping; Mateo and his dad in Lidia's kitchen, where his dad was teaching them how to make pegao; Mateo hanging streamers for Penny's first birthday party; Mateo, Lidia, and Penny smiling in the backseat of Abuelita's car; Mateo in his graduation cap and gown, hugging Lidia, who brought him flowers and balloons. Lidia clicks out of the photos. Memory lane is too painful when she knows he's still out there, alive. She stares at his profile picture, a photo she took of him in his bedroom where he was looking out the window, waiting for the mailman to deliver his Xbox Infinity.

This time tomorrow, Lidia will put up a status about her best friend passing. People will reach out to her and offer their condolences, much like they did when Christian passed. And after everyone remembers Mateo, whether as the boy in their homeroom or at their lunch table, they'll rush over to his page and leave comments like a digital memorial. How they hope he rests in peace. How he was too young to go. How they wish they'd taken the time to talk to him while he was alive.

Lidia will never know how Mateo is spending his End Day, but she hopes her best friend finds whatever he's looking for.

RUFUS

9:41 a.m.

We stumble across seven abandoned pay phones in some ditch, underneath a highway leading north toward the Queensboro Bridge.

"We gotta go in there."

Mateo is about to protest, but I hold up my finger, shutting that down real fast.

I drop my bike on the ground, and we crawl through an opening in the chain-link fence. There are rusty pipes, stuffed garbage bags that smell like old food and shit, and trails of blackened gum snaking around the pay phones. There's graffiti of a Pepsi bottle beating the crap out of a Coca-Cola bottle; I take a picture, upload it to Instagram, and tag Malcolm so he knows he was with me on my End Day.

"It's like a graveyard," Mateo says. He picks up a pair of sneakers.

"If you find any toes in there, we're jetting," I say.

Mateo inspects the insides of the sneakers. "No toes or other body parts." He drops the sneakers. "Last year I bumped into this guy with a bloody nose and no sneakers."

"Homeless dude?"

"Nope. He was our age. He got beat up and robbed so I gave him my sneakers."

"Of course you did," I say. "They don't make them like you."

"Oh, I wasn't looking for a compliment. Sorry. I'm curious what he's up to now. Doubt I'd recognize him since he had so much blood on his face." Mateo shakes his head, like it'll make the memory go away.

I crouch over one pay phone, and in blue Sharpie there's a message by where the receiver used to be: I MISS YOU, LENA. CALL ME BACK.

Pretty damn hard for Lena to call you back, Person, without an actual phone.

"This is a crazy find," I say, mad lit as I move on to the next pay phone. "I feel like Indiana Jones right now." Mateo smiles my way. "What?"

"I watched those movies obsessively as a kid," Mateo says. "Forgot about it until now." He tells me stories about how his dad would hide treasure around the apartment—how the treasure was always a jar of quarters they used for laundry. Mateo would wear his cowboy hat from his Woody costume and use a shoelace as a lasso. Whenever he got close to finding the jar, his dad would put on this Mexican mask a neighbor bought him and he would throw Mateo onto the couch for an epic fight.

"That's awesome. Your pops sounds cool."

"I got lucky," Mateo says. "Anyway, I hijacked your moment. Sorry."

"Nah, you're fine. It's not some huge, big, worldly moment. I'm not about to go off on how removing pay phones from street corners is the start of universal disconnection or some nonsense like that. I think this is just really dope." I snap some photos with my phone. "It is crazy, though, right? Pay phones are gonna stop being a thing. I don't even know anyone's phone number."

"I only know Dad's and Lidia's," Mateo says.

"If I was locked up behind bars, I would've been extra screwed. Knowing someone's number isn't gonna matter anyway. You'll no longer be a quarter away from calling someone." I hold up my phone. "I'm not even using a real camera! Cameras that use film are going extinct too, watch."

"Post offices and handwritten letters are next," Mateo says.

"Movie rental stores and DVD players," I say.

"Landlines and answering machines," he says.

"Newspapers," I say. "Clocks and wristwatches. I'm sure someone's working on a product for us to automatically know the time."

"Physical books and libraries. Not anytime soon, but eventually, right?" Mateo is quiet, probably thinking about those Scorpius Hawthorne books he mentioned in his profile. "Can't forget about all the endangered animals."

I definitely forgot about them. "You're right. You're totally right. It's all going away, everyone and everything is dying. Humans suck, man. We think we're so damn indestructible and infinite because we can think and take care of ourselves, unlike pay phones or books, but I bet the dinosaurs thought they'd rule forever too."

"We never act," Mateo says. "Only react once we realize the clock is ticking." He gestures to himself. "Exhibit A."

"Guess that marks us next on the list," I say. "Before the newspapers and clocks and wristwatches and libraries." I lead us out through the fence and turn around. "But you do know no one actually uses landlines anymore, right?"

TAGOE HAYES

9:48 a.m.

Death-Cast did not call Tagoe Hayes because he isn't dying today, but he'll never forget what it was like seeing his best friend receive the alert. The look on Rufus's face will haunt Tagoe far longer than any of the gore he's seen in his favorite slasher films.

Tagoe and Malcolm are still at the police station, sharing a holding cell that is twice the size of their bedroom.

"I thought for sure it was gonna smell like piss here," Tagoe says. He's sitting on the floor because the bench is too shaky, creaking every time he shifts.

"Just vomit," Malcolm says, biting his nails.

Tagoe plans on throwing these jeans out when he gets home. He removes his glasses, letting Malcolm and the desk officer blur. He's been known to do this every now and again, so everyone knows when he wants a time-out from whatever is happening around him. The only time it ever pissed Malcolm off was when Tagoe did this during a game of Cards Against Humanity; Tagoe never admitted it was because the card he'd drawn from the deck was making fun of suicide, which made him think about the man who'd abandoned him.

Thinking about if Rufus is alive and well makes Tagoe's neck ache.

Tagoe suppresses his tic often because his neck jerking around every other minute is not only uncomfortable, but it also makes him look unapproachable and wild. Rufus once asked him what that urge feels like, so Tagoe got Rufus, Malcolm, and Aimee to hold their breath and not blink for as long they could. Tagoe didn't have to do the exercise with the Plutos to know the relief they were in for once they breathed out and blinked. His tic was as natural to him as breathing and blinking. But as his neck pulls him in directions, Tagoe feels little cracks, and he always imagines his bones crumbling with every turn.

He puts his glasses back on. "What would you do if you got the call?"

Malcolm grunts. "Probably same thing as Roof. Except I wouldn't invite my ex-girlfriend whose boyfriend I just jumped to my funeral."

"That's no doubt where he went wrong," Tagoe says.

"What about you?" Malcolm asks.

"Same."

"Do you . . ." Malcolm stops. It's not like when Malcolm was helping Tagoe defeat writer's block as he was working on *Substitute Doctor* and was shy about his pitch about the demon doctor wearing a stethoscope that could read his patients' minds—that was a great idea. This is something sure to piss him off.

"I wouldn't look for my mom or find out how my dad died," Tagoe says.

"Why not? If I knew more about the asshole who burned my home down, I'd get into my first fight," Malcolm says.

"I only care about the people who wanna be in my life. Like Rufus. Remember how he was nervous about coming out to us because he didn't wanna stop sharing a room with us since we had so much fun? That's someone who wants to be in my life. And I wanna be there for his. However much of it is left."

Tagoe takes off his glasses and lets his neck run wild.

KENDRICK O'CONNELL

10:03 a.m.

Death-Cast did not call Kendrick O'Connell because he isn't dying today. He may not be losing his life, but he's just lost his job at the sandwich shop. Kendrick keeps his apron, not giving a shit. He leaves the shop, lighting a cigarette.

Kendrick has never been lucky. Even when he struck gold last year, when his parents finally divorced, it wasn't long before his luck ran dry. His mother and father were as good a fit for each other as an adult's foot in a child's shoe; even at nine years old Kendrick recognized this. Kendrick didn't know much back then, but he was pretty sure love didn't mean that your father slept on the couch and that your mother didn't care when her husband was caught cheating on her with younger girls in Atlantic City. (Kendrick has a problem with minding his own damn business, and could possibly be happier if he were a little more ignorant.)

The first child support check came just in time since

Kendrick needed new sneakers; the front soles of his old pair had split, and his classmates made fun of him relentlessly because his shoes "talked" every time he walked—open, close, open, close. Kendrick begged his mother for the latest Jordans, and she spent three hundred dollars on them because Kendrick "needed a victory." At least that's what she told his paternal grandfather, who is a terrible man—but that's not a story of any importance here.

Kendrick felt ten feet tall in his new sneakers . . . until four six-foot-tall kids jumped him and stole them off his feet. His nose was bleeding and walking home in his socks was painful, all resolved by this boy in glasses who gave Kendrick a packet of tissues he'd had in his backpack and the sneakers off his feet in exchange for nothing. Kendrick never saw him again, never got his name, but he didn't care about that. Never getting his ass kicked again was the only thing that mattered.

That's when Damien Rivas, once his classmate, now a proud dropout, made Kendrick strong. It took Kendrick one weekend with Damien to learn how to break the wrist of anyone who swung at him. Damien sent him out on the street, unleashing him like a fierce pit bull onto other unsuspecting high schoolers. Kendrick would walk up on someone, clock them, and lay them out in one hit.

Kendrick became a Knockout King, and that's who he is today.

A Knockout King without a job.

A Knockout King with no one to hit, since his gang disbanded after their third, Peck, got a girlfriend and tried to live his life right.

A Knockout King in a kingdom of people who keep taunting him with their purposes in life, straight begging to get their jaws dislocated.

MATEO

10:12 a.m.

"I know I'm not supposed to have any more ideas. . . ."

"Here we go," Rufus says. He's riding his bike alongside me. He wanted me to get on that death trap with him. I didn't do it before and I'm not doing it now. But I couldn't let my paranoia keep him from riding himself. "What are you thinking?"

"I want to go to the cemetery and visit my mom. I only know her through my dad's stories and I'd like to spend some time with her," I say. "That phone booth graveyard did a number on me, I guess." My dad normally visited my mom alone because I was too nervous to make the trip. "Unless there's something else you want to do."

"You really wanna go to a cemetery on the day you're gonna die?"

"Yeah."

"I'm game. What cemetery?"

"The Evergreens Cemetery in Brooklyn. It's close to the neighborhood where my mom grew up."

We're going to take the A train from Columbus Circle station to Broadway Junction.

We pass a drugstore and Rufus wants to run in.

"What do you need?" I ask. "Water?"

"Just come on," Rufus says. He wheels his bike down the aisles and stops when he finds the bargain toys. There are water blasters, modeling clay, action figures, handballs, scratch-and-sniff erasers, and Legos. Rufus picks up a set of Legos. "Here we go."

"I'm confused. . . . Oh."

"Gear up, architect." Rufus heads to the front counter. "You're gonna show me what you got." I smile at this little miracle, one I doubt I would've thought to grant myself. I pull out my wallet and he flicks it. "Nah, this is on me. I'm paying you back for the Instagram idea."

He buys the Legos and we head out. He puts the plastic bag in his backpack and walks beside me. He tells me about how he always wanted a pet, but not like a dog or cat because his mother was deathly allergic, but instead something badass like a snake or fun like a bunny. As long as both snake and bunny never had to be roommates, I would've been cool with it.

We reach the Columbus Circle subway stop. He carries his bike down the stairs, and then we swipe our way in, catching the A train right before it departs.

"Good timing," I say.

"Could've been here sooner if we rode the bike," Rufus jokes. Or I think he's joking.

"Could've been at the cemetery sooner if a hearse carried us."

Like the train we took in the middle of the night, this one is also pretty empty, maybe a dozen people. We sit with our backs to a poster for the World Travel Arena. "What were some of the places you wanted to travel to?" I ask.

"Tons of places. I wanted to do cool stuff, like surfing in Morocco, hang gliding in Rio de Janeiro, and maybe swimming with dolphins in Mexico—see? Dolphins, not sharks," Rufus says. If we were living past today, I get the sense he'd be mocking the Deckers swimming with sharks for a long time. "But I also wanted to take photos of random sites around the world that aren't getting enough credit because they don't have cool history like the Leaning Tower of Pisa or the Colosseum, but are still awesome."

"I really like that. What do you think is—"

The train's lights flicker and everything shuts off, even the hum of the fans. We're underground and we're in total darkness. An announcement on the overhead tells us we're experiencing a brief delay and the system should be up and running again shortly. A little boy is crying as a man curses about another train delay. But this feels really wrong; Rufus and I have bigger things to worry about than getting somewhere late. I didn't observe any suspicious characters on the train, but we're stuck now. Someone could stab us and no one would know until the lights flash back on. I scooch toward Rufus, my leg against him, and I shelter him with my body because maybe I can buy him time, enough time to see the Plutos if they manage to get released today, maybe I can even shield him from death, maybe I can go out as a hero, maybe Rufus will be the exception to the Death-Cast-is-always-right record.

There's something glowing beside me, like a flashlight.

It's the light from Rufus's phone.

I'm breathing really hard and my heart is pounding and I don't feel better, not even when Rufus massages my shoulder. "Yo, we're totally cool. This happens all the time."

"No it doesn't," I say. The delays do, but the lights turning off isn't common.

"You're right, it doesn't." He reaches into his backpack and pulls out the Legos, pouring some of them into my lap. "Here. Build something now, Mateo."

I don't know if he also believes we're about to die and wants me to create something before I do, but I follow his lead. My heart is still pounding pretty badly, but I stop shaking when I reach for the first brick. I have no clue what I'm building, but I allow my hands to keep aimlessly laying down the foundation with the bigger bricks because there's a literal spotlight on me in an otherwise completely dark train car.

"Anywhere you wanted to travel to?" Rufus asks.

I'm suffocated by the darkness and this question.

I wish I was brave enough to have traveled. Now that I don't have time to go anywhere, I want to go everywhere: I want to get lost in the deserts of Saudi Arabia; find myself running from the bats under the Congress Avenue Bridge in Austin, Texas; stay overnight on Hashima Island, this abandoned coal-mining facility in Japan sometimes known as Ghost Island; travel the Death Railway in Thailand, because even with a name like that, there's a chance I can survive the sheer cliffs and rickety wooden bridges; and everywhere else. I want to climb every last mountain, row down every last river, explore every last cave, cross every last bridge, run across every last beach, visit every last town, city, country. Everywhere. I should've done more than watch documentaries and video blogs about these places.

"I'd want to go anywhere that would give me a rush," I answer. "Hang gliding in Rio sounds incredible."

Halfway through my construction, I realize what I'm building—a sanctuary. It reminds me of home, the place where I hid from exhilaration, but I recognize the other side of the coin too, and know my home kept me alive for as long as it did. Not only alive, but happy too. Home isn't to blame.

When I finally finish, in the middle of a conversation with Rufus about how his parents almost named him Kane after his mother's favorite wrestler, my eyes close and my head drops. I snap back awake. "Sorry. You're not boring me. I like talking to you. I, uh, I'm really tired. Exhausted, but I know I shouldn't sleep because I don't have time for naps." This day is really sucking everything out of me, though.

"Close your eyes for a bit," Rufus says. "We're not moving yet and you might as well get some rest. I'll wake you up when we get to the cemetery. Promise."

"You should sleep," I say.

"I'm not tired."

That's a lie, but I know he's going to be stubborn about this.

"Okay."

I rest my head back while holding the toy sanctuary in my lap. The light is no longer on me. I can still feel Rufus's eyes on me, though it's probably in my head. At first it feels weird, but then nice, even if I'm wrong, because it feels like I have a personal guardian looking out for my time.

My Last Friend is here for the long run.

RUFUS

10:39 a.m.

I gotta take a photo of Mateo sleeping.

That sounds creepy, no shit. But I gotta immortalize this dreamy look on his face. That doesn't sound any less creepy. Shit. It's the moment, too, I want. How often do you find yourself on a train that's having a blackout with an eighteen-year-old kid and his Lego house as he's on his way to the cemetery to visit his mother's headstone? Exactly. That's Instagram-worthy.

I stand to get a wider shot. I aim in the darkness and take his picture, the flash blinding me. A moment later, no joke, the train's lights and fans come back and we continue moving.

"I'm a wizard," I mutter. No shit, I discover I have superpowers on my End Day. I wish someone got that on camera. I could've gone viral.

The picture is dope. I'll upload it when I have service.

It's good I got the photo of Mateo sleeping when I did—yeah, yeah, creepy, we established that—because his face is shifting, his left eye twitching. He looks uneasy and he's breathing harder. Shaking. Holy shit, maybe he's epileptic. I don't know, he never told me anything like that. I should've asked. I'm about to call out for someone on the train who might know what to do if he's having a seizure when Mateo mutters "No," and repeats it over and over.

Mateo is having a nightmare.

I sit beside him and grab his arm to save him.

MATEO

10:42 a.m.

Rufus shakes me awake.

I'm no longer on the mountain; I'm back on the train. The lights are on and we're moving.

I take a deep breath as I turn to the window, as if I'm actually expecting to find boulders and headless birds flying my way.

"Bad dream, dude?"

"I dreamt I was skiing."

"That's my bad. What happened in the dream?"

"It started with me going down one of those kiddy slopes."

"The bunny slope?"

I nod. "Then it got really steep and the hills got icier and I dropped my ski poles. I turned around to look for them and I saw a boulder coming for me. All of a sudden it got louder and louder and I wanted to throw myself off to the side into this mound of snow, but I panicked. I was supposed to turn down another hill where I saw my Lego sanctuary, except it was as big as a cabin, but my skis disappeared and I flew straight off the mountain while headless birds circled overhead and I kept falling and falling."

Rufus grins.

"It's not funny," I say.

He shifts closer to me, his knee knocking into mine. "You're okay. I promise you don't have to worry about boulders chasing you or flying off a snowy mountain today."

"And everything else?"

Rufus shrugs. "You're probably good on the headless birds, too."

It sucks that that was the last time I'll ever dream.

It wasn't even a good one.

DELILAH GREY

11:08 a.m.

Infinite Weekly has secured Howie Maldonado's final interview.

Delilah herself hasn't.

"I know everything about Howie Maldonado," Delilah says, but her boss, Senior Editor Sandy Guerrero, isn't having it.

"You're too new for a profile this important," Sandy says, walking toward a black car sent over by Howie's people.

"I know I work in the absolutely worst cubicle with the most ancient computer, but that doesn't mean I'm not qualified to at least assist you with this interview," Delilah says. She comes off as ungrateful and arrogant, but she won't take it back. She'll move far in this industry by knowing her worth—and by landing a byline in this piece. It may have been Sandy's industry status that persuaded the publicist to choose *Infinite Weekly* over *People* magazine, but Delilah grew up with not only the Scorpius Hawthorne books, but also the films, all eight of them, which nurtured her love for this medium. From fangirl to paid fangirl.

"Howie Maldonado won't be the last person to die, I'm pleased to report," Sandy says, opening the car door and removing her sunglasses. "You have your whole life ahead of you to eulogize celebrities."

Delilah still can't believe how low Victor sank last night with that prank Death-Cast alert.

Sandy gives Delilah's colorful hair a once-over, and Delilah wishes she'd respected her editor's hints to dye it brown again, if only to gain her favor right now.

"Do you know how many MTV Movie Awards Howie has won?" Delilah asks. "Or which sport he played competitively as a child? How many siblings he has? How many languages he speaks?"

Sandy doesn't answer a single question.

Delilah answers them all: "Two awards for Best Villain. Competitive fencing. Only child. He speaks English and French. . . . Sandy, please. I promise I won't let my passion get in your way. I will never have another chance to meet Howie."

His death can be life-changing for her career.

Sandy shakes her head and releases a deep breath. "Fine. He's agreed to interview, but there are no guarantees. Obviously. We've reserved a private dining area in Midtown and we're still awaiting confirmation from his publicist that Howie has agreed to this setup. The earliest Howie may see us is at two."

Delilah is ready to sit in the car with her when Sandy shakes her finger.

"There's still time before we meet," Sandy says. "Please find me a copy of Howie's book, the one he *wrote*." The sarcasm in Sandy's voice is so sharp she doesn't need air quotes. "I'll be a hero if I get a copy signed for my son." Sandy closes the door and lowers her window. "I'd stop wasting time if I were you."

The car takes off and Delilah pulls out her phone, walking toward the street corner while looking up phone numbers for nearby bookstores. She trips off the curb and lands flat in the street, a car honking as it approaches her. The car brakes, a couple feet away from her face. Her heart runs wild and her eyes tear up.

But she lived because Delilah isn't dying today. People fall all the time.

Delilah is no exception, she reminds herself, even if she's not a Decker.

MATEO

11:32 a.m.

The clouds are gathering as we walk into Evergreens Cemetery. I haven't been here since I was twelve, the weekend of Mother's Day, and I cannot for the life of me tell you which of the entrances will help us reach her headstone fastest, so we're sure to be wandering for a bit. A breeze carries the smell of trimmed grass.

"Weird question: Do you believe in the afterlife?" I ask.

"That's not weird, we're dying," Rufus says.

"Right."

"Weird answer: I believe in two afterlives."

"Two?"

"Two."

"What are they?" I ask.

As we walk around tombstones—many so deeply worn that the names are no longer visible, others with crosses planted in them so high they look like swords in rocks—and under large pin oak trees, Rufus tells me his theory on the afterlives.

"I think we're already dead, dude. Not everyone, just Deckers. The whole Death-Cast thing seems too fantasy to be true. Knowing when our last day is going down so we can live it right? Straight-up fantasy. The first afterlife kicks off when Death-Cast tells us to live out our day knowing it's our last; that way we'll take full advantage of it, thinking we're still alive. Then we enter the next and final afterlife without any regrets. You get me?"

I nod. "That's interesting." His afterlife is definitely more impressive and thoughtful than Dad's—Dad believes in the usual golden-gated island in the sky. Still, the popular afterlife is better than no afterlife, like Lidia believes. "But wouldn't it be better if we already knew we were dead so we're not living in the fear of how it happens?"

"Nope." Rufus wheels his bike around a stone cherub. "That defeats the purpose. It's supposed to feel real and the risks should scare you and the goodbyes should suck. Otherwise it feels cheap, like Make-A-Moment. If you live it right, one day should be good. If we stay longer than that we turn into ghosts who haunt and kill, and no one wants that."

We laugh on strangers' graves, and even though we're talking about our afterlives, I forget for a second that this is where we'll end up. "What's the next level? Do you get on an elevator and rise up?"

"Nah. Your time expires and, I don't know, you fade or something and reappear in what people call 'heaven.' I'm not religious. I believe there's some alien creator and somewhere for dead people to hang out, but I don't credit all that as God and heaven."

"Me too! Ditto on the God thing." And maybe the rest of Rufus's theory is right too. Maybe I'm already dead and have been paired with a life-changer to spend my last day with as a reward for daring to do something new, like trying the Last Friend app. Maybe. "What does your after-afterlife look like?"

"It's whatever you want. No limitations. If you're into angels and halos and ghost dogs, then cool. If you wanna fly, you do you. If you wanna go back in time, knock yourself out."

"You've thought about this a lot," I say.

"Late-night chats with the Plutos," Rufus says.

"I hope reincarnation is real," I say. I'm already finding that this one day to get everything right isn't enough. This one life wasn't enough. I tap headstones, wondering if anyone here has been reincarnated already. Maybe I was one of them. I failed Past Me if so.

"Me too. I want another shot, but not counting on it. What's your afterlife look like?"

Coming up, there's a large tomb that resembles a pale blue teapot, and I know my mother's headstone is a few rows behind it. When I was younger I pretended this teapot tomb was a genie's lamp. Wishing for my mother to come back and complete my family never worked.

"My afterlife is like a home theater where you can re-watch your entire life from start to finish. And let's say my mother invited me into her theater—I could watch her life. I just hope someone knows what parts should fade to black so I'm not scarred my entire afterlife." I couldn't sell Lidia on this idea, but she did admit it sounded a little cool. "Oh! And there's also this transcript of everything you've ever said since birth and—"

I shut up because we've reached the corner, and in the space beside my mother's plot there's a man digging another grave while a caretaker installs a headstone with my name and dates of birth and death.

I'm not even dead yet.

My hands shake and I almost drop my sanctuary.

"And . . . ?" Rufus asks, quickly following with "Oh."

I walk toward my grave.

I know graves can be dug on an accelerated schedule, but it's only been eleven hours since I even got the alert. I know my final headstone won't be ready for days, but the temporary one isn't what's throwing me off. No one should ever witness someone digging their grave.

I'm hopeless too soon after believing Rufus is my life-changer. Rufus drops his bike. He walks up to the gravedigger and puts a hand on his shoulder. "Yo. Can we have a few minutes?"

The bearded gravedigger, dressed in a filthy plaid shirt, turns to me and then back to my mother's plot. "Is this the kid's mom?" He gets back to work.

"Yeah. And you're in the middle of digging his grave," Rufus says as trees rustle and a shovel scoops up earth.

"Yikes. My condolences all around, but me stopping ain't going to do anything, except slow me down. I'm knocking this out early so I can leave town and—"

"I don't care!" Rufus takes a step back, balling up his fists, and I'm scared he's about to try to take this guy on. "So help me . . . Give us ten minutes! Go dig the grave of someone who isn't standing right here!"

The other guy, the one who planted my headstone, drags the gravedigger away. They both curse about "Decker kids these days" but keep their distance.

I want to thank the men and Rufus, but I feel myself sinking, dizzy. I manage to stay upright and reach my mother's headstone.

ESTRELLA ROSA-TORREZ
JULY 7, 1969
JULY 17, 1999
BELOVED WIFE AND MOTHER
FOREVER IN OUR HEARTS

"Can I have a minute with my mom?" I don't even turn around because I'm stuck staring at her End Day and my birth date.

"I won't be far," Rufus says. It's possible he doesn't go very far, maybe only a couple of feet, or maybe he doesn't move at all, but I trust him. He'll be there when I turn around.

Everything has come full circle between my mother and me. She died the day I was born and now I'll be buried next to her. Reunion. When I was eight, I found it weird how she was credited as a "beloved" mother when the only mothering she did was carry me for nine months; ten years later, I know much better. But I couldn't wrap my head around her even feeling like my mom because she never had the chance to play with me, to open her arms as I took my first steps so I could crash into her, to teach me to tie my shoes, none of that or anything else. But then Dad reminded me, in a gentle way, that she couldn't do any of those things for me because the birth was complicated, "very hard," he said, and that she made sure I was okay instead of taking care of herself. That's definitely worthy of the "beloved" cred.

I kneel before my mother's headstone. "Hey, Mom. You excited to meet me? I know you created me, but we're still strangers when you think about it. I'm sure you've thought about this already. You've had a lot of time in your home theater where the credits start rolling because you died while I cried in some nurse's arms. Maybe that nurse could've helped with the severe bleeding if she hadn't been holding me. I don't know. I'm really sorry you had to die so I could live, I really am. I hope you don't send some border patrol to keep me out when I finally die.

"But I know you're not like that, because of Dad's stories. One of my favorites is the one where you were visiting your mother in the hospital, a few days before she died, and her roommate with Alzheimer's kept asking you if you wanted to hear her secret. You said yes and yes over and over even though you knew full well that she used to hide chocolate from her kids when they were younger because she had a sweet tooth." I place my palm on the headstone's face, and it's the closest I'll come to holding her hand. "Mom, am I going to be able to find love up there since I never got the chance to find it down here?"

She doesn't answer. There's no mysterious warmth taking over me, no voice in the wind. But it's okay. I'll know soon enough.

"Please look after me today, Mom, one last time, because I know I'm not already dead like Rufus thinks we are, and I would like to have my life-changing day. See you later."

I get up and turn to my open grave, which is maybe only three feet deep and uneven. I step in, sit down, and rest my back against the side the gravedigger hasn't finished with yet. I keep my toy sanctuary on my lap, and I must look like a kid playing with blocks in a park.

"Can I join you?" Rufus asks.

"There's only really room for one. Get your own grave."

Rufus steps inside anyway, kicks my feet, and squeezes in, resting one leg on one of mine so he'll fit. "No grave for me. I'm gonna be cremated like my family."

"Do you still have their ashes? We could scatter them somewhere. The 'Parting with Ashes' forum on *CountDowners* is really popular and—"

"The Plutos and I took care of that a month back," Rufus interrupts; I should try and rein in my stories about online strangers. "Scattered them outside my old building. I still felt mad empty afterward, but they're home now. I want the Plutos to scatter my ashes elsewhere."

"Where are you thinking? Pluto?"

"Althea Park," Rufus says.

"I love that park," I say.

"How do you know it?"

"I went there a lot when I was younger, always with my dad. He would teach me about different clouds, and I would shout out which clouds were in the sky while I was swinging toward them. Why do you like it there so much?"

"I don't know. I end up there a lot. It's where I kissed this girl, Cathy, for the first time. I went there after my family died, and after my first cycling marathon."

Here we are, two boys sitting in a cemetery as it begins drizzling, trading stories in my half-dug grave, as if we're not dying today. These moments of forgetting and relief are enough to push me through the rest of my day.

"Weird question: Do you believe in fate?" I ask.

"Weird answer: I believe in two fates," Rufus says.

"Really?"

"No." Rufus smiles. "I don't even believe in one. You?"

"How else do you explain us meeting?" I ask.

"We both downloaded an app and agreed to hang out," Rufus says.

"But look at us. My mom and your parents are dead. My father is out of commission. If our parents were around, we wouldn't have found ourselves on Last Friend." The app is designed mainly for adults, not teens. "If you can believe in two afterlives, you can believe in the universe playing puppet master. Can't you?"

Rufus nods as the rain comes down harder on us. He stands first and offers me a hand. I take it. The poetry you could write about Rufus helping me out of my grave isn't lost on me. I step out and walk over to my mother's headstone, kissing her inscribed name. I leave my toy sanctuary against the stone. I turn in time to catch Rufus snapping a photo of me; capturing moments really is his thing.

I turn to my headstone one last time.

HERE LIES
MATEO TORREZ, JR.
JULY 17, 1999

They'll add my End Day in no time: September 5, 2017.

My inscription, too. It's okay that there's a blank right now. I know what it will say and I know I'll make sure I've lived as I'm claiming: *He Lived for Everyone*. The words will wear away over time, but they'll have been true.

Rufus wheels his bike along the wet and muddy path, leaving tire tracks. I follow him, my insides feeling heavier with every footstep away from my mother and my open grave, knowing I'll be back soon enough.

"You sold me on fate," Rufus says. "Finish telling me about your afterlife."

I do.

PART THREE
The Beginning

It is not death that a man should fear,

but he should fear never beginning to live.

—Marcus Aurelius, Roman emperor

MATEO

12:22 p.m.

Twelve hours ago I received the phone call telling me I'm going to die today. In my own Mateo way, I've said tons of goodbyes already, to my dad, best friend, and goddaughter, but the most important goodbye is the one I said to Past Mateo, who I left behind at home when my Last Friend accompanied me into a world that has it out for us. Rufus has done so much for me and I'm here to help him confront any demons following him—except we can't whip out any flaming swords or crosses that double as throwing stars like in fantasy books. His company has helped me and maybe mine will help him through any heartache too.

Twelve hours ago I received the phone call telling me I'm going to die today, and I'm more alive now than I was then.

RUFUS

12:35 p.m.

I don't know where Mateo is leading me, but it's all good because the rain stopped and I'm recharged and ready to go after getting a strong power nap on the train ride back into the city. It sucks how I didn't dream, but no nightmares either. Win some, lose some.

I'm crossing out the Travel Arena because it's mad busy at this time of day, as Mateo pointed out, so if we're still alive in a few hours we have a better chance of not completely wasting away in lines. We have to wait for the herd to thin out, pretty much. Shitty way to think, but I'm not wrong. I hope whatever we're doing isn't some time-suck like Make-A-Moment. I'm betting it's charity work, or maybe he's been secretly chatting with Aimee and arranging a meet-up so she and I can make things right before I kick the bucket.

We've been in Chelsea for a solid ten minutes, in the park by the pier. I'm that guy I hate, the one who walks in the bike lane when there's clearly a lane for walkers and joggers. My karma score is gonna be jacked, legit. Mateo leads me toward the pier, where I stop.

"You gonna try and throw me over?" I ask.

"You've got an extra forty pounds on me," Mateo says. "You're safe. You said spreading your parents' and sister's ashes didn't do much for you. I thought maybe you could get some closure here."

"They all died on our way upstate," I say. Fingers crossed those road barriers our car flipped over, freak-accident style, have been repaired by now, but who knows.

"It doesn't have to be the crash site. Maybe the river will be enough."

"Not sure what I'm supposed to get out of this."

"I don't know either, and if you don't feel comfortable, we can turn around and do something else. Going to the cemetery gave me peace I wasn't expecting, and I want you to have that same wonder."

I shrug. "We're already here. Bring on the wonder."

There are no boats docked by the pier, which is a huge waste, like an empty parking lot. In July, I came by the pier a little farther uptown with Aimee and Tagoe because they wanted to see these waterfront statues, and came back there a week later because Malcolm missed out on account of food poisoning.

We walk across this arm of the pier. It's not made up of

planks, otherwise I'd be too nervous to go forward. I'm straight catching Mateo's paranoia, like a cold. The pier is all cement and sturdy, not some rickety mess that's gonna collapse under me, but feel free to put down a dollar on optimism tricking the shit out of me. We reach the end and I grab the steel-gray railing so I can lean out and see the river's currents doing their thing.

"How are you feeling?" Mateo asks.

"Like this whole day is a practical joke the world is playing on me. You're an actor and any minute now my parents, Olivia, and the Plutos are gonna run out the back of some van and surprise me. I wouldn't even be that pissed. I'd hug them and *then* kill them."

It's a fun thought, massacre aside.

"Seems pretty pissed to me," Mateo says.

"I've spent so much time being pissed at my family for leaving me, Mateo. Everyone's always running their mouth about survivor's guilt and I get it, but . . ." I've never talked about this with the Plutos, not even Aimee when we were dating, 'cause it's too horrible. "But I'm the one who left them, yo. I'm the one who got out the sinking car and swam away. I still think about if that was even me or some strong reflex. Like how you can't keep your hand on a hot stove without your brain forcing it away. It would've been mad easy to sink with them, even though Death-Cast hadn't hit me up yet. If it was that easy for me to almost die, maybe they should've worked harder to beat the odds and live. Maybe Death-Cast was wrong!"

Mateo comes closer and palms my shoulder. "Don't do this to yourself. There are entire forums on *CountDowners* for Deckers confident they're special. When Death-Cast calls, that's it. Game over. There isn't anything you could've done and there isn't anything they could've done differently."

"I could've driven," I snap, shaking off his hand. "Olivia's idea since I was tagging along. That way 'Decker hands' wouldn't be steering the car. But I was too nervous and too pissed and too lonely. I could've bought them a few more hours. Maybe they wouldn't have given up when things looked bad. Once I was out the car they just sat there, Mateo. No fight in them." They only cared about me getting out. "My pops reached for my door immediately, same time my mom did from behind. I could've opened my own door, it's not like my hand was jammed somewhere. I was dazed because our fucking car flew into the river, but I snapped out of it. They just gave up, though, once my door was open—*Olivia* didn't even gun for the escape."

I was forced to wait in the back of an ambulance with a towel that smelled like bleach around me as a team pulled their car out of the river.

"This was never your fault." Mateo's head is hanging low. "I'm going to give you a minute alone, but I'll be waiting for you. I hope that's what you want." He walks off, taking my bike with him, before I can answer.

I don't think a minute is enough—until I give in, crying harder than I have in weeks, and I hammer at the railing with the bottom of my fist. I keep going and going, hitting the railing because my family is dead, hitting it because my best friends are locked up, hitting it because my ex-girlfriend did us dirty, hitting it because I made a new dope friend and we don't even have a full day together. I stop, out of breath, like I just won a fight against ten dudes. I don't even want a picture of the Hudson, so I turn around and keep it behind, walking toward Mateo, who's wheeling my bike in pointless circles.

"You win," I say. "That was a good idea." He doesn't gloat like Malcolm would or taunt me like Aimee did whenever she won at Battleship. "My bad for snapping."

"You *needed* to snap."

He continues moving in his circle. I'm a little dizzy watching him.

"Truth."

"If you need to snap again, I'm here. Last Friends for life."

DELILAH GREY

12:52 p.m.

Delilah rushes to the only bookstore in the city that miraculously carries Howie Maldonado's science fiction novel, *The Lost Twin of Bone Bay*.

Delilah speeds toward the store, staying far away from the curb, ignoring the catcall from a balding man with a large gym bag, and rushing past two boys with one bike.

She's praying Howie Maldonado doesn't move up the interview before she can get there when she remembers there are greater stakes at play in Howie's dying life.

VIN PEARCE

12:55 p.m.

Death-Cast called Vin Pearce at 12:02 a.m. to tell him he's going to die today, which isn't that surprising.

Vin is pissed the beautiful woman with the colorful hair ignored him, pissed he never got married, pissed he was rejected by every woman on Necro this morning, pissed at his former coach who got in the way of his dreams, pissed at these two boys with a bike who are getting in the way of the destruction he's going to leave behind. The boy in the biker gear is so slow, taking up sidewalk space with the bike he's walking beside—bikes are meant to be ridden! Not carted around like a stroller. Vin barrels forward, no consequences in mind, bumping the boy's shoulder with his own.

The boy sucks his teeth, but his friend grabs his arm, holding him back.

Vin likes to be feared. He loves it in the outside world, but he loved it most in the wrestling ring. Four months ago, Vin began experiencing muscle pains, but refused to acknowledge his weaknesses. Lifting weights was a struggle with poor results; sets of twenty pull-ups became sets of four, on good days; and his coach pulled him out of the ring indefinitely because fighting would be impossible. Illnesses have always run through his family—his father died years ago after being diagnosed with multiple sclerosis, his aunt died from a ruptured ectopic pregnancy, and so on—but Vin believed he was better, stronger. He was destined for greatness, he was sure of it, like world championships and unbelievable riches. But chronic muscle disease pinned him down and he lost it all.

Vin walks inside the gym where he spent the past seven years training to become the next world heavyweight champion, the smell of sweat and dirty sneakers bringing back countless memories. The only memory that matters now is the one where his coach made him pack up his locker and suggested a new career route, like being a ringside commentator or becoming a coach himself.

Insulting.

Vin sneaks down to the generator room and pulls a homemade bomb out of his gym bag.

Vin is going to die where he was made. And he's not dying alone.

MATEO

12:58 p.m.

We pass a shop window with classic novels and new books sitting in children's chairs, like the books are hanging out in a waiting room, ready to be bought and read. I could use some lightness after the threatening grill of that man with the gym bag.

Rufus takes a picture of the window. "We can go in."

"I won't be longer than twenty minutes," I promise.

We go inside the Open Bookstore. I love how the store name is hopeful.

This is the best worst idea ever. I have no time to actually read any of these books. But I've never been in this store before because I usually have my books shipped to me or I borrow them from the school library. Maybe a bookshelf will topple over and that's how I go out—painful, but there are worse ways to die.

I bump into a waist-high table while eyeing an antique

clock on top of a bookshelf, knocking over their display copies of back-to-school books. I apologize to the bookseller—Joel, according to his name tag—and he tells me not to worry and assists me.

Rufus leaves his bike in the front of the store and follows me as I tour the aisles. I read the staff recommendations, all different genres praised in different handwriting, some more legible than others. I try avoiding the grief section, but two books catch my eye. One is *Hello, Deborah, My Old Friend*, the biography by Katherine Everett-Hasting that caused some controversy. The other is that bestselling guide no one shuts up about, *Talking About Death When You're Unexpectedly Dying*, written by some man who's still alive. I don't get it.

They have a lot of my favorites in the thriller and young adult sections.

I pause in front of the romance section, where they have a dozen books wrapped in brown paper stamped "Blind Date with a Book." There are little clues on what the book is to catch your interest, like the profile of someone you meet online. Like my Last Friend.

"Have you ever dated anyone?" Rufus asks.

The answer feels obvious. He's nice for giving me the benefit of the doubt. "Nope." I've only had crushes, but it's embarrassing to admit they were characters in books and TV shows. "I missed out. Maybe in the next life."

"Maybe," Rufus says.

I sense there's something more he wants to say; maybe he wants to crack a joke about how I should sign up for Necro so I don't die a virgin, as if sex and love are the same thing. But he says nothing.

I could be totally wrong.

"Was Aimee your first girlfriend?" I ask. I grab the paper-wrapped book with an illustration of a criminal running away, holding an oversized playing card, a heart: "Heart Stealer."

"First relationship," Rufus says, playing with this spinner of New York City–themed postcards. "But I had things for other classmates in my old school. They never went anywhere, but I tried. Did you ever get close to someone?" He slides a postcard of the Brooklyn Bridge out the spinner. "You can send them a postcard."

Postcards.

I smile as I grab one, two, four, six, twelve.

"You had a lot of crushes," Rufus says.

I move for the cash register, where Joel assists me again. "We should send postcards to people, you know?" I keep it vague because I don't want to break the news to this bookseller that the customers he's ringing up are dying at seventeen and eighteen. I'm not going to ruin his day. "The Plutos, any classmates . . ."

"I don't have their addresses," Rufus says.

"Send it to the school. They'll have the address for anyone you graduated with."

It's what I want to do. I buy the mystery book and the postcards, thank Joel for his help, and we leave. Rufus said the key to his relationships was speaking up. I can do this with the postcards, but I have to use my voice, too.

"I was nine when I bothered my dad about love," I say, looking through the postcards again at places in my own city I never visited. "I wanted to know if it was under the couch or high up in the closet where I couldn't reach yet. He didn't say that 'love is within' or 'love is all around you.'"

Rufus wheels his bike beside me as we pass this gym. "I'm hooked. What did he say?"

"That love is a superpower we all have, but it's not always a superpower I'd be able to control. Especially as I get older. Sometimes it'll go crazy and I shouldn't be scared if my power hits someone I'm not expecting it to." My face is warm, and I wish I had the superpower of common sense because this isn't something I should've ever said out loud. "That was stupid. Sorry."

Rufus stops and smiles. "Nah, I liked that. Thanks for that story, Super Mateo."

"It's actually Mega Master Mateo Man. Get it right, side-kick." I look up from the postcards. I really like his eyes. Brown, and tired even though he got some rest. "How do you know when love is love?"

"I—"

Glass shatters and we're suddenly thrown backward through the air as fire reaches out toward a screaming crowd. *This is it.* I slam against the driver's side of a car, my shoulder banging into the rearview mirror. My vision fades—darkness, fire, darkness, fire. My neck creaks when I turn and Rufus is beside me, his beautiful brown eyes closed; he's surrounded by my postcards of the Brooklyn Bridge, the Statue of Liberty, Union Square, and the Empire State Building. I crawl toward him and tense as I reach out to him. His heart is pounding against my wrist; his heart, like mine, desperately doesn't want to stop beating, especially not in chaos like this. Our breaths are erratic, disturbed and frightened. I have no idea what happened, just that Rufus is struggling to open his eyes and others are screaming. But not everyone. There are bodies on the ground, faces kissing cement, and beside one woman with very colorful hair who's struggling to get up is another, except her eyes are skyward and her blood is staining a rain puddle.

RUFUS

1:14 p.m.

Yo. A little over twelve hours ago that Death-Cast dude hit me up telling me I'm a goner today. I'm sitting on a street curb, hugging my knees like I did in the back of the ambulance when my family died, straight shaken now over that explosion, the kind you only see in summer blockbusters. Police and ambulance sirens are blasting, and the firefighters are handling business on the burning gym, but it's too late for mad people. Deckers need to start wearing special collars or jackets, something that'll clue us in on not flocking in one place. That could've been me and Mateo if we were a minute or two slower. Maybe, maybe not. But I know this: a little over twelve hours ago, I got a phone call telling me I'm gonna die today, and I thought I made my peace with that, but I've never been more scared in my life of what's gonna go down later.

MATEO

1:28 p.m.

The fire has been put out.

My stomach has been screaming at me for the past twenty minutes to feed it, as if I can call time-out on my End Day to have another meal without wasting valuable time, and as if Rufus and I weren't almost just killed in an explosion that claimed other Deckers.

Witnesses are speaking to the cops and I don't know what they could possibly be saying. The explosion that destroyed the gym came out of nowhere.

I sit beside Rufus, his bike, and my bookstore bag. The postcards are scattered all around us and they can stay there on the ground. I don't have it in me to write anything when there are Deckers who've now found themselves in body bags, on the way to the morgue.

I can't trust this day.

RUFUS

1:46 p.m.

I gotta keep it moving.

I want more than anything to sit across from the Plutos and talk about nothing, but the next best thing to break me out of this mood is a bike ride. It's what I did after my parents and Olivia died, and when Aimee broke up with me, and this morning after beating down Peck and getting the alert. Once we're away from the chaos I get on the bike, flexing the brakes. Mateo dodges my gaze. "Please get on," I say. It's the first time I've spoken since being thrown in the air like a wrestler.

"No," Mateo says. "I'm sorry. It's not safe."

"Mateo."

"Rufus."

"Mateo."

"Rufus."

"Please, Mateo. I gotta ride after what went down and

I don't wanna leave you behind. We're supposed to be living, period. We know how this ends for both of us, but I don't wanna look back on any moment thinking we straight wasted it. This isn't some dream *and we won't wake up from this.*"

I don't know what else I can do. Get on my knees and beg? It's not my style, but I'll give it a go if it gets him to come with me.

Mateo looks seasick. "Promise to go slow, okay? Avoid going down any hills and through puddles."

"Promise."

I hand him the helmet, which he's refusing, but there's no way in hell I'm more at risk than he is. He straps the helmet on, hangs the bookstore bag from the handlebar, climbs on the rear pegs, and grips my shoulders.

"Is this too tight? I just don't want to fall, helmet or not."

"No, you're fine."

"Cool."

"Ready?"

"Ready."

I pedal, slowly, feeling the burn in my calves as I carry two people forward; it's like running up a hill. I find a good rhythm and put the police and corpses and destroyed gym behind us.

DEIRDRE CLAYTON

1:50 p.m.

Death-Cast did not call Deirdre Clayton because she isn't dying today, but she's going to prove them wrong.

Deirdre is on the ledge of her apartment building roof, eight stories high. There are two deliverymen watching her, either interested in catching her with the couch they're moving into the building or else placing bets on if she's a Decker or not. The blood and broken bones on the pavement will settle their wager.

This isn't the first time Deirdre has found herself higher than the world. Seven years ago, back when she was in high school and months after Death-Cast's services became available to the public, Deirdre was challenged to a fight after school, and when Charlotte Simmons and instigators and other students who only knew Deirdre as "that lesbian with the dead parents" arrived at what was supposed to be the battlefield, Deirdre was on the roof instead. She never understood how the way she loves could drag such hatred out of others, and she refused to stick around to find the love everyone hated her for. Except back then she had her childhood best friend to talk her down.

Today Deirdre is alone, knees wobbling, and crying because, as much as she wants to believe in better days, her job prevents her from doing so. Deirdre works at Make-A-Moment, where she's charging Deckers for thrills and fake experiences, fake *memories*. She doesn't understand why these Deckers aren't home with loved ones, particularly those two teen boys today, who, as they were leaving, talked about how underwhelming the virtual reality experience was. It's wasted time.

The boys from earlier reminded her of a short story she'd finished working on this morning, something for her eyes only that has kept her distracted in the quiet times at work. Her story is set in an alternate world where Death-Cast has another branch called Life-Cast, and this extension informs Deckers of when they will be reincarnated so their families and friends will know how to find them in their next life. It's centered around fifteen-year-old twin sisters, Angel and Skylar, who are devastated to learn one twin is about to die and immediately seek out Life-Cast's services to find out when Skylar will be reincarnated. Angel is upset because she won't be reunited with her sister for another seven years, when Skylar will be reincarnated as the son of some family in

Australia. Skylar dies saving her sister's life, and it ends with a devastated Angel depositing a hundred-dollar bill into an old piggy bank to start funding her way to Australia in seven years to welcome her sister back into the world—albeit as an infant boy.

Deirdre thought she would continue that story, but scratch that now. Life-Cast doesn't exist, and she's not waiting around for Death-Cast to let her know when her time is up. This is a world of violence and fear and children dying without having lived and she wants no part of it.

It will be so easy to jump. . . .

She stands on one foot, her entire body shaking, surely about to tumble forward any moment now. She once scaled a rooftop at work, in their virtual parkour station, but that was an illusion.

Death is prophesied in Deirdre's name, that of a heroine in Irish mythology who took her own life.

Deirdre looks down, ready to fly, when two boys on a bike turn the corner—they resemble the boys from earlier.

Deirdre reaches deep within herself, far past the place where lies and hopelessness come easily, and even beneath the very honest truth where she's okay with the impacting relief that comes with flying off this roof. She sees two boys living and this makes her feel less dead inside.

Intent may not be enough to cause her to actually die, she

knows this from the countless other mornings when she's woken up to ugliness, but when faced with the chance to prove Death-Cast wrong, Deirdre makes the right decision and lives.

MATEO

1:52 p.m.

This bike isn't the worst thing.

I squeeze Rufus's shoulder when he makes a sharp left, dodging some delivery guys who are staring up into the sky instead of moving a couch into a building, and we continue sailing down the street.

I felt really wobbly when he first got going, but as he picks up a good enough speed to throw a breeze our way, I appreciate the control I'm entrusting to him.

It's freeing.

I'm not expecting to go any faster than we are, but it's more exciting than the Make-A-Moment skydiving. Yeah, riding a bike is more thrilling than quote-unquote jumping out of a plane.

If I weren't such a coward, or a Decker, I would lean against Rufus, shifting my weight against him. I'd put my arms out and close my eyes, but it's too risky, so I keep holding him, which works for me, too. But when we reach our destination I'm going to do something small and brave.

RUFUS

2:12 p.m.

I slow down as we turn in to Althea Park. Mateo's hands slip off my shoulders and my bike is immediately lighter. I brake. I turn to see if he's broken his face or busted his head open despite the helmet, but he's jogging toward me and a smile cracks on his face; he's all good. "Did you jump off?"

"I did!" Mateo takes off the helmet.

"You didn't want me riding the bike, and now you're going ahead and throwing yourself off one?"

"I was in the moment."

I wanna take full credit, but he's had this in him all along, always wanting to do something exciting, just being too scared to go out and do it.

"You feeling better?" Mateo asks.

"A little," I admit. I get off the bike. I limp toward the deserted playground as some college-age-looking dudes play handball in a nearby court, splashing in the puddles as they chase after the ball whenever someone misses. My basketball shorts are damp and dirty from the cemetery, same for Mateo's jeans, so the wet bench doesn't bother us when we sit. "I hate that we were there for that."

"I know. You never want to see someone die, even if you never knew them."

"It pulled me out of my bullshit zone. My whole I'm-ready-for-whatever-is-gonna-hit-us thing is bullshit, and I'm scared shitless. We could legit die in the next thirty seconds from rogue bullets or something, and I hate that. Whenever I get into this freaking-out headspace, I end up here. Never fails."

"But good times brought you here, too," he says. "Like finishing your first marathon." He takes a deep breath. "And having your first kiss with some girl."

"Yeah." That kiss bothers him, huh. I guess my gut was right. I stay shut for a solid stretch of time, only staring at squirrels climbing trees and birds chasing each other on foot. "Have you ever played Gladiator?"

"I know the game," he says.

"Good. Have you ever played?"

"I've seen others play."

"So no."

"No."

I stand, pull Mateo by his wrists, and lead him to the monkey bars. "I challenge you to a Gladiator match."

"I can't refuse, can I?"

"Definitely not."

"We just survived an explosion."

"What's a little more pain?"

Jungle gym Gladiator isn't crazy like an age-old coliseum match, but I've seen schoolmates get hurt before. Hell, I'm the reason some of them got hurt. Two players—gladiators—swing from the monkey bars into each other to try and knock their opponent down. It's the most barbaric childhood game, mad fun. We're both fairly tall, so we could just tiptoe and grab hold of the monkey bars, but I mini-hop and lift myself up, like I'm doing pull-ups. Mateo hops and takes hold but has zero upper-body strength, so he falls back on his feet ten seconds later. He jumps again and holds himself up this time. I count down from three as we swing toward each other, closing the small distance between us. I kick at him and he swerves to the side, almost falling. I lift my legs higher, throwing my legs around his midriff. He tries breaking out of my grapple as I rattle him, but no dice. My hands are kind of aching, so when he lets go, laughing, I fall with him onto the mat. I bang against the mat, shocks chasing each other around my body, but the pain doesn't kill me. We're side by side with each other, laughing while we massage our aching elbows and legs. Our backs are wetter and we keep slipping while trying to get up. Idiots. Mateo gets it together and helps me up.

"I won, right?" I say.

"I think it's a tie," he says.

"Rematch?"

"I'm good. I'm pretty sure I saw my life flash before my eyes when we were falling."

I smile. "Let me get real with you, Mateo." I say his name a lot, even though I'm obviously talking to him, because it's just cool, seriously—*Mateo.* "Past few months have been brutal. My life always felt over even without the alert. There were days I believed I could prove Death-Cast wrong and ride my bike into the river. But on top of being scared now, I'm pissed off because there's so much I'll never get to have. Time . . . other stuff, like—"

"You're not going to off yourself today, right?" Mateo asks.

"I'm safe from myself, I promise. I don't want everything over. Please promise you won't go dying before me. I can't see that."

"Only if you promise the same thing."

"We can't both promise this."

"Then I'm not promising my promise," Mateo says. "I don't want you to see me die, but I can't watch you die either."

"That's messed up. You're really gonna go down as the Decker who didn't promise to grant another Decker his dying wish?"

"Forcing myself to watch you die is not something I'll

promise you. You're my Last Friend, and it would wreck me."

"You don't deserve to die, Mateo."

"I don't think anyone deserves to die."

"Except serial killers, right?"

He doesn't answer because he probably thinks I won't like his answer. If anything, it only further proves my point: Mateo doesn't deserve to die.

A handball bounces our way, and Mateo races past me to catch it. This guy chases after the ball, but Mateo gets to it first and tosses it to him.

"Thanks," the guy says.

Homeboy is really pale, like he doesn't leave his apartment nearly enough. What a shitty, stormy day to come out and play. I'm guessing he's nineteen or twenty, but I'm not ruling out he's our age.

"No problem," Mateo says.

He's turning away when he sees my bike. "Nice! Is that a Trek?"

"It is. Got it for off-road races. Do you ride one?"

"Mine got wrecked—brake cable got busted and the seat clamp was all screwy. I'm buying another one when I get a job that pays more than eight an hour," he says.

"Take mine," I say. I can do this. I walk to my bike, which carried me through a brutal race and everywhere else I wanted to go, and wheel it toward this guy. "It's your lucky day, seriously. My friend isn't about me riding this thing, so you can have it."

"You serious?"

"You sure?" Mateo asks.

I nod. "It's yours," I tell the guy. "Have at it. I'm moving soon anyway and won't be able to bring it."

The dude throws the handball over to his friends, who've been shouting for him to come back and play. He sits on the bike and plays with the gears. "Wait. You didn't jack this from someone, right?"

"Nope."

"And it's not broken? Is that why you're leaving it behind?"

"It's not broken. Look, do you want it or not?"

"We good, we good. Can I pay you something?"

I shake my head. "We good," I say back.

Mateo gives the guy the helmet and he doesn't put it on before riding back to his friends. I get my phone out and snap photos of him riding my bike, his back to me as he stands on the pedals, while his friends play handball. It's a solid portrait of kids—a little older than me, but they're kids, don't fight me on that—too young to be worried about shit like Death-Cast alerts. They know their day is going to end like it usually does.

"Good move," Mateo says.

"I got one last ride out of it. I'm set." I take more photos: the ongoing handball match, the monkey bars where we played Gladiator, the long yellow slide, the swings. "Come."

I almost go back for my bike before remembering I've just given it up. I feel lighter, like my shadow just quit his day job, walked off, and threw up a peace sign. Mateo follows me to the swings. "You said you'd come here with your dad, right? Naming clouds and shit? Let's swing."

Mateo sits on the swing, holds on for dear life—I know—takes a few steps, and propels forward, his legs looking like they're about to kick over a building. I get a picture before joining him on the swing, my arms wrapped around the chains, and I manage to take some pictures. Puts me and my phone at risk—again, I know—but for every four blurry shots I snap a good one. Mateo points out the dark nimbus clouds, and I'm straight wowed I get to live in this moment with someone who doesn't deserve to die.

It'll storm again soon, but for now we go back and forth, and I wonder if he's thinking two Deckers sharing swings might mean the entire thing will collapse and kill us, or if we'll swing so high we'll fly and fall out of life, but I feel safe.

We slow down and I shout to him, "The Plutos gotta scatter me here."

"Your place of change!" Mateo shouts while the swing throws him backward. "Any other big changes today? Besides the obvious?"

"Yeah!"

"What?"

I smile over at him as our swinging comes to a stop. "I

gave up my bike." I know what he's really asking, but I don't take the bait. He's gotta make a move himself, I'm not robbing him of that moment, it's too big. I stay seated as he stands. "Weird how this is the last time I'll be in this park—with flesh and a heart that works."

Mateo looks around; it's his last time here too. "You ever hear about those Deckers who turn into trees? Sounds like a fairy tale, I know. The Living Urn offers Deckers the opportunity to have their ashes put in a biodegradable urn containing a tree seed that absorbs nutrients and stuff from their ashes, which I thought was fantasy but nope. Science."

"Maybe instead of having my ashes just scattered on the ground some dog is going to shit on, I could live on as a tree?"

"Yeah, and other teens will carve hearts into you and you can produce oxygen. People like air," Mateo says.

It's drizzling so I get up from the swing, the chain rattling behind me. "Let's get somewhere dry, weirdo."

Coming back as a tree would be pretty chill, like I'm growing up in Althea Park again, not that I'll say that out loud because yo, you can't go around telling people you wanna be a tree and expect them to take you seriously.

DAMIEN RIVAS

2:22 p.m.

Death-Cast did not call Damien Rivas because he isn't dying today, which he considers a shame because he's not very impressed with the way he's been living his life lately. Damien has always been an adrenaline junkie. New roller coasters every summer he met the required height. Stealing candy from drugstores and cash from his father's pouch. Fighting those who are the Goliath to his David. Starting a gang.

Playing a game of darts against himself isn't exactly thrilling.

Talking to Peck on the phone isn't exciting either.

"Calling the cops is some little bitch shit," Damien says, loud enough for his speakerphone. "Getting me to call the cops goes against everything I stand for."

"I know. You only like the cops when they're called on you," Peck says.

Damien nods, like Peck can see him. "We should've handled that ourselves."

"You're right," Peck says. "The cops never even got Rufus. They're probably giving up because he's a Decker."

"Let's get you some justice," Damien says. Excitement and purpose surge through him. He's been living away from the edge all summer and now he's inching closer and closer to his favorite place in the world.

He imagines Rufus's face where the dartboard is. He throws the dart and hits bull's-eye—right between Rufus's eyes.

MATEO

2:34 p.m.

It's raining again, harder than back at the cemetery. I feel like the bird I looked after as a kid, the one pummeled by the rain. The one that left its nest before it was ready.

"We should go inside," I say.

"Scared of catching a cold?"

"Scared of becoming a statistic who gets struck by lightning." We hang out underneath the awning of this pet store, puppies in the window distracting us from figuring out our next move. "I have an idea to honor your explorer side. Maybe we can ride the train back and forth. There's so much I never got to see in my own city. Maybe we'll stumble into something awesome. Forget it, that's stupid."

"That's not stupid at all. I know exactly what you're talking about!" Rufus leads the way to a nearby subway station. "Our city is gigantic, too. Someone can live here their entire life and never walk every block in every borough. I once dreamt I was on some intense cycling trip where my tires had this glow-in-the-dark paint on them and I was aiming to make the city light up by midnight."

I smile. "Did you succeed?" There's actual race-against-the-clock suspense in this dream.

"Nah, I think I started dreaming about sex or something and woke up from that," Rufus says. He's probably not a virgin, but I don't ask because it's not my business.

We're heading back downtown. Who knows how far we'll go. Maybe we'll ride the train until the very last stop, catch a bus, ride that to an even farther stop. Maybe we'll end up in another state, like New Jersey.

There's a train, door open, at the platform and we run into it, finding an empty bench in the corner.

"Let's play a game," Rufus says.

"Not Gladiator again."

Rufus shakes his head. "Nope. It's a game called Traveler I used to play with Olivia. Make up a story about another passenger, where they're going and who they are." He shifts, his body leaning against mine as he discreetly points at a woman in blue medical scrubs under her jacket, holding a shopping bag. "She's going home to take a nap and then blast some pop music as she gets ready for her first day off in nine days. She doesn't know it yet, but her favorite bar is gonna be closed for renovations."

"That sucks," I say. Rufus turns to me, his wrist spinning,

encouraging me to go on. "Oh. She'll go back home, where she'll find her favorite movie on some cable network and catch up on emails to her friends during commercial breaks." He grins. "What?"

"She started her evening fairly adventurous," he says.

"She was taking a nap."

"So she'd have energy to party all night!"

"I figured she'd want to see what her friends are up to. She probably misses text messages and phone calls since she's usually too busy saving lives and delivering babies. She needs this, believe me." I nod at a girl with headphones bigger than fists and hair dyed platinum. She's drawing something colorful on her tablet with a blue stylus. I nod toward her. "She got the tablet for her birthday last week and she really wanted it for games and video-chatting with her friends, but she discovered this design app and experimented with it when she was bored. It's her new obsession."

"I like that," Rufus says. The train stops and the girl is scrambling to get her illustrated tote bag together. She runs out of the car right when the doors are closing—like an action movie sequence. "And now she's going home where she'll be late for a video chat with her friends because she's too busy getting this one idea right."

We keep playing Traveler. Rufus points out a girl with a suitcase who he thinks is running away, but I correct him. She's actually returning home after a big fight with her sister and they're going to repair their relationship. I mean, anyone with eyes can see that's what's happening. Another passenger, soaked, was having car trouble and had to ditch his van—no, wait, his Mercedes, Rufus corrects, because a train ride is a humbling experience for this rich guy. Some NYU students jump on the train with umbrellas by their sides, possibly coming from orientation, their whole lives ahead of them, and we play a flash round predicting who they'll become: a family court judge in a family of artists; a comedian in Los Angeles, where they'll appreciate her traffic jokes; a talent agent who won't make it big for a few years but will have her time to shine; a screenwriter for a children's TV show about monsters playing sports; a skydiving instructor, which is funny because he has this handlebar mustache that must look like it's smiling against the wind during every descent.

If someone else were playing Traveler, what would they predict for me and Rufus?

Rufus taps my shoulder, pointing at the exit as the doors open. "Hey, isn't this the stop where we spontaneously got our gym memberships?"

"Huh?"

"Yeah, it is! You wanted to be brolic after some dick bumped into you at the Bleachers concert," Rufus says, right when the doors close.

I haven't been to a Bleachers concert but I get the game now. "Wrong night, Rufus. The dude bumped into me at the Fun concert. Hey, this is the stop where we got tattoos."

"Yeah. The tattoo artist, Barclay—"

"Baker," I correct. "Remember? Baker the tattoo artist who quit medical school?"

"Riiiight. We caught Baker in a good mood and he gave us a Buy One, Get One Free deal. I got the bike tire on my forearm"—he taps his arm—"and you got . . . ?"

"A male seahorse."

Rufus looks so confused, like he might call time-out to see if we're still playing the same game. "Uh . . . remind me why you got that one again."

"My dad is really into male seahorses. He carried me through life solo, remember? I can't believe you forgot the meaning of the seahorse tattoo on my shoulder. No, wrist. Yeah, it's on my wrist. That's cooler."

"I can't believe you forgot where your tattoo is."

When we get to the next stop, Rufus throws us into the future: "Hey, this is where I normally get off for work. When I'm in the office, at least, and not in whatever resort around the world they send me to for review. It's wild I get to work in a building you designed and built."

"So wild, Rufus."

I look down at where my seahorse tattoo should be.

In the future, Rufus is a travel blogger and I'm an architect. We have tattoos we got together. We've gone to so many concerts he can't keep them straight in his head. I almost wish we weren't so creative in this moment, because these fake memories of friendship feel incredible. Imagine that—reliving something you never lived.

"We have to leave our mark," I say, getting up from my seat.

"We going outside to piss on fire hydrants?"

I put the blind-date book on the seat. "I don't know who will find this. But isn't it cool knowing someone will if we leave it here?"

"It's true. This is prime seating," Rufus says, getting up from the bench.

The train stops and the doors open. There has to be more to life than imagining a future for yourself. I can't just wish for the future; I have to take risks to create it.

"There's something I really want to do," I say.

"We out," Rufus says, smiling.

We get off the train before the doors close, almost bumping into two girls, and we take off out of the subway.

ZOE LANDON

2:57 p.m.

Death-Cast called Zoe Landon at 12:34 a.m. to tell her she's going to die today. Zoe was lonely, having only moved to New York eight days ago to begin classes at NYU *today*. She's barely unpacked her boxes, let alone made friends yet. But thankfully the Last Friend app was one click away. Her first message went to this boy Mateo, but he never responded. Maybe he died. Maybe he ignored her message. Maybe he found a Last Friend.

Like Zoe ultimately did.

Zoe and Gabriella get on the train right before the doors close, dodging two boys to do so. They rush to the bench in the corner, halting when they see a paper-wrapped object sitting there. Rectangular. Every time Zoe enters the subway, there are all these signs encouraging her to say something if she sees something—she's seeing *something*.

"This is bad," Zoe says. "You should get off at the next stop."

Gabriella, fearless because she didn't receive the alert today, picks up the object.

Zoe flinches.

"It's a book," Gabriella says. "Ooh! It's a surprise book!" She sits and eyes the illustration of a fleeing criminal. "I love this art."

Zoe sits next to her. She thinks the drawing is cute but respects Gabriella's opinion.

"It's my turn to tell you a secret," Gabriella says. "If you want."

Zoe shared all her secrets today with Gabriella. All the secrets she made her childhood best friends pinkie swear to never tell another soul. All the heartbreaking ones she always kept to herself because speaking up was too hard. Together, the two have laughed and cried, as if they've been best friends their entire lives. "Your secret dies with me," Zoe says. She doesn't laugh and neither does Gabriella, but she squeezes her hand to let her know she's going to be okay. A promise based on nothing but a gut instinct. Screw evidence of the afterlife.

"It's not a huge secret, but I'm Batman . . . of the Manhattan graffiti world," Gabriella says.

"Aw, you had me really excited, Batman . . . of the Manhattan graffiti world," Zoe says.

"I specialize in graffiti pushing Last Friends. In some places I'll draw with marker, like on menus and train posters, but my true love is graffiti. I've done tags for the Last Friends

I've met. Anywhere I can. In the past week, I've covered walls with the cute silhouettes from the app by McDonald's, two hospitals, and a soup spot. I hope everyone uses it." Gabriella taps her fingers against the book. At first look, Zoe thought the colors around her nails was a polish job gone terribly wrong, but she knows the truth now. "Anyway. I love art and I will tag a mailbox or something with your name."

"Maybe somewhere on the Broadway strip? I won't ever have my name in lights, but it'll be there," Zoe says. She pictures her request now. Her heart is full and empty at the thought.

Passengers look up from their newspapers and phone games and stare at Zoe. Indifference on one's face, pity on another's. Pure sadness from a black woman with this gorgeous afro. "Sorry to lose you," the woman says.

"Thank you," Zoe says.

The woman returns to her phone.

Zoe scoots closer to Gabriella. "I feel like I made this weird," she says, her voice quieter than before.

"Speak up while you can," Gabriella says.

"Let's see what that book is," Zoe says. She's curious. "Open it."

Gabriella hands Zoe the book. "*You* open it. It's your . . ."

"It's my End Day, not my birthday," Zoe says. "I don't need a gift and I'm not exactly going to read the book in the next . . ." Zoe checks her watch and feels dizzy. She has at most nine hours left—and she's a *very* slow reader. "Consider this gift left behind by someone else my gift to *you*. Thanks for being my Last Friend."

The woman across looks up. Her eyes widen. "I'm sorry to interrupt, but I'm just really happy to hear you're Last Friends. I'm happy you found someone on your End Day." She gestures to Gabriella. "And that you're helping make days full. It's beautiful."

Gabriella wraps an arm around Zoe's shoulders and pulls her close. The two thank the woman.

Of course Zoe meets the most welcoming New Yorkers on her End Day.

"Let's open it together," Gabriella says, returning their attention to the book.

"Deal," Zoe says.

Zoe hopes Gabriella continues befriending Deckers when she can.

Life isn't meant to be lived alone. Neither are End Days.

MATEO

3:18 p.m.

Seeing Lidia will be a huge risk, but it's one I want to take.

The bus pulls up and we allow everyone else to get on first before boarding. I ask the bus driver if he received the alert today and he shakes his head. This ride should be safe. We can still die on the bus, yeah, but the odds of the bus being completely totaled and killing us while leaving everyone else severely injured seem pretty low.

I borrow Rufus's phone so I can call Lidia. My phone's battery is dying, down close to thirty percent, and I want to make sure the hospital can reach me in case my dad wakes up. I move to a different seat near the back of the bus and dial Lidia's number.

Lidia picks up almost instantly, but there's still this pause before she answers, a lot like in the weeks after Christian died. "Hello?'

"Hi," I say.

"Mateo!"

"I'm sorry, I—"

"You blocked my number! I taught you how to do that!"

"I had to—"

"How could you not tell me?"

"I—"

"Mateo, I'm your fucking best fucking friend—Penny, don't listen to Mommy—and you don't fucking tell me you're dying?"

"I didn't want—"

"Shut up. Are you okay? How are you doing?"

I've always thought Lidia is like a coin being flipped in the air. Tails is when she's so pissed it's like she's turning her back on you and heads is when she sees you at her clearest. I think we've landed on heads, but who knows.

"I'm okay, Lidia. I'm with a friend. A new friend," I say.

"Who is this? How'd you meet her?"

"The Last Friend app," I say. "His name is Rufus. He's a Decker too."

"I want to see you."

"Me too. That's why I'm calling. Any chance you could drop off Penny somewhere and meet me at the Travel Arena?"

"Abuelita is already here. I called her—freaking the fuck out—hours ago and she came home from work. I'll go to the arena, right now, but please get there safely. Don't run. Walk slowly, except when you're crossing the street. Only cross when it's your light and only when there isn't a car in sight, even if they're stopped at a red light, or parked along the sidewalk. Actually, do not move. Where are you right now? I'm coming for you. Do not move unless someone around you looks shady."

"I'm on a bus with Rufus already," I say.

"Two Deckers on one bus? Do you have a death wish? Mateo, those odds are insane. That thing could topple over."

My face burns a little. "I don't have a death wish," I quietly say.

"I'm sorry. I'm shutting up. Please be careful. I have to see you one la— I have to see you, okay?"

"You'll see me and I'll see you. I promise."

"I don't want to hang up," she says.

"Me either."

We don't hang up. We could, and should, probably use this time to talk about memories or find things to apologize for in case I can't keep my promise, but nope, we talk about how Penny just hit herself on the head with a big toy and isn't crying, like the little soldier she is. A new memory to laugh over is just as good as reflecting on an old one, I think. It may even be better. I don't want to kill Rufus's phone battery in case the Plutos reach out, so Lidia and I agree to hang up at the same time. Pressing *End* kills my mood and the world feels heavier again.

PECK

3:21 p.m.

Peck is getting the gang back together.

The gang with no name.

Peck got his nickname because there's no power behind his punches. More annoying than harmful, like a bird pecking on you. If you want someone laid out, sic the Knockout King on them. Peck is good with stomping someone out if the occasion calls for it, but Damien and Kendrick don't keep him around because he's an extra body. Peck's access to an end-all weapon makes him valuable.

He walks toward his closet, feeling Damien's and Kendrick's eyes on his back. From here on it's like a Russian nesting doll, designed that way by Peck. He opens the closet, wondering if he has it in him. He opens the hamper, wondering if he's okay never seeing Aimee again, knowing she'll never forgive him if she ever finds out he's responsible. He opens the last box, a shoebox, knowing he's got to respect himself for once.

Peck will gain respect by unloading this gun into the one who disrespected him.

"What we do now?" Damien asks.

Peck opens up Instagram, goes on Rufus's profile, and is pissed to find more comments from Aimee saying how much she misses him. He keeps refreshing the account, over and over.

"We wait."

MATEO

3:26 p.m.

The rain turns to drizzle when the bus stops outside the World Travel Arena at Thirtieth and Twelfth. I step off the bus first and behind me there's a squeak and "FUCK!" I turn in time to grab onto the steps' railing so Rufus doesn't fall face-first out of the bus and take me with him. He's a little muscular, so the weight hurts my shoulders, but Rufus helps situate us both.

"Wet floor," Rufus says. "My bad."

We're here.

We're safe.

We have each other's back. We'll stretch this day out as long as possible, like we're the summer solstice.

The Travel Arena has always reminded me of the Museum of Natural History, except half as big and with international flags fixed along the edges of the dome. The Hudson River is a couple blocks away, which I don't point out to Rufus. The maximum capacity of the arena is three thousand people, which is more than perfect for Deckers, their guests, those with incurable diseases, and anyone else looking to enjoy the experience.

We decide to get our tickets while waiting for Lidia.

A staff member assists us. The three lines are organized by urgency, as in, those with sicknesses versus those of us dying today by some unknown force versus bored visitors. It's easy figuring out our line with one look at the others. The line to our right is full of laughter, selfies, texting. The line to our left has none of that. There's a young woman with a scarf wrapped around her head leaning against her oxygen tank; others are wheezing terribly; some are disfigured or badly burned. The sadness chokes me, not only for them, and not even for myself, but for the others ahead of us in our line who were woken up from their safe lives and will hurtle into danger in the next few hours, maybe even minutes. And then there are those who never got this far in the day.

"Why can't we have a chance?" I ask Rufus.

"A chance at what?" He's looking around, taking pictures of the arena and the lines.

"A chance at another chance," I say. "Why can't we knock on Death's door and beg or barter or arm-wrestle or have a staring contest for the chance to keep living? I'd even want to fight for the chance to decide how I die. I'd go in my sleep." And I would only go to sleep after I lived bravely, as the kind of person someone would want to wrap their arm around, who would maybe even nuzzle against my chin or shoulder, and go on and on about how happy we were to be alive with each other without question.

Rufus lowers his phone and looks me in the eyes. "You really think you can beat Death in an arm-wrestling match?"

I laugh and look away from him because the eye contact is warming my face. An Uber pulls up and Lidia storms out of the backseat. She's frantically looking around for me, and even though today isn't her End Day, I'm still nervous when a bike rider almost clips her, like he'll knock her unconscious and she'll find herself in the hospital with Dad.

"Lidia!"

I run out of line as her eyes find me. I almost trip in my excitement, like I haven't seen her in years. She throws her arms around me and squeezes, almost as if she herself has pulled me out of a sinking car, or caught me after I've fallen out of a crashing plane. She says everything in this hug—every thank-you, every I-love-you, every apology. I squeeze her back to thank her, to make her feel my love, to apologize, and everything else that falls deep inside and skirts outside these realms. It's the sweetest moment in our friendship since she handed me Penny as a newborn—Lidia steps back and slaps me hard across the face.

"You should've told me." Lidia pulls me back into another hug.

My cheek stings, but I dig my chin into her shoulder, and she smells like whatever cinnamon thing she must've fed Penny today because she hasn't changed out of the baggy shirt I last saw her in. In our hug we sway and I search for Rufus in line and he's clearly shocked by the slap. It's weird how Rufus doesn't know this is Lidia at her core, how, like I said, she's a coin constantly flipping. It's strange how I've only known Rufus for a day.

"I know," I tell Lidia. "You know I'm sorry and I was only trying to protect you."

"You're supposed to be with me forever," Lidia cries. "You're supposed to be around to play bad cop when Penny brings a crush home for the first time. You're supposed to keep me company with card games and bad TV marathons when she leaves for college. You're supposed to be around to vote for Penny to become president because you know she's such a control freak already that she won't be happy until she's ruling the country. God knows she'll sell her soul to take over the whole world, and you're supposed to be there to help me stop her from making Faustian deals."

I don't know what to say. I go back and forth between nodding and shaking my head because I don't know what to do. "I'm sorry."

"It's not your fault." Lidia squeezes my shoulder.

"Maybe it is. Maybe if I wasn't hiding I'd have street smarts or something. It's early to be blaming myself, but maybe it's going to be my fault, Lidia." This day has sort of felt like being thrust out into the wilderness with all the supplies I'd need to survive and no idea how to even make a fire.

"Shut your face," Lidia demands. "This is not your fault. We failed you."

"Now you shut your face."

"That's the rudest thing you've ever said," Lidia says with a smile, like I've had promise to be mean all along. "The world isn't the safest place ever, we know that because of Christian and everyone else dying on the daily. But I should've shown you some risks are worth it."

Sometimes you have a child who you love more than anything, unexpectedly. This was one way she showed me. "I'm taking risks today," I say. "And I want you here because it's so much harder for you to break out and be adventurous with Penny in your life. You've always wanted to see the world, and since we're not going to get a chance in this lifetime to go on road trips, I'm happy we can travel together right now." I hold her hand. I nod toward Rufus.

Lidia turns to Rufus with the same nervous face she had when we were sitting in her bathroom with her pregnancy test. And just like then, before she flipped over the stick to see the result, she says, "Let's do this." She squeezes my hand, which Rufus focuses on.

"Hey, what's up?" Rufus asks.

"Better days, obviously," Lidia says. "This fucking sucks. I'm so sorry."

"Not your fault," Rufus says.

Lidia stares at me like she's still surprised I'm in front of her.

We reach the front of the line. The teller, dressed in a cheerful yellow vest, solemnly smiles. "Welcome to the World Travel Arena. Sorry to lose you three."

"I'm not dying," Lidia corrects.

"Oh. Cost for guests is going to be one hundred dollars," the teller says. He looks at me and Rufus. "Suggested donation is one dollar for Deckers."

I pay for all our tickets, donating an extra couple hundred dollars in the hope that the arena remains open for many, many years. What the arena provides for Deckers seems incomparable, way better than the Make-A-Moment station. The teller thanks us for our donation and doesn't seem surprised by it; Deckers are always throwing their money around. Rufus and I receive yellow wristbands (for healthy Deckers) and Lidia an orange one (visitor), and we proceed in.

We stay close, not wandering too far from one another. The main entrance is a little crowded as Deckers and visitors look up at the gigantic screen listing all the regions you can visit, and the different kinds of tours available: Around the World in 80 Minutes, Miles of Wilds, Journey to the Center of the United States, and more.

"Should we go on a tour?" Rufus asks. "I'm game for any of them except You, Me, and the Deep Blue Sea."

"The Around the World in 80 Minutes tour starts in ten," I say.

"I'd love that," Lidia says, her arm locked in mine. She turns to Rufus, embarrassed. "Sorry, oh my god, sorry. Really, it's whatever you two want. I don't get a vote. Sorry."

"It's okay," I say. "Rufus, you cool with this?"

"Around the world we go, yo."

We find Room 16 and settle into a double-decker trolley with twenty other people. Rufus and I are the only Deckers with yellow wristbands. There are six Deckers with blue wristbands. Online, I've followed many Deckers with incurable illnesses who take it upon themselves to travel the real countries and cities while they still have time. But those who can't afford to do so settle for the next best thing with the rest of us.

The driver stands in the aisle and speaks through her headset.

"Good afternoon. Thank you for joining me on this wonderful tour, where we'll travel the world in eighty minutes, give or take ten. I'm Leslie and I'll be your tour guide. On behalf of everyone at the World Travel Arena, I offer my condolences to you and your family. I hope our trip today manages to put a smile on your face and leaves a wonderful memory for any guests joining you.

"If at some point you'd like to linger in any region, you're more than welcome to, but please be advised the tour will have to keep moving if we're to finish traveling the world in under eighty minutes. Now, if everyone would please fasten your seat belts, we'll take off!"

Everyone buckles up and we set off. I'm no cartographer, but even I know the destination grid behind each seat—looking similar to the electronic maps on the subway—isn't geographically correct. Still, it's an unbelievable time with unbelievably convincing replicas in each room, made even better by Lidia sharing fun facts about each location she learned from her own studies. We move down a railway where we can see Deckers and guests enjoying themselves, some even waving at us like we're not all tourists here.

In London, we pass the Palace of Westminster, where a myth says it's illegal to die there, but my favorite part is hearing the bell of Big Ben chime, even if seeing the hands on the clock snaps me back into reality. In Jamaica, we're greeted by dozens of large butterflies, the Giant Swallowtail, as people sitting on the floor eat special dishes, like ackee and saltfish. In Africa, we see a giant fish tank with inhabitants from Lake Malawi, and I'm so enraptured by the blues and yellows swimming around that I almost miss the live feed on the wall of a lioness carrying her cub by the scruff of its neck. In Cuba, we see guests competing against Cubans in dominoes, and a line for sugar cubes, and Rufus cheers for his roots. In Australia, there are exotic flowers, kite races, and complimentary koala plush toys for any children. In Iraq, the sounds of the national bird, the chucker partridge, play over the speakers discreetly hidden behind the merchant carts offering beautiful silk scarves and shirts. In Colombia, Lidia tells us about the country's perpetual summer, and we're tempted to grab a drink from the juice vendors. In Egypt, there are only two pyramid replicas, and since the room has a dry heat, the employees are offering Nile River–brand water bottles. In China, Lidia jokes about how she heard reincarnation is forbidden here without government permission, and I don't want to think about that so I focus on the lit-up skyscraper replicas and people playing table tennis. In South Korea, we see a couple of orange-yellow robots used in classrooms—"robo-teachers," they're called—and Deckers having their faces made up. In Puerto Rico, the trolley stops for its forty-second break. Rufus tugs at my arm and ushers me elsewhere, Lidia following.

"What's going on?" I ask over the chorus of tiny tree frogs—it's unclear if they're actually here or just recordings—and the sounds of wildlife are so jarring, since I'm only used to sirens and cars honking, that hearing the people talking by the rum cart comforts me.

"We talked about how you wanted to do something exhilarating if you ever had the chance to travel, right?" Rufus says. "I've been keeping an eye out for something on this tour, and look." He points at the sign by a tunnel: Rainforest Jump! "I don't know what it means, but it's gotta be better than that fake skydive earlier."

"You went skydiving?!" Lidia asks. Her tone is both are-you-crazy and I'm-super-jealous. She's possessive in the most nurturing, big-sister way possible.

The three of us walk along the beige tiles, sprinklings of actual sand around, to the tunnel. An arena employee hands us a brochure for the El Yunque Rainforest Room and offers us an audio tour, while admitting we'll miss out on some of the more natural music of the area if we do. We pass on the headphones and walk through the tunnel, where the air is moist and warm.

The crowding trees withstand the drizzle as an artificial sunlight filters through the thick leaves. We walk around the twisting trunks, going off the beaten path toward the trilling croaks of more tree frogs. Dad told me stories about how when he was my age he'd race up the trees with his friends, catch frogs and sell them to other kids who wanted pets, and sometimes just sit with his thoughts. The deeper we go, the more the frog song is replaced by the sounds of people and a waterfall. I mistake the latter for a recording until we pass through a clearing and I find water spilling off a twenty-foot-high cliff into a pool with shirtless Deckers and lifeguards. This must be the advertised rainforest jump.

Don't know why I thought it was going to be something lamer, like jumping from rock to rock on even ground.

I've seen so much already that the idea of leaving this arena is sharper than that of this day ending, like being ripped out of a dream you've waited your entire life to have. But I'm not dreaming. I'm awake, and I'm going for it.

"My daughter hates the rain," Lidia tells Rufus. "She hates anything she can't control."

"She'll come around," I say.

We walk toward the edge of the cliff where Deckers are jumping. A petite girl with a blue wristband, a headscarf, and floaties does something dangerous at the very last second—she turns around and falls backward, like someone pushed off a building. A lifeguard below whistles and the others swim to the center where she's splashed through. She returns to the surface, laughing, and it looks like the lifeguards are scolding her, but she doesn't care. How could anyone on a day like today?

RUFUS

4:24 p.m.

For all the mouth I ran about being brave, I'm not sure about this jump. I haven't set foot onto a beach or gone inside a community pool since my family died. The closest I've come to big bodies of water like this before today was when Aimee was fishing in the East River, and that led to a nightmare of me fishing for my family's car in the Hudson River, reeling up their skeletons in the clothes they died in, reminding me how *I* abandoned *them*.

"You're all good to go here, Mateo. Gonna have to veto this for myself."

"You should skip this too," Lidia tells him. "I know I have no real say here, but veto, veto, veto, veto."

Mad props to Mateo for getting in line anyway; I want this for him. There aren't any more croaking frogs, so I know he heard me. This kid has changed. I know you're paying attention, but look at him—he's in line to leap off a cliff and I bet you anything he can't even swim. He turns and waves us over, like he's inviting us to a line for a roller coaster.

"Come on," Mateo says, eyeing me. "Or we can go back to Make-A-Moment and swim around one of their pools if you want. I honestly think you'll feel better about everything if you get back in the water. . . . Me coaching you through something is weird, right?"

"It's a little ass-backward, yeah," I say.

"I'll make it short. We don't need those Make-A-Moment stations and their virtual realities. We can make our own moment right here."

"In this artificial rainforest?" I smile back.

"I made no claims to this place being real."

The arena attendant tells Mateo he's next.

"Is it cool if my friends and I jump together?" Mateo asks.

"Absolutely," she responds.

"I'm not going!" Lidia says.

"Yes you are," Mateo says. "You'll regret it if you don't."

"I should push you off the cliff," I tell Mateo. "But I won't because you're right." I can take on my fear, especially in a controlled environment like this with lifeguards and arm floaties.

No one planned for a swim, so we strip down to our underwear and yo, I had no idea how damn skinny Mateo is. He avoids looking my way—which I find funny—unlike

Lidia, in nothing but her bra and jeans, who's looking me up and down.

They attendants give us our gear—I'm calling the floaties "gear" because it sounds less cute—and we slip it on. The attendant tells us to jump when we're comfortable, which shouldn't be too long since a line is forming behind us.

"Count of three?" Mateo asks.

"Yeah."

"One. Two . . ."

I grab Mateo's hand and lock my fingers in his. He turns to me with flushed cheeks and grabs Lidia's hand.

"Three."

We all look ahead and below, and we jump. I feel like I'm falling through the air faster, dragging Mateo with me. Mateo shouts, and in the few seconds I have left before hitting the water I shout too, and Lidia cheers. I hit the water, Mateo still beside me, and we're underwater for only a few seconds, but I open my eyes and see him there. He's not panicking, and it reminds me of how settled my parents looked after they set me up for freedom. Lidia has disconnected; she's already out of sight. Mateo and I float back to the top with our hands still locked, lifeguards flanking us. I move toward Mateo, laughing, and I hug him for this freedom he's forced onto me. It's like I've been baptized or some shit, ditching more anger and sadness and blame and frustration beneath the surface, where they can sink to who-cares-where.

The waterfall pummels the water around us, and a lifeguard ushers us to the hill.

An attendant at the bottom of the hill offers us towels and Mateo wraps his around his shoulders, shivering. "How do you feel?" he asks.

"Not bad," I say.

We don't bring up the hand-holding or anything like that, but hopefully he gets where I'm coming from now in case he had any doubts. We head on up to the top of the hill, drying ourselves with towels, and retrieve our clothes and get dressed. We exit through the gift shop, where I catch Mateo singing along with the song on the radio.

I corner Mateo as he picks up one of the "Farewell!" cards offered here. "You made me jump and now it's your turn."

"I jumped with you."

"Not what I'm talking about. Come with me to this underground dance club place. Deckers go there to dance and sing and chill. You down?"

OFFICER ANDRADE

4:32 p.m.

Death-Cast did not call Ariel Andrade because he isn't dying today, but since he's an officer of the law, getting the call is his greatest fear every night when the clock strikes midnight. Especially since losing his partner two months ago. He and Graham could've been a buddy-cop movie, the way they handled business and traded dad jokes over beers.

Graham is always on Andrade's mind, and today is no exception, with these foster kids in the holding cell who are acting out because their brother is a Decker. You don't need matching DNA for someone to be your brother, Andrade knows this. And you definitely don't need the same blood to lose a part of yourself when someone dies.

Andrade doesn't believe the Decker, Rufus Emeterio, who he stopped pursuing in the early-morning hours, is going to be trouble—if he's even still alive. He's always had a sixth sense for Deckers who will spend their final hours creating chaos. Like the Decker responsible for Graham's death.

On the day Graham received his alert, he insisted on spending his End Day working. If he could die saving lives, it was a better way to go than one last lay. The officers were pursuing a Decker who was signing up for Bangers, the challenge for online feeds that has had a heartbreaking amount of daily hits and downloads the past four months. People tune in every hour to watch Deckers kill themselves in the most unique way possible—to go out with a bang. The most popular death wins the Decker's family some decent riches from an unknown source, but for the most part, it's just a bunch of Deckers who don't kill themselves creatively enough to please the viewers and, well, you don't exactly get a second shot. Graham's attempts to prevent a Decker from riding his motorcycle off the Williamsburg Bridge only got himself killed.

Andrade is doing his damn best to get that snuff channel terminated by the end of the year. No way in hell he can share a beer with Graham in heaven without getting this job done. Andrade wants to focus on his real work, not babysitting. That's why he has their foster parents signing release forms this very second. Let them go home with firm warnings so they can sleep.

And grieve.

Maybe even find their friend if he's still alive.

If you're close enough to a Decker when they die, you won't be able to put words to anything for the longest time. But few regret spending every possible minute with them while they were still alive.

PATRICK "PECK" GAVIN

4:59 p.m.

"Maybe he's dead already."

Peck has notifications turned on for Rufus's Instagram, but stays personally locked on anyway. "Come on, come on. . . ."

Peck wants Rufus dead, of course. But he wants to deliver the killing blow.

RUFUS

5:01 p.m.

The line for Clint's Graveyard isn't as long as it was last night when I was headed back to Pluto. Not even gonna start speculating if this means everyone is inside or if they've gone and died already. It's gotta be the greatest club, hands down, for Mateo. They better let me in even though I don't turn eighteen for another few weeks.

"Weird coming to a club at five," Lidia says.

My phone goes off and I'm banking on it being Aimee when I see Malcolm's dead-ass ugly profile pic. "The Plutos! Oh shit."

"Plutos?" Lidia asks.

"His best friends!" Mateo says, which doesn't really scratch the surface on who they are to me, but I let it slide because this is so wild even Mateo is tearing up for me. I bet I'd be the same way if his dad called him right now.

I answer FaceTime, walking away from the line. Malcolm

and Tagoe are together, legit surprised I answered. They're smiling at me like they wanna tag-team bang me.

"ROOF!"

"Holy shit," I say.

"You're alive!" Malcolm says.

"You're not locked up!"

"They can't hold us," Tagoe says, fighting for space so he can be seen too. "You see us?"

"Screw all of this. Roof, where you at?" Malcolm is squinting, looking beyond my head. I have no idea where they're at either.

"I'm at Clint's." I can give them a better goodbye. I can hug them. "Can you guys get here? Soon?" Making it past five has been a fucking miracle, but time is running out, no doubt. Mateo is holding Lidia's hand, and I want my best friends here too. All of them. "Can you grab Aimee too? Not that asshole Peck. I'll beat his ass again." If there was a lesson I was supposed to learn here, I didn't. Dude ruined my funeral and got my friends locked up, I get to deck him again and don't try to tell me I'm wrong.

"He's lucky you're still alive," Malcolm says. "We'd be spending our night hunting him down if you weren't."

"Don't leave Clint's," Tagoe says. "We'll be there in twenty minutes. Smelling like prison." Funny how Tagoe swears he's a hardened criminal now.

"I'm not going anywhere. I'm here with a friend. Just

get here, all right?'

"You better be there, Roof," Malcolm says.

I know what he's really saying. I better be alive.

I take a photo of the sign for Clint's Graveyard and upload it to Instagram in full color.

PATRICK "PECK" GAVIN

5:05 p.m.

"Got him," Peck says, hopping off his bed. Clint's Graveyard. He puts the loaded gun in his backpack. "We gotta be fast. Let's go."

PART FOUR

The End

No one wants to die. Even people who want to go to heaven don't want to die to get there. And yet death is the destination we all share. No one has ever escaped it. And that is as it should be, because Death is very likely the single best invention of Life. It is Life's change agent. It clears out the old to make way for the new.

—Steve Jobs

MATEO

5:14 p.m.

This day has some miracles.

I found a Last Friend in Rufus. Our best friends are joining us on our End Day. We've overcome fears. And we're now at Clint's Graveyard, which receives high praise online, and this could be the perfect stage for me if I outgrow my insecurities—in the next few minutes.

From all the movies I've seen, bouncers are normally stubborn in their ways and absolutely intimidating, but here at Clint's Graveyard there's a young woman wearing a fitted cap backward welcoming everyone.

The young woman asks for my ID. "Sorry to lose you, Mateo. Have fun in there, okay?" I nod. I drop some cash into a plastic donations container and wait for Rufus to pay his way in. The girl eyes him up and down and my face heats up. But then Rufus catches up to me and pats my shoulder and the burn is different, like when he grabbed my hand back at the Travel Arena.

Music is booming from the other side of the door and we wait for Lidia.

"You good?" Rufus asks.

"Nervous and excited. Mainly nervous."

"Regret making me jump off a cliff yet?"

"Do you regret jumping?"

"No."

"Then no."

"Are you gonna have fun in there?"

"No pressure," I say. There's a difference between jumping off a cliff and having fun. Once you jump off a cliff, there's no undoing it, there's no stopping midair. But having the kind of fun that seems daring and embarrassing in front of strangers requires a special bravery.

"There's no pressure," Rufus says. "Just our last few hours left on this planet to die without any regrets. Again, no pressure."

No regrets. He's right.

My friends stand behind me as I pull open the door and walk into a world where I immediately regret not having spent every minute possible. There are strobe lights, flashing blues, yellows, and grays. The graffiti on the walls was marked by Deckers and their friends, sometimes the last piece of themselves the Deckers have left behind, something that immortalizes them. No matter when it happens, we all have our endings. No one goes on, but what we leave behind keeps us alive for someone else. And I look at this crowded room of people, Deckers and friends, and they are all living.

A hand closes on mine, and it's not the same one that grabbed mine less than an hour ago; this hand carries history. The hand I held when my goddaughter was born, and the many mornings and evenings after Christian died. Traveling that world-within-a-world with Lidia was incredible, and having her here in this moment, a moment I couldn't buy, makes me happy despite every reason to be down. Rufus comes up beside me and wraps an arm around my shoulders.

"The floor is yours," Rufus says. "The stage, too, when you're game."

"I'm getting there," I say. I have to get there.

Onstage there's a teenager on crutches singing "Can't Fight This Feeling" and, as Rufus would say, he's absolutely killing it. There are a couple people dancing behind him—friends, strangers, who knows, who cares—and this energy elevates me. I guess I could call this energy freedom. No one will be around to judge me tomorrow. No one will send messages to friends about the lame kid who had no rhythm. And in this moment, how stupid it was to care hits me like a punch to the face.

I wasted time and missed fun because I cared about the wrong things.

"Got a song in mind?"

"Nope," I say. There are plenty of songs I love: "Vienna" by Billy Joel; "Tomorrow, Tomorrow" by Elliott Smith. "Born to Run" by Bruce Springsteen is one of Dad's favorites. All these songs have notes I have no chance of hitting, but that's not what's stopping me. I just want the song to be *right*.

The menu above the bar is illustrated with a skull and crossbones, and it's striking to see the skull smiling. *Last Day to Smile*, it reads. The drinks are all alcohol-free, which makes sense since dying isn't an excuse to sell alcohol to minors. There was a huge debate a couple years ago about whether or not Deckers eighteen and up should be allowed to purchase drinks. When lawyers presented percentages about teenagers dying from alcohol poisoning and drunk driving, it was ruled things would remain as they have been—legally. It's still really easy to get liquor and beer, is my understanding; always has been, always will be.

"Let's grab a drink," I say.

We push past the crowd, strangers dancing against us as we try to clear a path. The deejay calls up a bearded guy named David to the stage. David rolls onto the stage and announces he's singing "A Fond Farewell" by Elliott Smith; I don't know if he's a Decker or singing for a friend, but it's beautiful.

We reach the bar.

I'm not in the mood for a GrapeYard Mocktail. Definitely not Death's Spring.

Lidia orders a Terminator, this ruby-red mocktail. They serve her quickly. She takes a sip, scrunching her face like she's eaten a handful of sour candy. "Do you want?"

"I'm good," I say.

"I wish this had some kick to it," Lidia says. "I can't be sober when I lose you."

Rufus orders a soda and I do the same.

Once we have our drinks, I raise my glass. "To smiling while we can." We clink glasses and Lidia is biting her quivering lower lip while Rufus, like me, is smiling.

Rufus cuts through our circle and he's so close his shoulder is pressed against mine. He talks directly into my ear since the music and cheers are so loud. "This is your night, Mateo. Seriously. You sang to your dad earlier and stopped when I came in. No one is judging you. You're holding yourself back and you have to go for it." That David guy finishes his song and everyone applauds, and it's not some faint applause either; you would think there's a rock legend performing up there.

"See? They just wanna see you having fun, living it up."

I smile and lean in to his ear. "You have to sing with me. You choose the song."

Rufus nods and his head leans against mine. "Okay. 'American Pie.' Can we make that happen?"

I love that song. "It's happening."

I ask Lidia to watch our drinks as Rufus and I run up to

put in a request with the deejay. Before we reach the deejay, a Turkish girl named Jasmine sings "Because the Night" by Patti Smith and it's amazing how someone so tiny can demand such attention and ignite this level of excitement. A brunette girl with a wide smile—a smile you don't expect to find on someone dying—requests a song and steps away. I tell DJ LouOw our song and he compliments our choice. I sway a little to Jasmine's performance, bopping my head when I feel it's appropriate. Rufus is smiling, watching me, and I stop, embarrassed.

I shrug and pick it all up again.

I like being visible this time.

"The time of my life, Rufus," I say. "I'm having it. Right now."

"Me too, dude. Thanks for reaching out to me over Last Friend," Rufus says.

"Thanks for being the best Last Friend a closet case could ask for."

The brunette from earlier, Becky, is called to the stage and she performs Otis Redding's "Try a Little Tenderness." We're next in the queue and we wait by the stage's sticky steps. When Becky's song is reaching its close, the nerves finally hit me—the *next*-ness of it all. But nothing prepares me for the moment when DJ LouOw says, "Rufus and Matthew to the stage." Yes, he gets my name wrong, much like Andrea from Death-Cast so many hours ago it feels like it could've been a different day—I've lived a lifetime today and this moment is my encore.

Rufus rushes up the steps and I chase after him. Becky wishes me luck with the sweetest smile; I pray she's not a Decker, and if she is, I hope she passes without any regrets. I shout back, "Great job, Becky!" before turning around. Rufus drags two stools center stage for our pretty lengthy song. Good call because my knees are trembling as I walk across the stage, spotlight in my eyes and a buzzing in my ears. I sit down beside him and DJ LouOw sends someone over to hand us microphones, which makes me feel mighty, like I've been handed Excalibur in a battle my army was losing.

"American Pie" begins to play and the crowd cheers, like it's our own song, like they know who we are. Rufus squeezes my hand and lets go.

"*A long, long time ago . . .* ," Rufus begins, "*I can still remember . . .*"

"*How that music used to make me smile,*" I join in. My eyes are tearing up. My face is warm—no, hot. I find Lidia swaying. A dream couldn't possibly capture the intensity of this moment.

"*. . . This'll be the day that I die. . . . This'll be the day that I die. . . .*"

The energy in the room changes. Not just my confidence despite how off-key I am, no, our words are actually connecting with the Deckers in the audience, sinking deep past their skin and into their souls, which are fading, like a firefly turning off, but still very present. Some Deckers sing along and I'm sure if they were allowed to have lighters in here, they'd whip them out; some are crying, others are smiling with closed eyes, hopefully lost in good memories.

For eight minutes Rufus and I sing about a thorny crown, whiskey and rye, a generation lost in space, Satan's spell, a girl who sang the blues, the day the music died, and so much more. The song ends, I catch my breath, and I breathe in everyone's roaring applause, I breathe in their love, and it energizes me to grab Rufus's hand while he's bowing. I drag him offstage, and once we're behind the curtain, I look him in the eyes and he smiles like he knows what's about to go down. And he's not wrong.

I kiss the guy who brought me to life on the day we're going to die.

"Finally!" Rufus says when I give him the chance to breathe, and now he kisses me. "What took you so long?"

"I know, I know. I'm sorry. I know there's no time to waste, but I had to be sure you are who I thought you were. The best thing about dying is your friendship." I never thought I would find someone I could say words like this to. They're so broad yet deeply personal, and it's a private thing I want to share with everyone, and I think this is that feeling we all chase. "And even if I never got to kiss you, you gave me the life I always wanted."

"You took care of me too," Rufus says. "I've been so damn lost the past few months. Especially last night. I hated all the doubts and being so pissed off. But you gave me the best assist ever and helped me find myself again. You made me better, yo."

I'm ready to kiss him again when his eyes move away from mine, beyond the stage and into the audience. He squeezes my arm.

Rufus's smile is brighter. "The Plutos are here."

HOWIE MALDONADO

5:23 p.m.

Death-Cast called Howie Maldonado at 2:37 a.m. to tell him he's going to die today.

His 2.3 million Twitter followers are taking it the hardest.

For the greater part of the day, Howie stayed in his hotel room with a team of security guards outside his door, all armed; fame gave him this life, but it won't keep him alive. The only people allowed inside his hotel room were his lawyers, who needed wills created, and his literary agent, who needed his next contract signed before Howie could kick it. Funny how a book he didn't write has more of a future than he does. Howie answered phone calls from costars, his little cousin whose popularity in school is tied to Howie's success, more lawyers, and his parents.

Howie's parents live in Puerto Rico, where they moved back after Howie's career took off. Howie desperately wanted them to remain in Los Angeles, where he lives now, offering to take care of every last bill and splurge, but his parents' love for San Juan, where they first met, was too great. Howie can't help but be bothered by the fact that his parents, while clearly devastated, are going to be fine without him. They've already grown used to living without him, to watching his life from afar—like fans.

Like strangers.

Howie is currently in a car with more strangers. Two women from *Infinite Weekly* for a final interview. He's only doing this for the fans. Howie knows he could've lived another ten years and everything he shares about himself would've never been enough. They're ravenous for "content," as his publicists and managers say. Every haircut. Every new magazine cover. Every tweet, no matter how many typos.

Howie's tweet last night was a picture of his dinner.

He's already sent out one last tweet: *Thank you for this life.* Attached is a photo, taken by himself, smiling.

"Who are you on your way to see?" the older woman asks. Sandy, he believes. Yes, Sandy. Not Sally like his very first publicist. Sandy.

"Is this part of the interview?" Howie asks. Whenever he does these pieces, his answers require zero focus, so he normally hops on his phone and scrolls through Twitter and Instagram. But keeping up with the outpouring of love, including messages from the author of the Scorpius Hawthorne series, is ten times more impossible than usual.

"It could be," Sandy says. She lifts the tape recorder. "Your call."

Howie wishes his publicist were here with him to shut down this question herself, but he wrote her a big check, had it sent down to her hotel room, and encouraged her to stay far away from him, as if he were infected with a zombie virus.

"Pass," Howie says. It's no one's business that he's on his way to see his childhood best friend and first love, Lena, who's flown in from Arkansas to see him one last time. The girl who could've been more than a friend if he didn't live in the spotlight. The girl he'd once missed so much he'd write her name around the city, like on pay phones and coffee tables, never signing his name. The girl who loves the quiet life her husband gives her.

"Very well," Sandy says. "What's your proudest accomplishment?"

"My art," Howie says, fighting back an eye roll. The other woman, Delilah, stares at him like she's seeing past his bullshit. Howie would be intimidated if he wasn't busy being distracted by her beautiful hair, which resembles the northern lights, and the fresh bandage on her forehead, which is covering up a Scorpius Hawthorne–like wound.

"Where do you think you would be without the Draconian Marsh role?" Sandy asks.

"Literally? Back in San Juan with my parents. Professionally . . . Who can say."

"Better question," Delilah speaks up. Sandy is pissed and Delilah speaks over her. "What do you regret?"

"Excuse her," Sandy says. "I'm firing her and she's getting out at the next red light."

Howie turns his attention to Delilah. "I love what I did. But I don't know who I am beyond the voice of a Twitter account and the evil face for a franchise."

"What would you have done differently?" Delilah asks.

"I probably wouldn't have done that shitty college-bait film." Howie smiles, surprised by his own humor on his last day ever. "I would've only done what meant a lot to me. Like the Scorpius films. That adaptation was one of a kind. But I should've used those fortunes to spend time with the people who mean a lot to me. Family and friends. I got caught up reinventing myself so I could land different roles and not be the evil wizard kid. For fuck's sake, I'm in town to meet a publisher for another book I didn't write."

Delilah eyes the copy of Howie's book, unsigned, sitting between her and her boss.

Former boss. It's unclear.

"What would've made you happy?" Delilah asks.

Love comes to mind, immediately, and it surprises him like a lightning bolt on a day with clear forecasts. Howie never felt lonely, because he could go online at any moment and find himself flooded with messages. But affection from millions and intimacy from that one special person are completely different beasts.

"My life is a double-edged sword," Howie says, not speaking of his life as if it's already over as other defeated Deckers do. "I am where I am because my life moved as fast as it did. If I didn't land that gig, maybe I would be in love with someone who loves me back. Maybe I would've been an actual son and not someone who thought being a bank account was enough. I could've taken time to learn Spanish so I could speak with my grandma without my mom translating."

"If you weren't successful and had all those things instead, would that have been enough for you?" Delilah asks. She's sitting at the edge of her seat. Sandy is invested too.

"I think so—"

Howie shuts up as Delilah's and Sandy's eyes widen.

The car jerks and Howie closes his eyes, a deep sinking in his chest, like every time he's been on a roller coaster, scaling higher and higher, past the point of no return, and he's falling at incredible speed. Except Howie knows he's not safe.

THE GANG WITH NO NAME

5:36 p.m.

Death-Cast did not call this gang of boys today, and they're living as if this means their lives can't be over while they're alive. They run through the streets, not caring about traffic, as if they're invincible against speeding cars and completely untouchable by the law. Two boys laugh when one car bangs into another, spinning out of control until it crashes against the wall. The third is too focused on reaching his target and pulling the handgun out of his backpack.

DELILAH GREY

5:37 p.m.

Delilah is still alive. She doesn't have to test Howie's pulse to know he isn't. She saw the way his head banged against the reinforced window, heard the sickening crack that will stay with her forever—

Her heartbeat runs wild. In a single day, the same day when she received a call informing her she will die today, Delilah has not only survived an explosion by a bookstore, but also a car accident caused by three boys running through the street.

If Death wanted her, Death had two shots.

Delilah and Death won't be meeting today.

RUFUS

5:39 p.m.

I wanna keep holding Mateo's hand, but I gotta hug my people. I move through the crowd, pushing Deckers and others aside to get to the Plutos. We all hit *Pause* on ourselves—and press *Play* at the exact same second, like four cars moving at a green light. We group hug, four Plutos coming together in the Pluto Solar System embrace I've been wanting for over fifteen hours, ever since I ran out of my own damn funeral.

"I love you guys," I say. No one cracks homo jokes. We're past that. They shouldn't be here, but taking risks is the name of the game today and I'm playing it. "You don't smell like prison, Tagoe."

"You should see my new ink," Tagoe says. "We've seen shit."

"We didn't see shit," Malcolm says.

"You guys ain't shit," I say.

"Not even house arrest," Aimee says. "Damn shame."

We pull apart, but stay really close, as if the crowd is forcing us to squeeze up against each other. They're all staring at me. Tagoe looks like he wants to pet me. Malcolm looks like he's seeing a ghost. Aimee looks like she wants another hug. I don't let Tagoe treat me like a dog or shout "Boo!" at Malcolm, but I move in and hug the hell out of Aimee.

"My bad, Ames," I say. I didn't know I was sorry until I saw her face. "I shouldn't have shut you out like that. Not on a damn End Day."

"I'm sorry too," Aimee says. "There's only one side that matters to me and I'm sorry I was trying to play both. We didn't have nearly as much time as we should've, but you'll always be more important. Even after . . ."

"Thanks for saying that," I say.

"I'm sorry I had to say something so obvious," Aimee says.

"We're all good," I say.

I know I helped Mateo live his life, but he helped me get mine back in shape. I wanna be remembered as who I am right now, not for that dumbass mistake I made. I turn and Mateo and Lidia are standing shoulder to shoulder. I pull him over by his elbow.

"This is my Last Friend, Mateo," I say. "And this is his number one, Lidia."

The Plutos shake hands with Mateo and Lidia. Solar systems are colliding.

"Are you scared?" Aimee asks us both.

I grab Mateo's hand and nod. "It'll be game over, but we won first."

"Thanks for taking care of our boy," Malcolm says.

"You're both honorary Plutos," Tagọe says. He turns to Malcolm and Aimee. "We should get badges made."

I give the Plutos a beat-by-beat play of my End Day, and I fill them in on how color found its way to my Instagram.

"Elastic Heart" by Sia comes to an end. "We should be out there. Right?" Aimee says, nodding toward the dance floor.

"Let's do this."

Mateo says it before I can.

MATEO

5:48 p.m.

I grab Rufus's hand and drag him to the dance floor right as a young black guy named Chris takes the stage. Chris says he's about to perform an original song called "The End." He raps about final goodbyes, nightmares we want to wake up from, and the inevitable squeeze of Death. If I weren't standing here with Rufus and our favorite people, I would be depressed. But instead we're all dancing, something else I never thought I would get to do—not just dancing, but dancing with someone who challenges me to live.

The beat pulses through me and I follow the lead of others, bopping my head and bouncing my shoulders. Rufus does a mock Harlem Shake to either impress me or make me laugh, and it works on both counts, mainly because his confidence is glowing and admirable. We close the space between us, our hands still very much to our sides or in the air, but we're dancing against each other. Not always in sync, but who cares. We remain pressed together as more people flood the dance floor. Yesterday Mateo would've found this claustrophobic, but now? Don't ever move me.

The song changes and now it's superfast, but Rufus stills me and puts a hand on my hip. "Dance with me."

I thought we were dancing already. "Am I doing it wrong?"

"You're great. I meant a slow dance."

The beat has only increased, but we place our hands on each other's shoulders and waist; my fingers dig into him a little, the first time I'm getting to touch someone else like this. We take it slow, and out of all the ways I've lived today, maintaining eye contact with Rufus is really hard; it's easily become the most intense intimacy ever I've ever experienced. He leans in to my ear, throwing me into this weird phase where I'm relieved to be free of his gaze but also miss his eyes and the way he looks at me, like I'm good enough, and Rufus says, "I wish we had more time. . . . I wanna ride bikes through empty streets and spend a hundred dollars at an arcade and take the Staten Island ferry just to introduce you to my favorite snow cones."

I lean in to his ear. "I want to go to Jones Beach and race you to the waves and play in the rain with our friends. But I want quiet nights, too, where we talk about nonsense while watching bad movies." I want us to have history, something longer than the small window of time we're actually sharing, with an even longer future, but the dying elephant in the room crushes me. I rest my forehead against his, the both of us sweating. "I have to talk to Lidia." I kiss Rufus again before we break through the crowd. He grabs my hand from behind, following me through the path I'm clearing.

Lidia sees us holding hands right as Rufus lets go and I take hers in mine, leading her toward the bathrooms, where it's a little quieter. "Don't slap me," I say, "but I'm obviously into Rufus and he's into me and I'm sorry for never telling you someone like Rufus is someone I would be into. I thought I had more time to accept myself, you know, even though I never really saw anything ugly or wrong about it. I think I was waiting around for a reason—something beautiful and awesome to accompany any declaration. It's Rufus."

Lidia raises her hand. "I still want to slap you, Mateo Torrez." She wraps her arms around me instead. "I don't know this Rufus character, and I'm not sure how well you know him either after one day, but—"

"I don't know every detail about his past. But what I've gotten out of him in one day is more than I feel like I ever deserved. I don't know if that makes sense."

"What am I going to do without you?"

This loaded question is the reason I didn't want anyone to know I was dying. There are questions I can't answer. I cannot tell you how you will survive without me. I cannot tell you how to mourn me. I cannot convince you to not feel guilty if you forget the anniversary of my death, or if you realize days or weeks or months have gone by without thinking about me.

I just want you to live.

On the wall there are markers of many colors, most of them dried out, hanging from rubber cords. I find a bold orange marker that works and I tiptoe to reach this blank space where I write: *MATEO WAS HERE AND LIDIA WAS BY HIS SIDE, AS ALWAYS.*

I hug Lidia. "Promise me you'll be okay."

"It would be a huge lie."

"Please lie to me," I say. "Come on, tell me you'll keep moving. Penny needs you at one hundred percent, and I need to know you'll be strong enough to take care of the future global leader."

"Damn it, I can't—"

"Something is wrong," I say. My heart is pounding. Aimee is standing between Rufus and the Plutos and three guys who are yelling over her. Lidia grabs my hand, like she's trying to drag me backward a bit, to save my life before I can get caught up in this. She's scared she's going to have to watch me die and I am too. The shorter guy with the bruised face pulls out a gun—who could want to kill Rufus like this?

The guy he jumped.

Everyone notices the gun and pandemonium rages in the club. I run toward Rufus, guests charging into me as they run for the door. I get knocked down and people are stepping on me and this is how I'm going to die, a minute before Rufus gets shot to death, maybe even the same minute. Lidia is screaming at everyone to stop and back off, and she's helping me up. There haven't been any gunshots yet, but everyone is steering clear of the circle. This stampede is impossible to get through and I can't reach Rufus and I'm not going to be able to touch him again while he's still alive.

RUFUS

5:59 p.m.

I wanna get at Aimee, thinking she led him here, but she's standing between me and his gun. I know she's not gonna die today, but that don't make her bulletproof. I don't know how Peck knew to find me here, with his goons and a gun, but this is it for me.

I can't be stupid. I can't be a hero.

I don't wanna make peace with this—maybe if I had a gun pointed at me before I met Mateo and got my Plutos back, yeah, whatever, pull the trigger. But my life is stepping its game up.

"You not talking shit now, huh?" Peck asks. His hand is shaking.

"Don't do this. *Please.*" Aimee shakes her head. "This will end your life too."

"You begging for him, right? You don't give a shit about me."

"I will never give a shit about you if you do this."

She better not be saying this just to calm him down, because I will haunt the hell out of these two if they actually stay together. I wanna take my shot at hiding behind Malcolm for a second and dashing toward Peck, but that's not gonna get me far.

Mateo.

He's coming up behind Peck and I shake my head at him, which Peck sees. Peck turns and I run at him because Mateo's life is threatened. Mateo punches Peck in the face, which is straight unbelievable, and it doesn't send Peck to the floor or nothing like that, but we got a chance now. Peck's homie swings at Mateo and is about to rock his head off his shoulders, but he pulls back at the last second, like he recognizes him—I don't know, but Mateo finally steps back. Peck lunges for Mateo and I charge at him, but Malcolm beats me to it, running into Peck and his boy like a train, carrying them through the air as the gun drops, and he slams them against the wall.

The gun doesn't go off, we all good.

Peck's other boy goes for the gun and I kick him in the face as he goes to grab it, and Tagoe jumps on top of him. I grab the gun. I can try and end Peck for good and keep Aimee safe from him. I point the gun at him as Malcolm clears away. Mateo is looking at me the way he did when I caught up with him after he ran away from me. Like I'm dangerous.

I unload the gun.

All the bullets find their way into the wall.

I grab Mateo and we jet because Peck and his people are here to kill and we're the ones most likely to find a knife in our necks or bullets in our heads.

This day is doing me dirty on goodbyes.

DALMA YOUNG

6:20 p.m.

Death-Cast did not call Dalma Young because she isn't dying today, but if they had, she would've spent the day with her half sister, and maybe even a Last Friend—she created the app, after all.

"I promise you don't want to work for me," Dalma says, her arm interlocked with her half sister's as they cross the street. "*I* don't want to work for me. This job has become such a *job*."

"But this internship is so stupid," Dahlia says. "If I'm going to work this hard in tech, I might as well get paid triple what I'm receiving now." Dahlia is the most impatient twenty-year-old in New York. She refuses to slow down and is always ready to move from one phase of her life to the next. When she started dating her last girlfriend, she brought up getting married within a week. And now she wants to turn her tech internship into a Last Friend job. "Whatever.

How did the meetings go? Did you get to meet Mark Zuckerberg?"

"Meetings went really well," Dalma says. "Twitter may launch the feature as soon as next month. Facebook may need a little more time."

Dalma is in town meeting with developers from both Twitter and Facebook. This morning, she pitched a new Last Message feature that will allow respective users to prepare their final tweets/statuses so their online legacy is more meaningful than, say, their thoughts on a popular movie or some viral video of someone else's dog.

"What do you think your Last Message would be?" Dahlia asks. "I'll probably go with that *Moulin Rouge!* quote about how the greatest thing in the world is to love and be loved in return and yadda blah whatever."

"Yeah, you seem truly passionate about that quote, sis," Dalma says.

Dalma has given thought to this question, of course. Last Friend has been an incredible resource over the past two years, since its prototype stage, but she'll forever be horrified by the eleven Last Friend serial killings last summer. She was tempted to sell the app, wash the blood from her hands. But there have been so many instances where the app has done good, like this afternoon on the train when she overheard a conversation between two young women, smiling at each other when one said she was so grateful she reached out over

Last Friend, and learning the other loves the movement so much she tags the city with graffiti to promote the app.

Her app.

Before Dalma can answer, two teen boys run past her. One with a buzz cut, brown complexion shades lighter than her own, and another with glasses, fuller brown hair, and light tan skin like Dahlia's. The first teen trips, the other helping him up, and they take off again, who knows where. She wonders if they're half siblings with only a mother in common too. Maybe they're lifelong friends constantly up to no good and constantly lifting each other up.

Maybe they've just met.

Dalma watches the teens run off. "My Last Message would be to find your people. And to treat each day like a lifetime."

MATEO

6:24 p.m.

We're in the clear, sinking against a wall, like earlier when I was breaking down after running away from Lidia's. I want to be somewhere safe, like a locked room, not out here where people can hunt down Rufus. Rufus holds my hand and wraps his arm around my shoulders, holding me close.

"Props on punching Peck," Rufus says.

"First time I've ever hit anyone," I say. I'm still in shock from all my firsts—singing in public, kissing Rufus, dancing, punching someone, hearing bullets that close.

"Though you really shouldn't punch people with guns," Rufus says. "You could've gotten yourself killed."

I stare out into the street, still trying to catch my breath. "Are you criticizing how I saved your life?"

"I could've turned around and you would've been dead. I'm not having that."

I have no regrets. I go back in time and imagine myself

being a little slower, maybe tripping, and losing valuable time and losing my valuable friend as bullets rip apart his beautiful heart.

I almost lost Rufus. We have less than six hours left, and if he goes first, I'll be a zombie who's well aware his head is on the chopping block. The connection I have with Rufus isn't what I expected when I met him around three in the morning.

This day is unimaginably rewarding and still so, so impossible.

I'm tearing up and there's no stopping there. I finally cry because I want more mornings.

"I miss everyone," I say. "Lidia. The Plutos."

"Me too," Rufus says. "But we can't risk their lives again."

I nod. "The suspense of everything is killing me. I can't take being out here." My chest is tight. There's a huge difference between living fearlessly, like I've finally been doing, and knowing you have something to fear while you're out living. "Will you hate me if I want to go home? I want to rest in my bed where everything is safe and I want you to come with me, but inside this time. I know I spent my life hiding there, but I did my best to live, too, and I want to share this place with you."

Rufus squeezes my hand. "Take me home, Mateo."

THE PLUTOS

6:33 p.m.

Death-Cast did not call these three Plutos because they aren't dying today, but their fourth *did* receive the alert and that's just as devastating. The Plutos almost witnessed the death of their best friend, Rufus, as a gun was pulled on him. Rufus's Last Friend appeared out of nowhere like a superhero and punched Peck in the face, saving Rufus's life—for a little while longer, at least. The Plutos know Rufus won't survive the day, but they didn't lose him to a violent act from someone who had it out for him.

The Plutos stand together on the curb outside Clint's Graveyard as a cop car speeds off down the street, taking the gang with no name away.

The two boys cheer and hope they spend more time behind bars than they did today.

The girl regrets her role in all of this. But she's relieved her insecure, jealous boyfriend didn't deliver the killing blow. Ex-boyfriend.

While they're not facing Death themselves, tomorrow everything changes for the Plutos. They will have to restart, something they've grown used to doing; their youth is packed with more history than most teens their age. The death of their friend, however it unfolds, will stay with them forever. Entire lives aren't lessons, but there are lessons in lives.

You may be born into a family, but you walk into friendships. Some you'll discover you should put behind you. Others are worth every risk.

The three friends hug, a planet missing from their Pluto Solar System—but never forgotten.

RUFUS

7:17 p.m.

We pass the plot where Mateo buried that bird this morning, back when I was still a stranger on a bike. We should be freaking out, big-time, because we're gonna be on our way out soon too, like old meat, but I'm keeping it together by Mateo's side and he seems chill too.

Mateo leads the way into his building. "If there's nothing else you want to do, Roof, I thought we could visit my dad again."

"You just call me 'Roof'?"

Matco nods, and his face scrunches up like he's told a bad joke. "Thought I would try it out. That okay?"

"Definitely okay," I say. "That's a good plan, too. I'm cool with resting for a bit before making that run." Part of me can't help but wonder if Mateo is bringing me home so we can have sex, but it's probably safe to assume sex isn't on the brain for him.

Mateo is about to press the elevator button until he remembers we're not about that, especially not this late in the game. He opens the stairwell door and cautiously goes up. The silence is mad heavy between us, step by step. Wish I could challenge him to a race to his apartment, like he imagined for us at Jones Beach, but that's a surefire way to never actually reach the apartment.

"I miss . . ." Mateo stops on the third floor. I think he's about to bring up his dad, maybe Lidia. "I miss when I was so young I didn't know to be afraid of death. I even miss yesterday when I was paranoid and not actually dying."

I hug him because that says everything when I actually don't have anything to say. He squeezes me back before we go up the last flight of steps.

Mateo unlocks his front door. "I can't believe I'm bringing a boy home for the first time and there's no one here for you to meet."

How wild would it be if we go in and his dad is on the couch, waiting for him?

We go inside and no one is here except us.

Hope not.

I tour the living room. Not gonna front, I got myself a little nervous, like some old family-friend-turned-enemy is about to pop out because they figured the place was vulnerable with Mateo's dad in a coma. Everything seems good. I look at Mateo's class photos. There's a bunch of photos of him without glasses.

"When'd you have to get glasses?" I ask.

"Fourth grade. I was only teased for about a week, so I was lucky." Mateo stares at his senior photo, cap and gown, and it's like he's looking at a mirror and finding some sci-fi alternate-universe version of himself. I should capture it on camera because it's dope, but the look on his face only makes me wanna hug him again. "I bet I disappointed my dad by signing up for online classes. He was so proud of me when I graduated, and I'm sure he was hoping I would change my mind, get off the internet, and have the typical college experience."

"You'll get to tell him everything you've done," I say. We won't hang around here long. It'll mean a lot to Mateo if we see his dad again.

Mateo nods. "Follow me."

We go down a short hall and into his room.

"So this is where you've been hiding from me," I say. There are books all over the floor, like someone tried robbing the place. Mateo doesn't seem freaked by it.

"I wasn't hiding from *you*." Mateo crouches and puts the books into piles. "I had a panic attack earlier. I don't want my dad knowing I was scared when he comes home. I want him to believe I was brave all the way through."

I get down on my knees and pick up a book. "Is there a system here?"

"Not anymore," Mateo says.

We put the books back on his shelves and pick up some little trinkets off the floor.

"I don't like the idea of you being scared either."

"It wasn't that bad. Don't worry about old me."

I look around his room. There's an Xbox Infinity, a piano, some speakers, a map I pick up off the floor for him. I'm flattening it out with my fist, thinking about all the dope places Mateo and I have been together, when I spot a Luigi hat on the floor between his dresser and bed. I grab the hat and he grins as I put it on his head.

"There's the guy who hit me up this morning," I say.

"Luigi?" Mateo asks.

I laugh and pull out my phone. He doesn't smile for the camera, he's legit just smiling at me. I haven't felt this good about myself since Aimee.

"Photo-shoot time. Go jump on your bed or something."

Mateo rushes to the bed and leaps, falling face-first. He gets up and jumps and jumps, turning to the window quickly as if some freak bounce accident will launch him out there like a catapult.

I don't stop taking photos of this awesome, unrecognizable Mateo.

MATEO

7:34 p.m.

I'm out of character and Rufus is loving it. I'm loving it too.

I stop bouncing and stay seated at the edge of the bed, trying to catch my breath. Rufus sits beside me and grabs my hand. "I'm going to sing something for you," I say. I don't want to let go of his hand but I promise myself I'll put both of mine to good use.

I sit in front of my keyboard. "Get ready. This is a once-in-a-lifetime performance." I look over my shoulder. "Feeling special yet?"

Rufus fakes being unimpressed. "I'm feeling okay. A little tired, actually."

"Well, wake up and feel special. My dad used to sing this for my mother, though his voice is much better than mine."

I play the keys for Elton John's "Your Song" with a pounding heart, though my face isn't as hot as it was back at Clint's Graveyard. I'm not kidding when I tell Rufus to feel special.

I'm off-key and I don't care because of him.

I sing about a man making potions in a traveling show, how my gift is my song, sitting on the roof, keeping the sun turned on, the sweetest eyes I've ever seen, and so much more. I turn during a quick break and catch Rufus filming me on his phone. I smile his way. He comes over and kisses me on my forehead while I sing with him by my side: "*I hope you don't mind, I hope you don't mind, that I put down in words . . . how wonderful life is now you're in the world. . . .*"

I finish and Rufus's smile is a victory. He's tearing up. "You *were* hiding from me, Mateo. I always wanted to stumble into someone like you and it sucks that I had to find you through a stupid app."

"I like the Last Friend app," I say. I get his sentiment, but I wouldn't change how I met Rufus. "There I was, looking for some company, and I found you and you found me, and we chose to meet up because of gut instinct. What would've been the alternative? I can't guarantee I would've ever left here, or that our paths would've crossed. Not with one day left. It would make for a great story, yeah, but I think the app puts you out there more than anything else. For me, it meant admitting I was lonely and wanted to connect with someone. I just wasn't counting on what I have with you."

"You're right, Mateo Torrez."

"It happens every now and again, Rufus Emeterio." It's the first time I've said his last name out loud and I hope I've pronounced it right.

I go to the kitchen and return with some snacks. It's childish, but we play house. I smear peanut butter on crackers for him—after confirming he's not allergic—and serve them with a glass of iced tea. "How was your day, Rufus?"

"The best," he says.

"Me too," I say.

Rufus pats the edge of the bed. "Get over here." I sit down beside him and we get comfortable, linking our arms and legs together. We talk more about our histories, like how whenever he was acting out his parents would force him to sit in the middle of the room with them, kind of like how my dad would tell me to go take a shower and calm down. He tells me about Olivia and I tell him about Lidia.

Until it stops being about the past.

"This is our safe space, our little island." Rufus traces an invisible circle around us. "We aren't moving from here. We can't die if we don't move. You got me?"

"Maybe we'll smother each other to death," I say.

"Better that than whatever the hell is off our island."

I take a deep breath. "But if for some reason this plan doesn't work, we need to promise to find each other in the afterlife. There has to be an afterlife, Roof, because it's the only thing that makes dying this young fair."

Rufus nods. "I will make it so easy for you to find me. Neon signs. Marching bands."

"Good, because I might not have my glasses," I say. "Not sure if they'll ascend with me."

"You're positive about a movie theater in the afterlife but not if you'll have your glasses? Seems like an oversight in your heavenly blueprint." Rufus removes my glasses and puts them on. "Wow. Your eyes suck."

"You taking my glasses isn't helping my case here." My vision is hazy and I can only make out his skin tone, but none of his features. "I bet you look stupid."

"Let me take a photo. Actually, lean in with me."

I can't see anything, but I look straight, squinting, and smile. He puts the glasses back on my face and I check out the photo. I look like I've just woken up. Rufus wearing my glasses is a welcome intimacy, like we've known each other for so long that this kind of silliness comes easily to us. I wasn't ever counting on this.

"I would've loved you if we had more time." I spit it out because it's what I'm feeling in this moment and was feeling the many moments, minutes, and hours before. "Maybe I already do. I hope you don't hate me for saying that, but I know I'm happy.

"People have their time stamps on how long you should know someone before earning the right to say it, but I wouldn't lie to you no matter how little time we have. People waste time and wait for the right moment and we don't have that luxury. If we had our entire lives ahead of us I bet you'd get tired of me telling you how much I love you because I'm positive that's the path we were heading on. But because we're about to die, I want to say it as many times as I want—I love you, I love you, I love you, I love you."

RUFUS

7:54 p.m.

"Yo. You know damn well I love you too." Man, it actually hurts how much I mean this. "I don't talk out of my dick, you know that's not me." I wanna kiss him again because he resurrected me, but I'm tight. If I didn't have common sense, if I hadn't fought so hard to be who I am, I would do some dumb shit again and punch something because I'm so pissed. "The world is mad cruel. I started my End Day beating up someone because he's dating my ex-girlfriend and now I'm in bed with an awesome dude I haven't known for twenty-four hours. . . . This sucks. Do you think . . . ?"

"Do I think what?" Twelve hours ago Mateo would've been nervous asking me a question; he would've done it, but he would've looked away. Now he doesn't break eye contact.

I hate to ask it, but it might be on his mind too. "Did finding each other kill us?"

"We were going to die before we knew each other," Mateo says.

"I know. But maybe this is how it was always written in stone or the stars or whatever: Two dudes meet. They fall for each other. They die." If this is really our truth, I get to punch whatever wall I want. Don't try and stop me.

"That's not our story." Mateo squeezes my hands. "We're not dying because of love. We were going to die today, no matter what. You didn't just keep me alive, you made me live." He climbs into my lap, bringing us closer. He hugs me so hard his heart is beating against my chest. I bet he feels mine. "Two dudes met. They fell in love. They lived. That's our story."

"That's a better story. Ending still needs some work."

"Forget about the ending," Mateo says in my ear. He pushes his chest away from mine so he can look me in the eye. "I doubt the world is in the mood for a miracle, so we know not to expect a happily-ever-after. I only care about the endings we lived through today. Like how I stopped being someone afraid of the world and the people in it."

"And I stopped being someone I don't like," I say. "You wouldn't have liked me."

He's tearing up and smiling. "And you wouldn't have waited for me to be brave. Maybe it's better to have gotten it right and been happy for one day instead of living a lifetime of wrongs."

He's right about everything.

We rest our heads on his pillows. I'm hoping we die in our sleep; that seems like the best way to go.

I kiss my Last Friend because the world can't be against us if it brought us together.

MATEO

8:41 p.m.

I wake up feeling invincible. I don't check the time because I don't want anything to shatter my survivor spirit. In my head, I'm already in another day. I have beat Death-Cast's prediction, the first person in history to do so. I put my glasses back on, kiss Rufus's forehead, and watch him resting. Nervous, I reach for his heart, and I'm relieved it is still beating: he's invincible too.

I climb over Rufus and I bet he would kill me himself if he caught me leaving our safe island, but I want to introduce him to Dad. I leave the room and go to the kitchen to prepare tea for us. I set the pot over the stove's burner and check the cabinets for tea selections and decide on peppermint.

When I switch on the burner, my chest sinks with regret. Even when you know death is coming, the blaze of it all is still sudden.

RUFUS

8:47 p.m.

I wake up choking on smoke. This deafening fire alarm makes it mad hard to think. I don't know what's happening, but I know this is the moment. I reach over to wake up Mateo, but my hand finds no one in all this darkness, just my phone, which I pocket.

"MATEO!"

The fire alarm is drowning out my cries, and I'm choking, but I still call for him. Moonlight beams through the window, and that's all the light I have to work with. I grab my fleece and wrap it around my face while crawling on the floor, reaching out for Mateo, who's gotta be somewhere here on the floor and not anywhere near the source of the smoke. I shake off thoughts of Mateo burning because no, that's not happening. Impossible.

I get to the front door and open it, allowing some of the black smoke to spill out. I cough and cough, choke and choke, and the fresh air is what I need, but the panic is doing its damn best to keep me down and out for the final count. Breathing is so fucking hard. There are some neighbors out here, no one Mateo ever shared any stories about. There are so many things he hasn't gotten around to telling me. It's okay: we still have a few more hours together once I find him.

"We've already called the fire department," one woman says.

"Someone get him water," some man says, patting my back as I continue choking.

"I got a note from Mateo earlier," another man says. "Said he was going to be passing and not to worry about the stove. . . . When did he come home? I knocked earlier and he wasn't there!"

I beat the cough out of my system, the best I can, at least, before pushing the man aside with more strength than I'd have bet I had. I run back inside the burning apartment and straight toward the orange glow of the kitchen. The apartment is blasting with a heat I've never known, the closest thing being when I was in Cuba vacationing with my family on Varadero Beach. I don't know why Mateo didn't stay in bed, we had a fucking deal. I don't know what problem the stove was having, but if I know Mateo, and dammit I do, I bet he was doing something nice for us, something that absolutely isn't worth his life.

Into the flames I go.

I'm about to run into the kitchen when my foot connects with something solid. I drop to my knees and grab whatever it is, and it's the arm that was supposed to be around me when I woke up. I grab Mateo, my fingers sink deep into boiled skin, and I'm crying hard as I find Mateo's other arm and drag him away from the fire, out of the smoke, and toward all the sons of bitches who are shouting at me from the doorway but weren't brave enough to run in and save some kids.

The hallway light hits Mateo. His back is badly burned. I turn him over, and half of his face is severely burned, the rest is deep red. I wrap my arm around his neck and cradle him, rocking back and forth. "Wake up, Mateo, wake up, wake up," I beg. "Why'd you get out of bed. . . . We, we said we wouldn't get out of . . ." He shouldn't have gotten out of bed and he shouldn't have ditched me in that home of fire and smoke.

Firefighters arrive. Neighbors try prying me away from Mateo and I swing at one, hoping that if I can deck one they'll all fuck off or find themselves kicked into Mateo's burning home. I wanna smack Mateo awake, but I shouldn't hit this face that's already been touched by flames. But this stupid Mateo kid isn't waking up, dammit.

A firefighter kneels beside me. "Let us get him in an ambulance."

I finally give in. “He didn’t receive the alert today,” I lie. “Get him to a hospital fast, please.”

I stay with Mateo as they cart him down the elevator, through the lobby, and outside toward the ambulance. A medic checks Mateo’s pulse and looks at me with sympathy and it’s fucking bullshit.

“We have to get him to the hospital, you see that!” I say. “Come on! Stop fucking around! Let’s go!”

“I’m sorry. He’s gone.”

“DO YOUR JOB AND GET HIM TO THE FUCKING HOSPITAL!”

Another medic opens the ambulance’s rear doors, but he doesn’t put Mateo in the back. He pulls out a body bag.

Hell no.

I snatch the body bag from his hand and throw it into the bushes because body bags are for corpses and Mateo isn’t dead. I return to Mateo’s side, choking and crying and dying. “Come on, Mateo, it’s me, Roof. You hear me, right? It’s Roof. Wake up now. Please wake up.”

9:16 p.m.

I’m sitting on the curb when the medics bag Mateo Torrez up.

9:24 p.m.

I'm receiving medical attention in the back of the ambulance as they rush me to Strouse Memorial. Sitting here reminds me of my family dying all over again. My heart is burning and I'm so pissed off at Mateo for dying before me. I don't wanna be here, I should find a rental bike or go for a run even if breathing hurts, but I also can't leave him like this.

I talk to the boy in the body bag about all the things we said we'd do together, but he can't hear me.

When we reach the hospital they split us up. They take me to Intensive Care and wheel Mateo off to the morgue for observation.

My heart is burning.

9:37 p.m.

I'm in a hospital bed getting good air from an oxygen mask and checking out all the love from the Plutos on my Instagram pics. There's no bullshit crying-face emojis, they know I'm not about that. Their messages on my last pic with Mateo are the ones that get me:

@tagoeaway: We will live it up for you, Roof! #Plutos4Life #PlutosForever

@manthony012: I love ya, bro. Catch ya at the next level. #Plutos4Life

@aimee_dubois: I love you and I'll look for you every day. #PlutoConstellation

They don't tell me to stay safe or nothing like that because they know what's what, but they're no doubt rooting for me.

They've left comments on all my pics, wishing they were with us at the Travel Arena and Make-A-Moment and the cemetery. Everywhere.

I open up my Plutos group chat and send them that painful text: Mateo is dead.

Their condolences spill in mad fast, it's dizzying. They don't ask for details, and I bet Tagoe is really fighting that urge to ask how it happened. I'm relieved he doesn't.

I need to close my eyes for a bit. Not a long time because I don't have that. But in case I don't wake up because of some complication, I shoot them one last text: Whatever happens to me, scatter me at Althea. Orbit each other so damn hard. I love you.

10:02 p.m.

I snap awake from the nightmare. Nightmare-Mateo was completely ablaze, blaming me for his death, telling me he would've never died if he hadn't met me. It sears into my mind, but I shake it off as nothing but a nightmare because Mateo would never blame anyone for anything.

Mateo is dead.

That was no way for him to go out. Mateo should've gone out saving someone, because he was such a selfless person. No, even if he didn't die a hero's death, he died a hero.

Mateo Torrez definitely saved me.

LIDIA VARGAS

10:10 p.m.

Lidia is home on her couch, eating comfort candy, letting Penny stay awake. Lidia's grandmother has gone to bed, exhausted from watching Penny, and Penny herself is winding down. She isn't cranky or whining, almost as if she knows to give her mother a break.

Lidia's phone rings. It's the same number Mateo called her from before, Rufus's. She answers: "Mateo!"

Penny looks at the door, but doesn't find Mateo.

Lidia waits for his voice, but he doesn't say anything.

". . . Rufus?" Lidia's heart races and she closes her eyes.

"Yeah."

It's happened.

Lidia drops the phone on the couch, punching the cushions, scaring Penny. Lidia doesn't want to know how it happened, not tonight. Her heart's already broken, she doesn't need every last piece shattered to bits. Tiny hands pull Lidia's hands away from her face, and, like earlier, Penny is tearing up because her mother is crying.

"Mommy," Penny says. This one word says everything to Lidia—fall apart, but piece herself back together. If not for herself, for her daughter.

Lidia kisses Penny's forehead and picks up the phone. "You there, Rufus?"

"Yeah," he says again. "I'm sorry for your loss."

"I'm sorry for your loss too," Lidia says. "Where are you?"

"I'm at the same hospital as his dad," Rufus says.

Lidia wants to ask him if he's okay, but she knows he won't be soon enough.

"I'm gonna visit him," Rufus says. "Mateo wanted to come out to him, but . . . we didn't make it. Should I tell his dad? Is it weird that it's me? You know him best."

"You know him really well too," Lidia says. "If you can't, I can."

"I know he can't hear, but I wanna tell him how brave his son was," Rufus says.

Was. Mateo is now a *was*.

"I can hear you," Lidia says. "Please tell me first."

Lidia holds Penny in her lap while Rufus tells her everything Mateo didn't get a chance to tell her himself tonight. Tomorrow she'll build the bookcase Mateo bought for Penny and put his pictures all around her room.

Lidia will keep Mateo alive the only way she can.

DELILAH GREY

10:12 p.m.

Delilah is writing the obituary based on the interview her boss didn't fire her over. Howie Maldonado may have wanted a different life, but the legacy Delilah has learned from him is an important one—life is about balances. A pie chart with equal slices in all areas of life for maximum happiness.

Delilah was positive she wouldn't be meeting Death today. But maybe Death simply has other plans for her. There's still a little under two hours left until midnight. In this time, she'll be able to see if it's been coincidence or a doomed fate pushing her back and forth all day, like wave after wave.

Delilah is at Althea, a diner named for the park across the street, where she first met Victor, and she's nearly done writing the obituary for the man she's mostly only ever known from afar, instead of confronting the man she loves in what could possibly be her final hours.

She pushes aside her notebook to make room so she can

spin the engagement ring Victor refused to take back last night. Delilah decides on a game. If the emerald is facing her, she'll give in and call him. If the band is facing her, she'll simply finish the obituary, go home, get a good night's rest, and figure out next steps tomorrow.

Delilah spins the ring and the emerald points directly at her; not even the slightest bit favoring her shoulder or other patrons.

Delilah whips out her phone and calls Victor, desperately hoping he's screwing with her. Maybe one of the many secrets regarding Death-Cast is they decide who dies, like some lottery no one wants to win. Maybe Victor went in to work, slid her name across Mr. Executive Executor's table, and said, "Take her."

Maybe heartbreak kills.

VICTOR GALLAHER

10:13 p.m.

Death-Cast did not call Victor Gallaher last night because he isn't dying today. Protocol for telling an employee about their End Day involves an administrator calling the Decker into their office "for a meeting." It's never obvious to the outside employees whether the person is dying or being terminated—they simply never return to their desk. But this is of little concern for Victor since he's not dying today.

Victor has been pretty depressed, more so than usual. His fiancée—he's still calling Delilah his fiancée because she still has his grandmother's ring—tried breaking up with him last night. Even though she claims it's because she's not in the same headspace he is, he knows it's because he hasn't been himself lately. Ever since starting at D-C three months ago, he's been in—for lack of a stronger word—a funk. He's on his way to the in-house therapist for all D-C employees, because on top of Delilah trying to end things with him, the weight of the job is killing him: the pleading he can't do anything about, the questions he has zero answers for—all of it is crushing. But the money is damn good and the health insurance is damn good and he'd really like things to be damn good with his fiancée again.

Victor walks into the building—undisclosed location, of course—with Andrea Donahue, a coworker who doesn't stop to admire the portraits of smiling Victorians and past presidents on the yellow walls. Death-Cast's aesthetic is not what you'd imagine it to be. No doom and gloom in here. It was decided the open floor plan should be less professional, and bright, like a day care, so the heralds wouldn't drive themselves crazy as they delivered End Day alerts in cramped cubicles.

"Hey, Andrea," Victor says, pushing the elevator button.

Andrea has been working at D-C since the beginning, at a job Victor knows she desperately needs, even though she hates it, because of the damn good pay for her kid's rocket-high tuition and damn good health insurance since her leg is busted. "Hi," she says.

"How's the kitty?" Small talk before and after shifts is encouraged by the D-C administrators; mini-opportunities to connect with those in possession of tomorrows.

"Still a kitty," Andrea says.

"Cool."

The elevator arrives. Victor and Andrea get on and Victor

quickly presses *Close* so he doesn't have to share the elevator with some of his coworkers who do nothing but ramble on about things that don't matter, like celebrity gossip and bad TV, on their way to basically ruin someone's life. Victor and Delilah call them "Switches" and they both hate that people like them exist.

His phone buzzes inside his pocket. He tries not psyching himself into thinking Delilah is calling and his heart races when he reads her name. "It's her," Victor tells Andrea, turning to her as if she's in the know. She's as interested in his life as he is in her new kitty. He answers the phone: "Delilah! Hi." A little desperate, sure, but this is love we're talking about.

"Did you do it, Victor?"

"Do what?"

"Don't mess with me."

"What are you talking about?"

"The End Day call. Did you have someone harass me because you're pissed? If you did, I won't report you. Just tell me now and we can forget about it."

Victor's spirit drops as he reaches the tenth floor. "You got the alert?" Andrea was about to get out, but stays on the elevator. Victor doesn't know if she's staying because she's concerned or interested, and he doesn't care. Victor knows Delilah isn't playing with his head. He can always tell when she's lying by the tone of her voice, and he knows she's accusing him of an actual threat she most certainly *would* report him for. "Delilah."

Delilah is quiet on the other end.

"Delilah, where are you?"

"Althea," she says.

The diner where they met—she still loves him, he knew it.

"Don't move, okay? I'm coming." He presses *Close* again, trapping Andrea in there with him. He presses *Lobby* thirty-something times, even as the elevator is already descending.

"I wasted the day," Delilah cries. "I thought . . . I'm so stupid, I'm so fucking stupid. I wasted the day."

"You're not stupid, you're going to be okay." Victor has never lied to a Decker before today. Oh shit, Delilah is a Decker. The elevator stops on the second floor and he bursts out, running down the stairs, losing cell service as he does so. He runs through the lobby, telling Delilah how much he loves her and how he's on his way. He checks his watch: two hours, exactly, but for all he knows, it could be over in two minutes.

Victor gets in his car and speeds to Althea.

RUFUS

10:14 p.m.

The last photo I'm throwing up on Instagram is the one of me with my Last Friend. It's the one we took in his bedroom where I'm wearing his glasses and he's squinting and we're smiling because we won some happiness before I lost him. I scroll through all my pictures, mad grateful for the pops of color Mateo gave me on our End Day.

The nurse wants me to stay in bed, but it's not only in my Decker rights to refuse assistance, there's no way in hell I'm camping out here when I gotta see Mateo's father.

I have less than two hours to live and I can't think of a better way to spend that time than respecting Mateo's final request to meet his father, but for real this time. I gotta meet the man who raised Mateo into the dude I fell in love with in less than a day.

I head to the eighth floor with the insistent nurse. Yeah, she's well intentioned and wants to assist, I get it. I just don't have much patience in me right now. I don't even hesitate when I get to the room. I march in.

Mateo's father isn't exactly what I pictured Mateo would look like in the future, but close enough. He's still sound asleep, completely unaware that his son won't be around to welcome him home if he ever wakes up. I don't even know what's left of their home. Hopefully the firefighters stopped the fire from spreading.

"Hey, Mr. Torrez." I sit down beside him. The same seat Mateo was in when he was singing earlier. "I'm Rufus and I was Mateo's Last Friend. I managed to get him out of the house, I don't know if he told you that. He was really brave." I pull my phone out of my pocket and I'm relieved when it powers on. "I'm sure you're really proud of him and you knew he had it in him all along. I've only known him for a day and I'm really proud of him too. I got to watch him grow up into the person he always wanted to be."

I scroll through the photos I took from the beginning of the day, skipping over the ones from my time before meeting Mateo and starting with my first color photo. "We did a lot of living today." I give him the full recap as I go from photo to photo: a sneaky shot of Mateo in Wonderland, which I never got to show him; the two of us dressed up like aviators at Make-A-Moment, where we went "skydiving"; the graveyard of pay phones where we discussed mortality; Mateo sleeping on the train, holding his Lego sanctuary; Mateo sitting inside his half-dug grave; the Open Bookstore window, minutes before we survived an explosion; that dude riding my bike I no longer wanted because Mateo was scared it would be the death of us, but not after one first and last ride together; adventures in the Travel Arena; outside of Clint's Graveyard, where Mateo and I sang and danced and kissed and ran for our lives; Mateo jumping around on his bed for me; and our last photo together, me in Mateo's glasses and he's squinting but so damn happy.

I'm happy too. Even now when I'm destroyed again, Mateo repaired me.

I play the video, which I could listen to on loop. "And here he was singing me 'Your Song,' which he said you sung too. Mateo acted like he was singing only because he wanted to make me feel special. I no doubt did, but I know he was singing for himself too. He loved singing even though he wasn't very good, ha. He loved singing and you and Lidia and Penny and me and everyone."

Mr. Torrez's heart monitor doesn't respond to Mateo's song or my stories. No skips, nothing. It's heartbreaking, this whole thing. Mr. Torrez stuck here alive, nowhere to go. Maybe it's an even bigger slap in the face than dying young. But maybe he'll wake up. I bet he'll feel like the last man in the world after losing his son, even though thousands will surround him every day.

There's a picture on top of the chest beside Mr. Torrez's

bed. It's Mateo as a kid, his dad, and a *Toy Story* cake. Kid Mateo looks so damn happy. Makes me wish I'd known him since childhood.

An extra week, even.

Extra hour.

Just more time.

On the back of the photo there's a message:

Thank you for everything, Dad.
I'll be brave, and I'll be okay.
I love you from here to there.
Mateo

I stare at Mateo's handwriting. He wrote this today and he delivered.

I need Mateo's dad to know about what his son was up to. I dig into my pocket and there's my drawing of the world from when Mateo and I first sat down this morning at my favorite diner. It's beat up and a little wet, but it'll do. I grab a pen from inside the chest drawer and write around the world.

Mr. Torrez,

I'm Rufus Emeterio. I was Mateo's Last Friend. He was mad brave on his End Day.

I took photos all day on Instagram. You gotta see how he lived. My username is @RufusonPluto. I'm really happy your son reached out to me on what could've been the worst day ever.

Sorry for your loss,

Rufus (9/5/17)

I fold up the note and leave it with the picture.

I head out the room, shaking. I don't go looking for Mateo's body. That's not what he would've wanted in my final minutes.

I leave the hospital.

10:36 p.m.

The hourglass is almost out of sand. It's getting creepy. I'm picturing Death stalking me, hiding behind cars and bushes, ready to swing his damn scythe.

I'm mad tired, not just physically, but straight emotionally drained. This is how I felt after losing my family. Full-force grief I have no chance pulling myself out of without time, which we know I don't have.

I'm making my way back to Althea Park to wait this night out. No matter how normal that is for me, I can't get myself to stop shaking 'cause I can be alert as all hell right now and it won't change what's going down mad soon. I also miss my family and that Mateo kid so much. And yo, there better be an afterlife and Mateo better make it easy to find him like he promised. I wonder if Mateo found his mother yet. I wonder if he told her about me. If I find my family first, we'll have our hug-it-out moment, and then I'll recruit them in my Mateo manhunt. Then who knows what comes next.

I throw on my headphones and watch the video of Mateo singing to me.

I see Althea Park in the distance, my place of great change.

I return my attention to the video, his voice blasting in my ears.

I cross the street without an arm to hold me back.

ACKNOWLEDGMENTS

I survived writing another book! And I definitely didn't do this alone.

As always, huge thanks to my agent, Brooks Sherman, for greenlighting my gut-punching pitches and for finding my book-shaped things the best homes. I'll never forgot how excited he was to hear I was writing a book titled *They Both Die at the End*, or how he texted me back around six a.m. when I finished the first draft. My editor, Andrew Harwell, deserves ten thousand raises for helping me turn this book-shaped thing into a "dark game of Jenga" his genius words, not mine. The countless rewrites for this book still weren't easy, and they would've been impossible without Andrew's attentive eye and thoughtful heart/brain.

Huge thanks to the entire HarperCollins team for embracing me. Rosemary Brosnan is a fierce joy in this universe. Margot Wood is always casting Epic witchcraft and wizardry. Thanks to Laura Kaplan for all things publicity, Bess Braswell and Audrey Diestelkamp for all things marketing, and Patty Rosati for all things School & Library. Janet Fletcher and Bethany Reis made me look smarter. Kate Jackson championed this book before even meeting me. And to the many people whose fingerprints are on this book, I look forward to meeting you and learning your names.

The Bent Agency, especially Jenny Bent, for championing my books.

The lovely team at Simon & Schuster UK, who've become my overseas family: Lucy Rogers, Hannah Cooper, Jack Noel, Jane Griffiths, Elisa Offord, and Laura Hough. Thank you for welcoming me and my books with mad love.

My assistant, Michael D'Angelo, for continuing to boss me around. And his crying selfies.

My friend group has grown because of words we wrote and that will never not be cool to me. My sister/work wife, Becky Albertalli, and my bro/fake husband, David Arnold-Silvera, for group chats and group hugs. Corey Whaley, the first person I hit up when I had the idea for this book in December 2012. My wealth of unbelievable friendships also includes Jasmine Warga, Sabaa Tahir, Nicola Yoon, Angie Thomas, Victoria Aveyard, Dhonielle Clayton, Sona Charaipotra, Jeff Zentner, Arvin Ahmadi, Lance Rubin, Kathryn Holmes, and Ameriie. And then the friends who have been there long before *More Happy Than Not*, like Amanda and

Michael Diaz, who have suffered me since the very beginning of our lives, and Luis Rivera, who is a literal lifesaver. Thank you all for always knowing when to get me away from the laptop and ultimately inspiring me to return to each story.

Lauren Oliver, Lexa Hillyer, and the entire Glasstown gang. I've never had the privilege of writing a book through the company, but I've learned so much about storytelling by working with this beyond-talented group.

Grateful for early feedback from Hannah Fergesen, Dahlia Adler, and Tristina Wright, to name a few.

My mom, Persi Rosa, and Gemini soul-sister, Cecilia Renn, my role models and cheerleaders who've always encouraged me to chase every dream (and every dude).

Keegan Strouse, who proved someone can change the game up on you in under twenty-four hours.

Every reader, bookseller, librarian, educator, and publishing badass who give us their everything to keep books alive. The universe sucks less because of all of you.

And, lastly, to every stranger who didn't call the cops on me when I asked them "What would you do if you found out you were about to die?" None of your answers inspired anything in this book, but wasn't it absolutely fun having a stranger make you observe your mortality?

THEY BOTH DIE AT THE END

COLLECTOR'S EDITION BONUS CONTENT

Turn the page for essays by the author, a map of the novel's characters and their connections, a look at the author's early outlines, an interview with Nicola Yoon and a sneak peek at *History Is All You Left Me.*

"THE TITLE SPOILS EVERYTHING"

Looking Back at *They Both Die at the End*

Adam Silvera

Ever since I announced the title of this book, I've had people ask me why I would spoil the ending. But did I? I mean, sort of, I guess. But the ending was never the point of the book. My first two books have some pretty strong twists, and I like to tell people that the big twist in *They Both Die at the End* is that there's no major twist at all. I laid out the cards, played the game by the rules of the title, and I never cheated. As much as we all want Mateo and Rufus to live forever, granting them some easy way out would've been a major disservice to their journey—and being inspired by their journey to treat our own days like lifetimes is what I believe to be the point of the book.

All my books so far have revolved around mortality because dying before my time, much like Mateo and Rufus unfortunately do, has always been my greatest fear. When touring for *They Both Die at the End* in Denmark, I was asked about my earliest experience with death, and I found myself rambling about being eleven years old in New York City when 9/11 happened—and the following month when my favorite uncle died in a plane crash. I doubt you're surprised to learn I avoided planes for over ten years. I still get nervous every time I have to fly. During my first book tour, I spent every morning calling and texting my favorite people and telling them that I loved them before I boarded each plane, *just in case. . . .*

This instinct has been with me for years, and that's how Death-Cast was born. Another question I regularly get from readers is if I would want Death-Cast's services if they were available today. Uh . . . HELL YEAH. I legit cannot think of any good reason why I wouldn't want to know if the day I was living was my End Day. I can't tell you how many times I paused writing this essay so I could finish doing laundry, or step out to pick up food, or because I simply needed fresh air and wondered if something unexpected would happen and prevent me from coming back to finish this (I'm not a fan of irony, friends). If something was going to happen, I would want to know so I could say *I love you*, and *thank you*, and *I'm sorry* to the appropriate people. I try to do this in my life today, but there's nothing like *knowing* for a fact to make sure I truly get it together, and that nothing gets left unsaid.

In a world where Death-Cast is real, I'd be a total Mateo. A total nervous wreck whose anxiety would prevent me from being adventurous on the off chance I'd set my death into motion for the following day. These feelings were something I had to work through so much that in the very first draft of this book, Mateo was the only narrator up until his passing, at which point Rufus carried the story until the end. Mateo grew, and I have, too. Today, I'm more like the bad-singing, Luigi hat-wearing, boy-kissing Mateo that he always wanted to be *and* got to be before time was up.

It's weird to be inspired by someone I created, someone based on my own fears and dreams, but I am. If Mateo—who feels so real to me—could do it, so can I. This isn't to claim I live a fearless life. Sure, I'm better since going on this journey with Mateo and Rufus. Even though my anxiety still weighs me down, I truly do live more now than I did before writing this book. Whenever I'm super nervous about doing something, like singing in front of friends because my voice sucks, or making the first move on a cute dude, or working my way through obstacle courses fifty feet in the air, I ask myself, "When you're on your deathbed, will you regret not doing this?" And the answer is usually yes. So I sing poorly, and I ask out cute dudes, and I hang on for dear life as I zip-line from tree to tree. When I'm on my deathbed, I want to be at peace with how I lived.

And this is just a little glimpse of how my journey has become a lot bolder because of Mateo and Rufus.

So yeah, maybe the title ruined the reading experience for some people. But I actually have a bigger spoiler for everyone: We all die at the end. Every single one of us. But once again, how we die, or the fact that we die isn't the point at all. I can't spoil the answer for this next question, but I hope it's one we keep on our minds daily: How did we live?

IMMORTALIZING MATEO AND RUFUS: HOW BOOKTOK GAVE THE BOYS A SECOND LIFE

". . . stories can make someone immortal as long as someone else is willing to listen . . ."
— They Both Die at the End

In August 2020, a mystery began.

I received an email from my original US editor, Andrew Eliopulos, that *They Both Die at the End* had seen a notable spike in sales three years after its original publication. We had no idea why. I assumed it was on some statewide summer reading list and would settle down as the school year began. But then the book popped back on both the *New York Times* bestseller list and the National Indie bestseller list. I thanked my readers for the support and admitted that I was clueless as to why this was happening.

Then readers told me they were seeing it on BookTok.

I had absolutely no idea what BookTok was.

I wondered if it was another app and quickly learned it was a subsection of TikTok, where readers were sharing book recommendations, reviews, and reactions. I legit had no idea this bookish corner of the universe existed, and I wasn't the only one. Publishers weren't familiar with BookTok yet, and no one thought TikTok could be used to market books. Then I found a TikTok video by @moongirlreads_ where the user, Selene (who is so lovely!), had recommended *They Both Die at the End* in her list for "Books that will make you SOB". That video went viral with millions of views, uploaded in early August. Mystery solved!

But it didn't stop there.

They Both Die at the End has now been living on bestseller lists across the world for over a year now, including hitting No. 1 in the US, UK, and Australia. It's been the top-selling YA book in 2021. And so much of that success is thanks to the fans on BookTok, this wonderful community whose hearts have been broken with Mateo and Rufus's twenty-four-hour love story.

I've watched so many videos of readers crying when they reach the end of the book. I've been tagged in so many requests and demands to pay for therapy bills to help them get over the deaths. And I've been super touched by all the messages about how many people are breaking free from their own binding ties and reaching for more daily fulfillment.

I want the best for all of you.

To all of you wonderful and powerful heroes of BookTok, thank you for loving Mateo and Rufus so much that you've grieved them, that you want to see them in the afterlife, that you want more for them and about them.

It's because of you that Mateo and Rufus will live on—both on the page and off it.

:) Adam

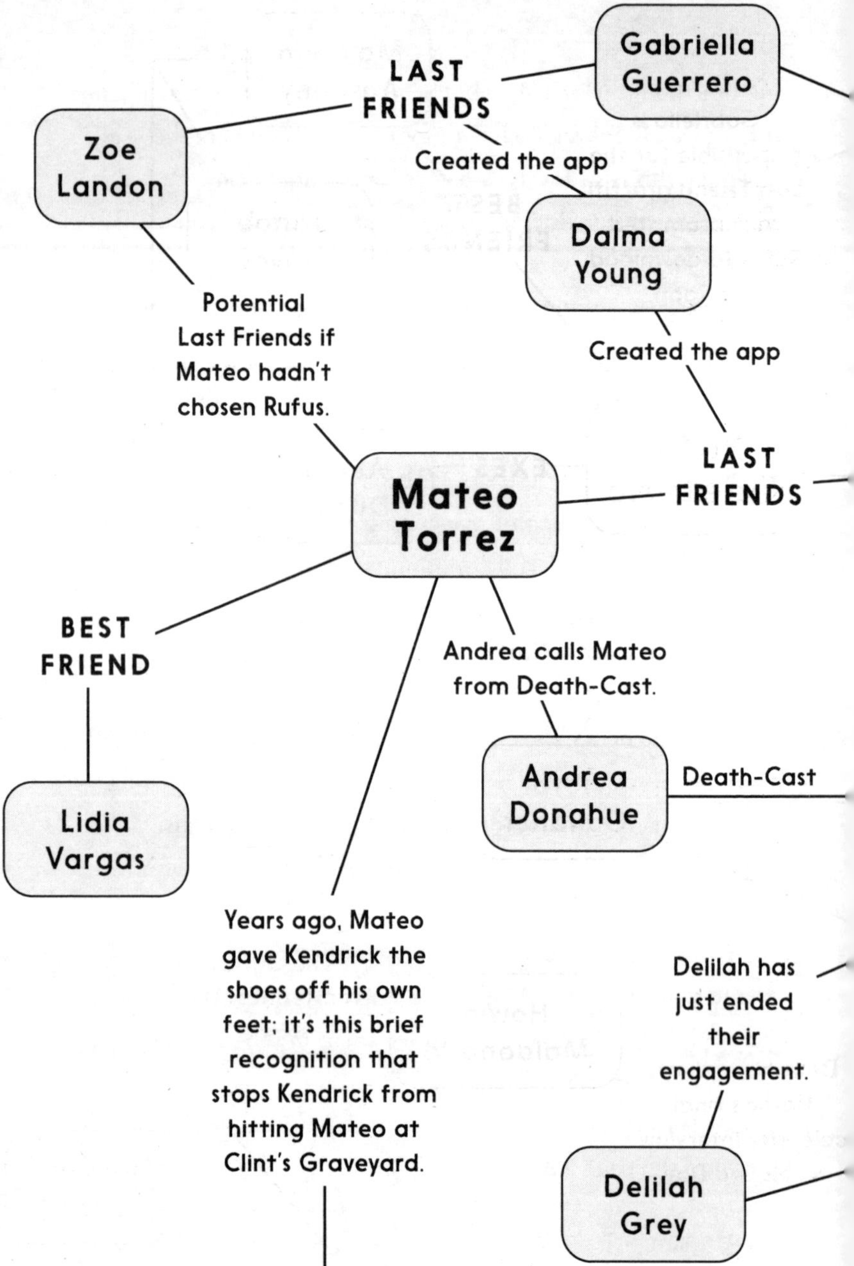

Gabriella Guerrero
LAST FRIENDS
Zoe Landon
Created the app
Dalma Young
Potential Last Friends if Mateo hadn't chosen Rufus.
Created the app
LAST FRIENDS
Mateo Torrez
BEST FRIEND
Andrea calls Mateo from Death-Cast.
Lidia Vargas
Andrea Donahue
Death-Cast
Years ago, Mateo gave Kendrick the shoes off his own feet; it's this brief recognition that stops Kendrick from hitting Mateo at Clint's Graveyard.
Delilah has just ended their engagement.
Delilah Grey

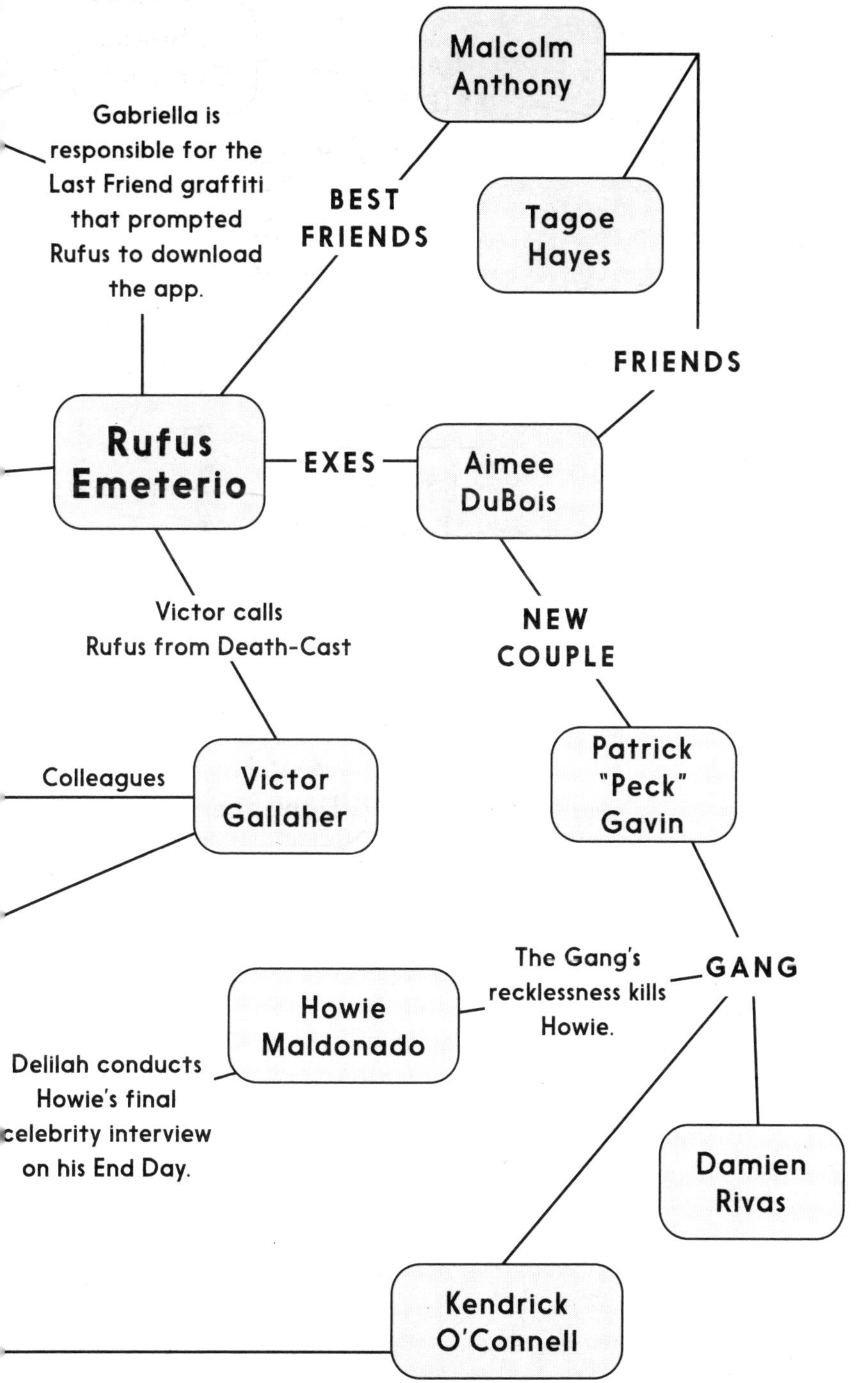

Malcolm Anthony
Gabriella is responsible for the Last Friend graffiti that prompted Rufus to download the app.
BEST FRIENDS
Tagoe Hayes
FRIENDS
Rufus Emeterio
EXES
Aimee DuBois
Victor calls Rufus from Death-Cast
NEW COUPLE
Patrick "Peck" Gavin
Colleagues
Victor Gallaher
The Gang's recklessness kills Howie.
GANG
Howie Maldonado
Delilah conducts Howie's final celebrity interview on his End Day.
Damien Rivas
Kendrick O'Connell

Adam Silvera's
early journal notes
for

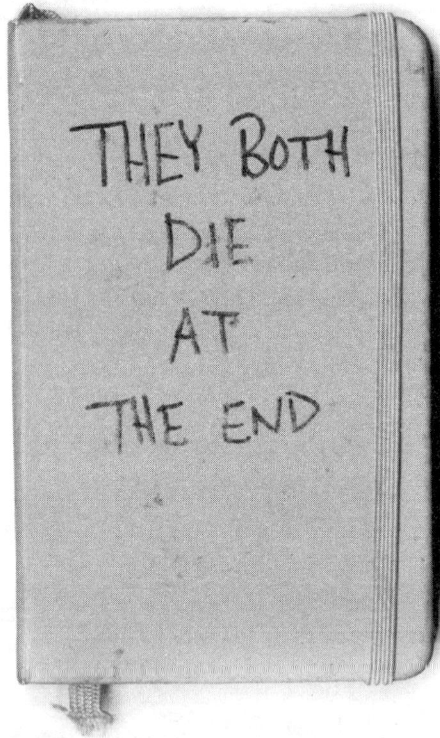

For every novel I write, I have a notebook where I jot down all my ideas, big and small. And in the case of *They Both Die at the End*, I outlined the entire book from start to finish before I wrote a single page. I'm excited to give you all a sneak peek at some of the changes (Mateo's name!) and what stayed true through every draft. Enjoy!

12:06

Wyatt Gonzalez recieves a phone call telling him he's about to die. The operator isn't very sympathetic. Wyatt feels sick but cannot get himself to cry. (Note: He doesn't cry because he doesn't know what he's missing until he meets Rufus, someone he could've seen himself living life with.) Wyatt does have a major freakout as he counts off all the ways he'll be unfulfilled. There will be unread books, unwatched movies, [illegible] cities on his map he'll never visit (he always wanted to be a traveller but was afraid of planes.), songs he'll never sing, piano he'll never play for friends, and deeper stuff, like growing up to become Adult Wyatt who does Adult things, like sex and drugs and marriage -

Wyatt finally leaves and sees a dead bird on the ground. He remembers that time he gave shelter to a bird in the rain which fallen out of its nest. He realizes by hiding himself in he probably had a chance to save this bird's life. "What else have I missed out on?"

Wyatt feeling guilty for a bird who probably had no warning except for a car horn (if even that) is just the kind of person he is.

And yet somehow, Wyatt isn't holding a funeral because a) he doesn't want the attention, and b) he believes it would be poorly attended.

Wyatt loves everyone.

Wyatt gets a bleep telling
him that Rufus is
looking at his profile, too.

Wyatt has a mini panic
attack. And before he
can decide whether or not
to say hi or close
the app, Rufus messages him.

Rufus: Hey Wyatt. I like your
hat.

(* LATER: Wyatt dies when
they go back to his house
to take photos of Wyatt with
his hat since its the first thing
they bonded over.) *

Wyatt is relieved Rufus
has said something to him,
but unsure how to reply.

12:00 P.M

A church bell strikes noon. Wyatt prays to his mother to make his day long and his death quick.

(small chapter - Like a paragraph.)

TRAVEL ARENA

There are temperature-specific generators in each "Country" and "State" and "City". Some of the activities include:

- swimming with dolphins in TK
- mountain climbing in TK
- safari ride-a-long in TK
- ice skating (on a "real" lake) in TK
- playing on the beach (sand imported from Bahamas)
- Watching bats fly out from under the bridge in Austin, TX.
- boat rides
- SPACE ROOM

it because he doesn't have to conform to Life's rules anymore, not when he's on his way out.

They make out, and it fades to black, and ~~it's~~ ~~[illegible]~~ what starts off as a nap turns into sex.. and then a nap.

*Wyatt and Rufus play House.

*Lidia keeps calling.

9:40 P.M

Wyatt wakes up and feels invincible. He kisses Rufus on his forehead while he sleeps. ~~He feels~~ (Maybe he doesn't feel invincible. Maybe he knows it's about to happen any minute left.)

In a couple short paragraphs, Wyatt reflects on how he just might survive, how he might beat this with Rufus. How he would love to beat it for at least one more day. (Wyatt is singing before he dies.)

Wyatt goes into the kitchen to make himself and Rufus some hot tea before they go see his Pa, when something goes terribly wrong with the oven, and Wyatt's life ends in a blaze.
(Before the fire comes, he realizes something bad is about to happen, and turns away.) # Like Carlito on the plane.

"It's not a heroes death. But Wyatt died a hero."
L Rufus.

9:48 P.M

"I wake up choking on black smoke." Rufus takes over the story. He searches frantically for Wyatt who isn't by his bedside. The fire alarm is going off. He leaves the bedroom where black smoke is completely obscuring his vision and chokes him

Rufus starts heading to the park where he always went whenever his life changed. This is by far the biggest change since losing his family, and he wonders if Wyatt is up there with his own mother, catching up, and then if they'll find Rufus's family before he joins them. Rufus would like the chance to introduce Wyatt to everyone.

Rufus then sees the park and gets chills.

"And then I cross the street without an arm to hold me back."

THE END! 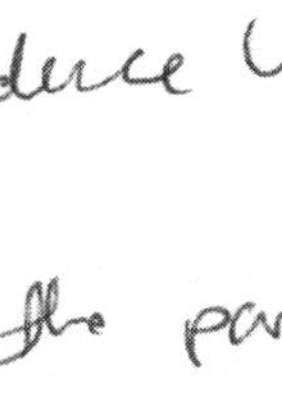

INTERVIEW WITH BESTSELLING AUTHOR AND FRIEND NICOLA YOON ABOUT *THEY BOTH DIE AT THE END*

Adam: My friend, hello! Thanks so much for agreeing to chat to me, I'm such a huge fan of you and your love stories. And you've somehow managed to not ban me from your life, even though my books have broken your heart many times.

Nicki: Hi, yes, hello. It really is remarkable that we're still friends after how much you've made me sob! I've decided to forgive you though and give you one last chance to write me a happily ever after book. Anyhoo, I have many questions about *They Both Die at the End*, so let's dive right in!

The Death-Cast universe you've created has so many interesting details that differentiate it from our own. How did you come up with the idea for things like the Last Friend app and the Make-A-Moment virtual reality station that filled out the world and made it feel real?

Adam: At the time of the novel, Death-Cast has only been around for a handful of years, so I didn't want anything to feel too impossible structurally. We already have virtual reality games and apps in the real world, but it came from asking how they would serve in this alternate universe. The Last Friend app came first because I was experimenting with dating apps when writing the book and I wanted to explore death through that lens. And then with Make-A-Moment, I thought about how badly I would want to do the riskiest things possible if I was unafraid of death, like skydiving. But I was also well aware in this Death-Cast world that skydiving could be how I die. So I created a virtual reality station that would scratch that itch for people. But just like virtual reality as we know it today, the technology will never match the real experience.

Nicki: One of the things I love so much about *They Both Die at the End* and *More Happy Than Not* is how the speculative element allows you to really explore all sorts of big meaning-of-life questions and emotions. In *More Happy Than Not*, we have memory alteration technology, which allows us, as readers, to consider how much of our own pasts we would change if we could. In *They Both Die at the End*, we have Death-Cast, which allows us to consider how we would choose to live our lives if we knew when they were going to end. I know you must've considered these questions yourself, so if you got the call from Death-Cast and decided to meet someone through the Last Friend app, what would you hope they'd be like?

Adam: Okay, for YEARS I've been asked what I would do if I got the End Day call, but I've never been asked who I would like to meet on the Last Friend app! I love this question, thank you. I would want to be paired with someone who is trustworthy. That's how I feel about all my relationships in general. I'd like for my Last Friend to be patient. I often think back to the scene in *They Both Die at the End* where Rufus is literally hanging around Mateo as he buries a dead bird. Rufus's clock is clicking too, and yet he's hanging around this stranger as Mateo does something that he would never take the time to do himself. I've always thought that moment speaks volumes about Rufus's character. A Rufus-type Last Friend would be wonderful, as would a Mateo-type, because he really does have an amazing heart that would inspire me to be a better person. Taking the time to be GOOD before you die is one of the best gifts you can leave behind for those who are living.

Nicki: So, given that you created such wonderful and caring characters in Rufus and Mateo, did you ever reconsider their fates? Also, did knowing their ultimate fate make any of the scenes in the book particularly difficult to write?

Adam: Never. Not once. A total of zero times. The title came to me before I knew who the boys even were, and the premise of two people who meet on the day they're going to die is something I never wanted to go rogue on. Especially with that title. I never wanted to cheat the reader. But, yes, falling for the characters as they fall for each other was brutal, especially when I wrote the scene where Mateo dies. My guiding light for writing Mateo was always, "Write the last person you want to see die." And then after watching this boy find such vibrancy, it was time to say goodbye. When Rufus cradles Mateo in the hallway, it was the first time I ever cried writing. There was no way I was going to write Rufus's death scene after experiencing that.

Nicki: Okay, let's shift away from death and despair just slightly. What was your favorite part of writing Rufus and Mateo's journey?

Adam: Hahaha! I love that you want to shift away from death and despair and here I am about to tell you how one of my very favorite scenes is when Mateo is sitting in his grave and Rufus joins him. Just two boys, sitting together in the earth, talking about living and dying. I knew I wanted to write that moment early on in the process. And from there on, I really love watching the characters grow individually and fall in love with each other.

Twenty-four-hour love stories can be really tricky. Did you find that to be the case in *The Sun Is Also A Star*?

Nicki: Yes, definitely tricky, but I love putting my characters into situations where they have to be real with each other fairly quickly. In *The Sun Is Also A Star,* the characters only have twelve hours to get to know each other. Natasha is a few hours away from being deported and Daniel is a few hours away from a life-changing college entrance interview. Because they have such limited time, they have to skip the small talk, i.e., the "What's your favorite color?" phase of the relationship and get to the good stuff quickly, the "What do you think the meaning of life is?" phase. I love watching my characters talk and fall in love with the other person's way of seeing the world. I also love watching them realize that when you fall in love with another person, you fall in love with yourself too.

Adam: I love that! Something else our books have in common is that we tell our same-day love stories with two narrators in first-person and then interconnected characters in third-person. We worked on these books at the same time and had no idea we were employing the same structure. What inspired you to take that approach?

Nicki: Great minds think alike, Adam! With *The Sun Is Also A Star,* I really wanted to explore the ways in which we, as human beings, are all connected. In our modern world, we tend to think we have nothing in common with strangers or with people with different backgrounds than ourselves. But that's not true at all. I put in those third-person sections so that I could show the ways in which Natasha and Daniel are connected to all the people in the world around them, even strangers. The other thing I really wanted to show was that, as the great Maya Angelou said in *Human Family*, "We are more alike, my friends, than we are unalike."

What drew you to that structure?

Adam: I had a more evolving journey with *They Both Die at the End*. In the very first draft, the entire story was told from Mateo's point of view up until his death. I always knew he was going to die first, at which point the narrating baton would be passed onto Rufus. I originally thought that would be a huge twist because readers naturally wouldn't assume the narrator would be the first to die. (You have to find twists where you can when your book's title spoils the ending!) But when I wrote Rufus after Mateo's death, I realized I didn't know him as intimately as I knew Mateo. I didn't know what he was doing when he got his End Day call, or how he reacted. So I went back in and wrote Rufus into the story so he could be just as dimensional as Mateo.

But my curiosity didn't stop there! What was going on with Lidia in the hours between when we first met her and then later at the Travel Arena? What about the Plutos after Rufus runs away from his funeral? What was it like to work at Death-Cast and tell perfectly healthy teenagers—amongst many other people—that they're about to die? Or

Dalma Young who created the Last Friend app? I loved getting glimpses into their lives and making the day feel even grander.

Nicki: Final question! Why do you think *They Both Die at the End* resonates so strongly with readers?

Adam: Every reader comes at it from a different angle, obviously, but it's probably safe to say that the book is universally asking people who they want to be in this life. If you got your End Day call today, would you be proud of the life you lived? Did you do things that brought you happiness? Were you good to people? If not, that's when I hear from readers saying they're looking to make changes in their lives after reading Mateo and Rufus's story.

Whenever the time comes when I find myself on my deathbed, I want to have as few regrets as possible. I've been getting better about that since writing the book. Just like Mateo, I love singing, but I don't have a great singing voice. But instead of singing alone in my shower, I did karaoke with you, your husband, David Yoon, and our friends Tahereh Mafi and Ransom Riggs. I had way more fun with our little YA author concert (that will never see the light of day), than singing by myself. And then when I was younger, I had a lot of anger in me like Rufus, but I never wanted that to be my defining characteristic. And Rufus showed me that there are actions you can take that will leave behind better legacies and a truer reflection of who you actually are.

Readers have told me the book has changed their views on how to live, and the same is true for me after writing it. I've become more daring in every corner of my life—writing and publishing the fantasy series (the Infinity Cycle) I've been imagining since I was a teenager, falling in love a lot of times, repairing friendships that mean the world to me etc. I'm so happy whenever someone tells me they're chasing down their dreams, or how they're honoring Mateo and Rufus in their own lives.

I think we're all understanding how short life is, and how important it is to live it while we can.

TURN THE PAGE FOR A SNEAK PEEK OF ANOTHER HEARTBREAKING BOOK FROM ADAM SILVERA, *HISTORY IS ALL YOU LEFT ME.*

TODAY

MONDAY, NOVEMBER 20TH, 2016

You're still alive in alternate universes, Theo, but I live in the real world, where this morning you're having an open-casket funeral. I know you're out there, listening. And you should know I'm really pissed because you swore you would never die and yet here we are. It hurts even more because this isn't the first promise you've broken.

I'll break down the details of this promise again. You made it last August. Trust me when I say I'm not talking down to you as I recall this memory, and many others, in great detail. I doubt it'll even surprise you since we always joked about how your brain worked in funny ways. You knew enough meaningless trivia to fill notebooks, but you occasionally slipped on the bigger things, like my birthday this year (May 17th, not the 18th), and you never kept your night classes straight even though I got you a cool planner with zombies on the cover (which you-know-who probably forced you to throw out). I just want you to remember things the way I do. And if bringing up the past annoys you now—as I know it did when you left New York for California—know that I'm sorry, but please don't be mad at me for reliving all of it. History is all you left me.

We made promises to each other on the day I broke up with you so you could do your thing out there in Santa Monica without me holding you back. Some of those promises took bad turns but weren't broken, like how I said I'd never hate you even though you gave me enough reasons to, or how you never stopped being my friend even when your boyfriend asked you to. But on the day we were walking to the post office with Wade to ship your boxes to California, you walked backward into the street and almost got hit by a car. I saw our endgame—to find our way back to each other when the time was right, no matter what—disappear, and I made you promise to always take care of yourself and never die.

"Fine. I'll never die," you said as you hugged me.

If there was a promise you were allowed to break, it wasn't that one, and now I'm forced to approach your casket in one hour to say goodbye to you.

Except it's not going to be goodbye.

I'll always have you here listening. But being face-to-face with you for the first time since July and for the last time ever is going to be impossible, especially given the unwanted company of your boyfriend.

Let's leave his name out of my mouth as long as possible this morning, okay? If I'm going to have any chance of getting through today, tomorrow, and all the days that follow, I think I need to go back to the start, where we were two boys bonding over jigsaw puzzles and falling in love.

It's what comes after you fell out of love with me that it all goes wrong. It's what comes after we broke up that's making me so nervous. Now you can see me, wherever you are. I know you're there, and I know you're watching me, tuned in to my life to piece everything together yourself. It's not just the shameful things I've done that are driving me crazy, Theo. It's because I know I'm not done yet.

HISTORY

SUNDAY, JUNE 8TH, 2014

I'm making history today.

Time is moving faster than this L train, but it's all good since I'm sitting to the left of Theo McIntyre. I've known him since middle school, when he caught my eye at recess. He waved me over and said, "Help me out, Griffin. I'm rebuilding Pompeii." A puzzle of Pompeii made up of one hundred pieces, obviously. I knew nothing of Pompeii at the time; I thought Mount Vesuvius was the hidden lair of some comic book overlord. Theo's hands had entranced me, sorting the puzzle pieces into groups according to shades before beginning, separating the granite roads from the demolished, ash-coated structures. I helped with the sky, getting the clouds all wrong. We didn't get very far with the puzzle that day, but we've been tight ever since.

Today's outing takes us from Manhattan to Brooklyn to see if the lost treasures in some flea market are as overpriced as everyone says they are. No matter where we are, Brooklyn or Manhattan, a schoolyard or Pompeii, I've planned on changing the game up on Theo on this even-numbered day. I just hope he's down to keep playing.

"At least we have the place to ourselves," I say.

It's almost suspicious how empty the subway car is. But I'm not questioning it. I'm too busy dreaming up what it would be like to always share this space and any other space with this know-it-all who loves cartography, puzzles, video animation, and finding out what makes humans tick. On a crowded train, Theo and I usually squeeze together when we sit, our hips and arms pressed against one another's, and it's a lot like hugging him except I don't have to let go as quickly. It sucks that Theo sits directly across from me now, but at least I get the very awesome view. Blue eyes that find wonder in everything (including train ads for teeth whitening), blond hair that darkens when it's wet, the *Game of Thrones* T-shirt I got him for his birthday back in February.

"It's a lot harder to people-watch without people," Theo says. His eyes lock on me. "There's you, I guess."

"I'm sure there will be some interesting people at the flea market. Like hipsters."

"Hipsters are characters, not people," Theo says.

"Don't hipster-shame. Some of them have real feelings underneath their beanie hats and vintage flannels."

Theo stands and does a bullshit pull-up on the rail; his brain gets him top marks, but his muscles can't carry him as high. He gives up and hops back and forth between the train benches like some underground trapeze artist. I wish he would somersault to my side and stay put. He holds on to the railing and stretches his leg to the opposite bench, and his shirt rises a little so I peek at his exposed skin peripherally while keeping my focus on Theo's grin. It might be my last day to do so.

The train rocks to a stop and we get off, finally.

Manhattan is home and all, so Theo never bad-mouths it, but I know he wishes more of its walls were stained with graffiti like they are here in Brooklyn, bright in the summer sun. Theo points out his favorites on the way to the flea market: a little boy in black and white walking across colorful block letters spelling out DREAM; an empty mirror demanding to find the fairest of them all in a crazy neat cursive that rivals Theo's perfect handwriting; an airplane circling Neptune, which is just fantastical enough that it doesn't give me flying anxiety; knights seated around Earth, like it's their round table. Neither of us have any idea what it's supposed to mean, but it's pretty damn cool.

It's a long, hot walk to the flea market, located by the East River. Theo spots a refreshment truck, and we spend five bucks each on cups of frozen lemonade, except there isn't enough of the sugary slush left so we're forced to chew ice to survive the heat.

Theo stops at a table with *Star Wars* goods. His face scrunches up when he turns to me. "Seventy dollars for that toy lightsaber?"

Theo's inside voice sucks. It's a problem.

The forty-something vendor looks up. "It's a recalled saber," she says flatly. "It's rare and I should be charging more." Her shirt reads PRINCESS LEIA IS NOT THE DAMSEL IN DISTRESS YOU'RE LOOKING FOR.

Theo returns her glare with an easy smile. "Did someone pull an Obi-Wan and cut someone's arm off?"

My knowledge on all things *Star Wars* is pretty limited, and the same goes for Theo's knowledge on all things *Harry Potter*. He's the only sixteen-year-old human I know who isn't caught up on everyone's favorite boy wizard. One night we argued for a solid hour over who would win in a duel between Lord Voldemort and Darth Vader. I'm surprised we're still friends.

"The battery hatch snaps off easily and children can't seem to keep them out of their damn mouths," the woman says. She isn't talking to Theo anymore. She's talking to an equally unhappy dude her age who can't figure out an R2-D2 alarm clock.

"Okay, then." Theo salutes her, and we walk away.

We stroll for a few minutes. (Six, to be exact.) "Are we done here?" I ask. It's hot, and I'm melting, and we've definitely seen that some of the treasures are way pricier than they legally should be.

"Hell no, we're not done," Theo says. "We can't leave empty-handed."

"So buy something."

"Why don't you buy *me* something?"

"You don't need that lightsaber."

"No, stupid, buy me something else."

"It's safe to assume you're buying me something too, right?"

"Seems fair," Theo says. He taps his dangerous watch. It is actually for-real dangerous, as in it's not safe to wear. I'm not even sure how or why it got made, because its sharp sundial hands have scratched unsuspecting people's bodies—mine included—enough times that he should throw it in a fireplace and kill it dead and then sue the manufacturer. He wears it anyway because it's different. "Let's meet at the entrance in twenty minutes. Ready?"

"Go."

Theo dashes away, nearly crashing into a bearded man with a little girl sitting on his shoulders. He is out of sight in seconds. I check the time on my phone—4:18, even minute—and I speed in the opposite direction, into an airy labyrinth full of people's relics for sale. I run past crates of old sneakers, crooked rows of smudged mirrors like a filthy funhouse, poles with floral pashminas that billow from a hidden fan, and buckets of seashells sold in tandem with paintbrushes.

The seashells are kind of cool, I guess, but they don't really scream "Theo!"

A minute or so later, I hit a grid of the market that *does* speak Theo's language. A dream catcher with a willow hoop dyed his favorite shade of green. An entire table of tiny ships inside bottles. He was recently reading up on their intricacies in the hopes of making one himself, except I know he wants his bottle to have a spaceship inside because he always has to put his Theo twist on things.

I still have all the time in the world—if the world only had twelve minutes to offer, at least. It's too bad he's not more of a fantasy fan, because the letter openers here are pretty boss and I'm sort of hoping he's found this table already and will surprise me with one, preferably the one designed like a sword sheath or this one with the bone handle. It's okay because I have all the time in the world . . . Actually, right now, no I don't, because according to my phone, I only have nine minutes, an odd number that's getting me really anxious, so I scratch my palm while running again. I somehow return to a world of more misses. Theo has no current use for breakfast-friendly pots and pans since he's pretty happy eating bowls of cereal with orange juice, and he definitely doesn't need gardening tools unless they come with instructions on how he can grow more video games and computer apps for free.

Then I hit the jackpot.

Puzzles.

I glance at my phone again: six minutes left. I'm no longer anxious; I'm excited. I know from being over at Theo's enough that he doesn't own any of these: a steampunk barn house gliding away on wings built of scraps from a satellite; Santa's sleigh being pulled by dolphins underwater (I don't want to know what's in those wrapped gifts, but I'd also love to hear Theo's guesses); a 3-D puzzle of a soccer ball, and the 3-D part is cool, but the sports part is less cool. I'm not sure where Theo stands on 3-D puzzles, but this doesn't seem like the one "to kick it off"—ha.

Boom, got it. The fourth one in the row on the table: Doomed Pirate Ship. The pirates are being thrown overboard by stormy weather and a raging sea; some try to climb back up, while another hangs from the plank. I know Theo will create a kick-ass story behind this one. The vendor drops the puzzle in a brown plastic bag and even though it costs nine bucks, I just shove a ten into her hands and jet back.

Theo is waiting by the exit, pressed against the wall to hide away in the shade, like a vampire who stayed out too late—too early? I don't blame him. We're both sweating. He looks at his sundial watch. "Two minutes to spare! Let's get the hell out of here before we go up in flames, or, worse, you get sunburn."

On the way back to the subway, the only clue I have of his gift is a box. It's a perfect cube. I have zero guesses as to what it is. Underground we're hidden from the sun, but the mugginess of a crowded platform is unbearable in its own way, like we've set up camp at the top of a volcano and zipped our tent shut. We somehow survive the six-minute wait, and once the train opens its doors, we race to the corner bench and sit before a couple of college-age-looking guys can take the seats for themselves. The air conditioner is on full blast, and I feel more like myself.

"Presents?" Theo asks, pointing at my bag with finger guns.

"You finished shopping first, so you go first," I say, inching my leg a little closer to his so our knees might accidentally touch.

"I'm not sure what kind of logic that is, but okay," Theo says.

He gives me the little box and whatever is inside doesn't weigh that much and slides back and forth as I toss it from hand to hand. I open it and pull out an ornament of none other than Ron Weasley, Harry Potter's best friend.

"What do you think?" Theo asks. "I know he's your favorite character, so you probably already have this, but I thought this one was cool, especially since he's got that seen-better-days roughness going on."

I nod. It's true: this Ron Weasley figurine is a little beat-up, the paint chipped on his red hair and black robe. But he's not my favorite character. It's an easy mistake because Ron is my favorite in the trio—sorry Harry, sorry Hermione—and it's not as if they make ornaments for characters that were only alive and important in one book. But Cedric Diggory is my absolute favorite character in the series, in any book, really. When Cedric died at the end of the Triwizard Tournament, I cried for way longer than I've ever admitted to anyone. Cedric's death is no doubt my most painful loss ever. But it's okay, it's not like I know for sure who Theo's favorite *Star Wars* character is. I want to say Yoda, but that sounds stupid, even to me. It's the thought that counts.

"This is awesome," I say. "And I don't own it already, so thanks." I wonder if the previous owner got over the series and pawned this little guy for fifty cents or something. One man's loss and all that, I guess. "Okay. Your turn." I'm missing the emptiness of the train we rode out, hyperalert that there are nameless spectators watching us exchange gifts and drawing their own conclusions about how we must be dating. It sucks that they're wrong. It double sucks that there's a chance Theo may be too scared to even be my friend after today.

Theo slides the puzzle out of the bag and his eyes widen. "Hell yes. Eight hundred pieces. You have to put this together with me."

"What's the story behind it?"

Theo studies it for a moment. "It's about the impending zombie-pirate apocalypse, obviously."

"Obviously. Tell me, how did the pirates get hit with the virus before anyone else?"

"The zombie virus has always existed, but the scientists knew it was best to keep it as far away from land as possible. They knew humans by nature are stupid and bored and would do something like unleash hell on the world if it meant not having to go to their dead-end jobs on Monday morning. Scientists contained the virus on an island—I'm redacting the name because I can't trust you with this secret, Griff—and they didn't account for the raging storm you see here destroying the island

and releasing the virus until it became airborne, hitting the traveling pirates first. Well, infecting the parrot of Captain Hoyt-Sumner first, who carried the virus onto *The Pillaging Mary.*"

Only then do I lose it and smile. "How the hell are you coming up with these names?"

"I didn't make it up, it's in all the textbooks. Read up on your future's history," Theo says.

"What's the parrot's name?"

"Fulton, but everyone calls her Rot Feathers after she makes all the pirates undead. They later renamed the ship *The Bloodcurdling Crawler,* which feels appropriate."

I really want to spend an hour inside his head, climbing all the different whirling clockwork gears.

"These zombie pirates are smart enough to rename their ship?" I ask him. "We're screwed."

"You better be my partner against the zombie pirates," Theo says. "I know how to save us."

Theo launches into different strategies we can employ to survive the apocalypse. We'll need to build a fortress somewhere up high, with cannons and other practical weapons, like military crossbows that shoot flaming arrows. Easy: I almost feel like I can already wield one from all the fantasy books I've read. Apparently, I'll also have to learn how to cook because Theo will be too busy keeping watch twenty-four/seven. He's pretty sure he'll have figured out the key to eternal unrest while the undead are among us—and won't have time to cook or we'll end up dinner ourselves.

"Sound good, Griff?"

"I can't promise the food I cook will even be edible, but desperate times call for desperate measures."

Theo holds out his hand and we shake on it, locking down our roles in the zombie-pirate apocalypse. Touching him gets my heart pounding, fast and heavy.

I let go. "I have to tell you something." The subway car is

rattling and loud, and the curious eyes have drifted. Everyone else is lost in their own worlds.

"There's something I have to tell you, too," Theo says.

"Who goes first?"

"Rock, paper, scissors?"

We both play rock.

"Same time?" Theo suggests.

"I don't think my thing is something to shout at the same time. You can go first."

"Trust me. I'm betting we're both going to say the same thing. It'll be easier this way," Theo says.

I'm not going to keep fighting him on this. Maybe what he has to say is worse than mine, and I won't feel as bad.

"Countdown from three?"

"Four."

Theo half-smiles, then nods. "Four, three, two, one."

"I think I might be crazy," I spit out while he says, "I like you."

Theo blushes, his half smile gone. "Wait, what?" He shifts his body around and stares out the train window, but we're underground, so all he'll see is darkness and his reflection. "I thought you were going to say you like me. Are you gay, Griff?"

"Yeah," I admit, for the first time ever, which somehow doesn't have my heart racing or my face heating up. All I know is, I would've lied to anyone else.

"Good. I mean, cool," Theo says. It seems like he's flirting with the idea of making eye contact again before keeping his gaze to the window. "Why were you scared to tell me? That you think you're crazy?"

"Right, that's the second thing. I think I might have OCD."

"Your room is too messy," Theo says.

"It's not about being organized. You know how lately I'm always forcing my way onto everyone's left side? It wasn't like that when we were kids. There's also my counting thing, where I prefer everything to be an even number, with a couple of exceptions, like one and seven. Volume, the timer on the microwave, how many chapters I read before putting a book down, even how many examples I use in a sentence. It's distracting, and I always feel *on*."

Theo nods. "I've felt like this before, too. Maybe not as intense, but I think it's just a sign of your genius. I'm pretty sure Nikola Tesla was obsessed with the number three and would sometimes walk around a block three times before entering a building. But, Griff, for all we know these compulsions might just turn out to be little quirks." His blue eyes find my face again, lit. "We can do some research later!"

Maybe he's right. Maybe I'm not just some delusional kid with a neck tic who scratches his palms whenever he's nervous, favors everyone's left side, tugs at his earlobe, and operates in evens. Maybe it's like autofocusing a camera, where I'm zooming in on one thing and missing everything else.

"It's been freaking me out a little bit, like I don't know who I'm going to be in the future. I'm scared something can grow from this and turn me into a Griffin who's too complicated for you to be friends with in a few years." I can't believe I'm unloading all this; it feels surreal, incredible, but I can't stop. Maybe confessing everything will jinx any illnesses.

Theo scoots closer to me. "I have real things to be worried about, dude, like if the zombie pirates are going to know how to use grappling hooks and matchlocks or if they're taking us down with teeth and nails. You don't scare me, and you'll never be too complicated for my friendship." Theo pats my knee. His hand rests there for a solid minute. "And I'm sorry if I forced you to come out just now—wait, am I the first person you've told?"

I nod, my heart pounding. "You didn't force me. Okay, actually, you did a little, but I wanted to tell you anyway. I just didn't have the balls or some huge speech. I was also a little scared I was wrong about my instincts for you. Delusions run on my mother's side of the family."

"You're not delusional," Theo says. "And you're not crazy."

He reaches for my hand, and it's not for a high five. I know the world hasn't changed, what goes up still has to come down, but the way I see the world has shifted a little to the right, moving forward, and I can now see it the way I've always wanted to. I hope I don't say or do anything that will force the world to shift counterclockwise again.

I squeeze Theo's hand, testing whatever it is we're doing here, and I feel like I'm answering a question I was never brave enough to ask.

"Stick with me here, okay?" Theo says.

"I'm not exactly about to walk off a moving train."

Theo lets go of my hand. I sink in a little, like I've failed him. "I've never told anyone this, but I've been dreaming up alternate universes for a couple of years. You know me, I'm always asking myself 'What if?'" He turns away for a second. "Lately I've been asking myself that more and more. A lot of the what-ifs are fun, but a lot of them are also really personal. Every night before I go to sleep, I find all the notes I've written on scrap paper or on my phone and I archive them in this journal. Dozens and dozens of alternate universes."

The train stops suddenly; passengers leave and others get on, giving us a little more breathing space—but once the doors close, Theo has my full attention again.

"I wrote one on the inside of my arm earlier, during the gift hunt," he continues. "I'm not going to show you yet. No spoilers. But it just reminded me of something. Every universe I've created lately, your face keeps popping up in it. And I thought that if you can't be cool with that, then I wouldn't hate you, but I might need some time for myself until we've had enough distance that I can imagine made-up worlds without you automatically appearing." Theo turns and above his left elbow is his handwriting—not the usual perfection because even *he* can't write on himself neatly—and he holds it closer.

The scrawl reads, *Alternate Universe: I'm dating Griffin Jennings and that's that.*

"I don't know if that makes sense to you at all, but I want that to be real," Theo says, still holding his arm out to me, as if to burn those messy letters into my memory. "If it can't, I understand and I hope we can still figure out how to be best friends. I just can't imagine never taking this shot." He lowers his arm, finally. "You've got to say something now."

I feel like someone has dropkicked me into an alternate universe of awesomeness. I can't believe this is a conversation I'm having, I can't believe I'm legit flirting with Theo and he's flirting back. This universe is clicking with me just fine. I can't tell him all these things, not yet, at least.

"I was going to," I say.

"Okay, but only say something if it's good. If it sucks, shut up."

"I've been freaking out for a while about this same thing, dude. I don't know when I would've manned up and said something, but it wouldn't have beat your bit about the alternate universes. I would've just said I like you."

"Were you going to at least mention how handsome I am?"

"Handsome seems like a strong word, but I would've talked about how you're cool to look at, sure."

"Good to know." I should tell him how much I like the sound of his writing, the words he puts down in his notebooks when he's hunched over his desk; I want to know what they are. I should tell him about the fantasies I've had where the next time I sleep over at his house and we share his bed, that we wouldn't have to use separate comforters and could maybe share one blanket one day without it being weird. I should tell him how fun it is to watch him flip an hourglass over and see if he can complete a massive puzzle by himself, and how I'm always rooting for him to succeed because I know how happy he is when he wins. I should tell him how much I appreciate the way he's been gravitating to my right lately. But I don't say any of this out loud right now because maybe I can admit this to him when it's happening in real time.

"Why today, Theo?"

"The photo Wade took of us yesterday," Theo says.

It hits me that I hadn't once thought of Wade during today's adventure. We're a three-dude squad, but I don't seem to get too anxious of the oddness versus evenness battle there, maybe because we always seem to make it work: it's the universe's one exception. Like yesterday afternoon, at Theo's place we played a *Super Smash Bros.* tournament—Theo and I versus Wade and the computer, teams forged by drawing names from Wade's fitted cap. It was close because Wade's really good with Bowser and the computer level was at its highest, but Theo and I won with Captain Falcon and Zelda. We stood up, victorious, and hugged each other as if we had just won a war against aliens or, even more fitting as of ten minutes ago, a war against the zombie pirates.

Wade had us pose. Theo and I faked our best serious faces, but we failed and cracked up.

"I saw us together and thought enough was enough. I've wanted to be with you for a while now. Wade's pic made it a little more unbearable not to be with you," Theo says.

"I feel the same way, I guess," I say. "What now? How do we lock this down? Probably a kiss or something, but I'm not in the mood." I trip over the last part because, honestly, it's a lie. I decide I'm swearing off lying because telling the truth can bring this kind of happiness, the kind that opens infinite alternate universes. I just really wish I had a piece of gum, but Wade is our squad's gum guy. "Maybe a handshake?"

We shake hands, and neither of us lets go.

"This is cool, but weird," I say.

"Very cool, very weird," Theo says. "But I think we fit, right?"

"No doubt, Theo."

I can't wait to see what happens next.

HAVE YOU READ?

HAVE YOU READ?

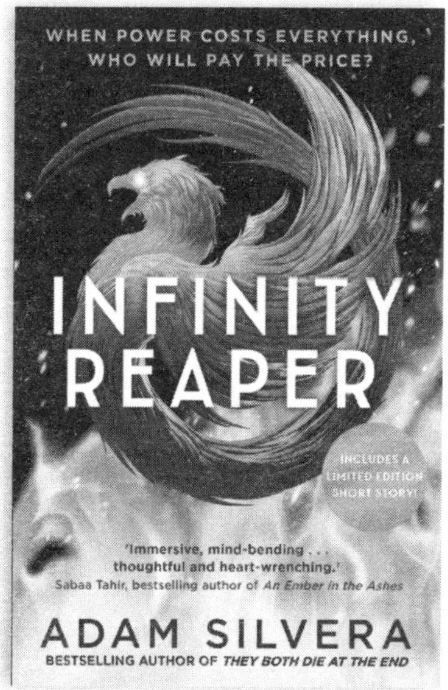

HAVE YOU READ?